One thing was certain. The woman was at the computer, working or beginning to, when she was killed.

Fitzgerald went back into the living area, moving around the woman's body, trying not to look. Her forehead had hit the table just to the side of the keyboard. By reaching around her body he could touch the keyboard. He took out his handkerchief, covered his index finger, pressed the space bar.

The screen saver vanished, replaced with an empty screen, an unnamed file of a word-processing program. He knew about that: empty screens. At the last moment of her life, the woman had been looking at one. He felt a surge of kinship—at the same time knew the difference, that a bullet had interrupted her flow of words. The woman had opened up a new file, meaning to write something, but had been stopped before she entered a word or named the file. Or was it the other way around? Had the killer been going to dictate something to her, waited until she was ready, then pulled the trigger?

———————— ★ ————————

"...amateur sleuth Fitzgerald...and girlfriend Mercy Virdon...make an engaging pair in this well-written mystery..."

—Publishers Weekly

"Fitzgerald is an unusual character...his air of intrigue keeps the reader turning pages."

—Harriet Klausner

Previously published Worldwide Mystery title by
RONALD WEBER

THE ALUMINUM HATCH

CATCH AND KEEP

RONALD WEBER

WORLDWIDE®

TORONTO • NEW YORK • LONDON
AMSTERDAM • PARIS • SYDNEY • HAMBURG
STOCKHOLM • ATHENS • TOKYO • MILAN
MADRID • WARSAW • BUDAPEST • AUCKLAND

CATCH AND KEEP

A Worldwide Mystery/June 2001

First published by Write Way Publishing, Inc.

ISBN 0-373-26388-0

Copyright © 2000 by Ronald Weber.
All rights reserved. No part of this book may be reproduced
or transmitted in any form or by any means, electronic or
mechanical, including photocopying, recording or by any
information storage and retrieval system, without permission
in writing from the publisher. For information, contact:
Write Way Publishing, Inc., P.O. Box 441278, Aurora, CO
80044 U.S.A.

All characters in this book are fictitious, and any resemblance to
actual persons, living or dead, is purely coincidental.

® and TM are trademarks of Harlequin Enterprises Limited.
Trademarks indicated with ® are registered in the United States
Patent and Trademark Office, the Canadian Trade Marks Office
and in other countries.

Printed in U.S.A.

For Dave, Dawn, Doug and Ann

ONE

THE PHONE WAS a relief. Even Phipps on the other end was better than an empty screen peering back at him, indifferent. "So," Phipps was asking, "you living well?"

"Well enough," Fitzgerald said.

"Catching fish?"

"Some."

"And writing a novel?"

"Trying to."

"Funny thing," Phipps said. "I've known a lot of newspaper guys tried to write a novel. Couldn't hack it. Not a single one."

"Encouraging."

"Don't get me wrong. A guy who won a lottery might get lucky again."

Some things never change. Phipps had lost his position, not his gift for insult. When Fitzgerald started on the *Detroit Free Press* Phipps was an assistant managing editor, a high-flyer on the way higher. Then he boozed his way down to the Sunday magazine, the paper's dustbin for hopeless cases. The magazine was on its last legs, advertising drying up to a trickle; when it folded, Phipps would fold with it. Fitzgerald felt no sympathy. Phipps was hard to like, even at his best. On the other hand, talking with him on the phone was a way of not writing a novel.

That morning Fitzgerald had tried something new. He took the laptop computer from the spare bedroom he used as an office and set up shop at the glass front of the A-frame, a view of the Borchard River through the cedars below, flashing gold in autumn sunlight. He sat in a leather armchair with the laptop on his lap—where, it dawned on him, it was meant to be—and a mug of fresh coffee on an end table beside him. The idea was that a change of setting might get him going.

Before, he worked on a card table in the bedroom facing a blank wall of knotty pine, no distractions, which only caused him to be acutely aware of the lack of distractions. Maybe, a striking view, a reverse effect would set in and he would make some headway. But no dice. The morning had been spent looking out at the Borchard and wondering if maybe the problem was the A-frame itself. He was renting it from Old Kent Bank, which had taken possession after the GM executive who built it as a vacation home was downsized and couldn't keep up the payments. Maybe, all wood and stone and perfectly situated, the place was too upscale for a writer. Maybe he should have found himself a simple cabin in the woods and settled down with pen and paper. Like Thoreau in *Walden*.

"Matter of fact," Phipps said, "this isn't a social call."

"Didn't think it was."

"I could use some help."

Fitzgerald pointed out that he was on leave of absence from the paper but Phipps plunged on. What he needed wouldn't take much time. It involved a stringer for the *Free Press*, a woman named Allison Thorne, who was working on an article for the Sunday magazine but had dropped out of contact. She couldn't be reached by phone. "A piece about fish," Phipps added. "Why I called you, the fish expert."

It seemed that an organization had formed on the Borchard River in opposition to catch and release fishing regulations, a group calling itself the Catch and Keep Alliance. The story was too Michigan north woods as far as Detroit was concerned, so when Allison Thorne sent a draft to the magazine Phipps had promptly rejected it. She was hurt by that, but not enough to give up on the story. She called Phipps and said she had evidence the catch and keep group had a connection with a Michigan militia outfit that was tied into the anti-government network in the country. Phipps' eyes lit up at that revelation. He gave her the green light to rework the article and submit a fresh draft. A little later she called again, said she was about ready to finish up. Phipps had gone ahead and scheduled the piece for publication.

"That was dumb," Fitzgerald said.

"Yeah?" Phipps snarled. "Since when were you an editor? We were running short on copy. I needed stuff." He switched tones then, explaining again. "I told her to get everything down cold—all the specifics. She said she was getting 'em."

"But she didn't?"

"She must have. Some guy from up there called the paper, bitched that Allison was pushing him, wanted her off his back. She must have found something."

"Not necessarily."

"Look," Phipps said, "if I knew the answers I wouldn't be calling. I'm asking you to find out." He gave Fitzgerald Allison Thorne's address, a county road in Cordlee.

"My address," Fitzgerald said, "it's Ossning. I'm not even sure where Cordlee is."

"You can't spare time from the novel?"

"That's not the point."

"Good."

"Wait a minute," Fitzgerald said before Phipps hung up. "You get the name of the caller who complained?"

Phipps rustled papers on his desk. "Max Ringwald."

"Okay, now what do I do if I find Allison Thorne?"

"Tell her to get the hell in touch. We've got deadlines."

"If I don't?"

"Then you get the hell in touch."

FITZGERALD HAD GOTTEN one thing settled about the novel—the name of his main character: Henry Walden. It wasn't original. It was the name Hemingway was going to give his dying writer in ''The Snows of Kilimanjaro'' before he reduced it to simply Harry. Hemingway surely had Henry Thoreau in mind, which was ironic because—so Fitzgerald had read somewhere—he didn't care much for Thoreau's work. Too literary or something.

Anyway, Fitzgerald liked the name. It had a nice ring to it. Henry Walden.

The problem was the rest of the novel. All he had for that were notes. He kept working them around, hoping the story would jell. It hadn't—or what had jelled was a story identical to his own. A political reporter for a city newspaper wins a state lottery—not one of the mammoth ones, just two million—and decides to pursue an ambition that has been gnawing at him a long time, which is to spend a year on a river in the north woods, fly fishing through all the seasons. So he settles half the money on his wife, the basis of a friendly divorce, and takes off from the paper and gets a place on a river and takes up serious fishing. He has two other ambitions, to read all of Thoreau and write a novel, and these he takes up, too.

Everything, in other words, goes according to plan.

Except one thing. He hadn't figured on meeting a woman and falling in love and asking her to marry him. Here was a complication he hadn't figured on—and a complication was a plot that after various ins and outs would be resolved. But how?

If he was going to write an autobiographical novel, he and Henry Walden one and the same, he had to live through the story before he knew how it came out. That would take time, and in the meantime all he would have for his novel were notes. The solution was to separate himself from

Henry Walden, spinning a plot from his imagination. But he couldn't get to first base with that.

Was that why newspapermen, stuck with facts, couldn't write novels?

FITZGERALD GOT fresh coffee and went back to the leather armchair, the laptop on his lap, and looked out through the cedars at the Borchard. It was one of Michigan's blue-ribbon trout streams, and since April he had fished it hard, rarely missing a day on the water. He fished through all the insect hatches and had gotten pretty good at picking up fish with nymphs and streamers when there weren't any hatches. In fact, he had gotten pretty good in general. The proof was that Calvin McCann and Verlyn Kelso took him with them to places on the South Branch of the river they had kept secret for years. They had even taken him to some beaver ponds back in the jack pines that were top secret.

Ahead was the short, heartbreaking north woods autumn with the maples along the river flashing flame-red among the pines, then the long winter of brutal cold and deep snow. He looked forward to all of it. He would keep a log fire going and tie flies and sip whiskey and read Thoreau and keep scratching away at his novel, and in late after-noons, a little stir-crazy in the A-frame, he would drive to the Borchard Hotel in Ossning for a drink at the bar while he waited for Mercy Virdon to get off work.

There were plenty of outdoor things to do as well—cross-country skiing on the DNR trails and ice fishing on the lakes that dotted the county and steelhead fishing in the rivers that emptied into Lake Michigan. Half the people in Michigan got out during the winter and went to Florida, leaving it just fine for the other half who liked the quiet and the lack of tourists and the short days and long black nights.

Long black nights.

It was the presence of the woman he loved, Mercy, who tied his life together, who caused him to anticipate the change of seasons, anticipate everything, as optimistic as Thoreau. But for the time being Mercy was gone, and would be for the rest of the month. She was in a Department of Natural Resources seminar at Michigan State in East Lansing, driving back to Ossning on weekends but otherwise gone, leaving Fitzgerald alone in the A-frame, fishing out what was left of the season and trying to make headway with his novel and failing.

He shut down the laptop and sat for a while in the leather chair, sipping coffee, looking out at the Borchard. He still liked the name: Henry Walden. But Phipps had given him another name, one that wasn't made up, the real name of a real person with a real life.

A name for a newspaperman who was on leave of absence and couldn't write a novel.

TWO

If FITZGERALD CAME this time of day, only old-timers left in the Six-Grain Bakery after the morning rush, it meant he didn't want coffee. He wanted to talk. With one hand Bonnie Pym fluffed her hair, currently a soft brown, with the other adjusted her apron. The apron didn't do much as far as spilled coffee went but it showed she still had the waist of a girl.

Fitzgerald came across the street from where he parked his Grand Cherokee, wearing gray corduroy trousers, a blue button-down shirt, and a Detroit Tigers baseball cap. It was what he usually wore—what set him apart from every other unattached man in town. He still looked like he came from a city. The others looked like they came from Ossning and planned to remain there.

When he entered the bakery Bonnie gave him a wink, then went over to refresh the coffee of the old-timers. Fitzgerald took a table in a shaft of sunlight near the front window and began leafing through a copy of the *Call,* the Ossning weekly. Bonnie watched him out of the corner of her eye. He seemed absorbed, as if there was something in the local rag worth knowing about.

"Hey, sugar," she said when she came over to his table. "Somebody die?"

Fitzgerald looked up at her and smiled. "Not exactly." Then he said, "It's funny, Bonnie. I read the sports page and I kind of get to know these kids. All the town's high school heroes. I follow their careers, root for them, want them to do well. At the same time there's some sadness.

It's their moment in the sun. After that it's jobs in the paper mill or at the government trough. All downhill.''

"Tell me about it," Bonnie sighed.

"'The mass of men lead lives of quiet desperation.'''

"That's in there?''

"Somewhere else. A book by Thoreau."

"I don't know," Bonnie said. "Maybe you shouldn't read the paper. Life's tough enough."

Fitzgerald pushed aside the *Call,* leaned back from the table, gave her his full attention.

"Like 'em?" Bonnie asked. She turned from side to side so he had a view of each one. The earrings, linked copper hoops at the end of Navajo-blue chains, nearly touched her shoulders.

"Nice."

"Know where I got 'em? Yard sale. Isn't that something?''

"It is." Fitzgerald asked then if she knew a woman named Allison Thorne.

"Something about her in the paper?''

"No," Fitzgerald said but didn't explain.

Bonnie shook her head. She didn't know anyone by that name. But she knew a guy with the last name—Thorne. He was a hell-raiser who lived back in the pines.

"Cordlee?''

"Haven't the faintest." Bonnie angled a hip to the side, swinging it beneath the apron. "How come you're interested?''

"Someone I know is. The woman I mentioned, she lives near Cordlee. You happen to know where that is?''

"Ask Calvin."

"He'd know?''

"His cabin down there, the address is Cordlee. Unless he's gone to New Zealand already.''

"Not until the end of October," Fitzgerald told her.

"Verlyn's keeping the Kabin Kamp open an extra two weeks to accommodate some Japanese tycoons coming up from Detroit. Calvin's guiding them on the South Branch. It'll be late in the season but he'll get them into brookies and a few browns."

"Calvin can always find fish." Bonnie shifted her weight to the other hip and changed the subject. "Mercy still downstate?"

"Afraid so."

"That why you want to know about Allison Thorne?"

Fitzgerald smiled and said, "I told you. Someone else does."

"That's what they all say."

"Sometimes it's true."

Bonnie smiled back at him and said, "You need anything, you know where to find me."

"I do."

"It ain't Cordlee, sugar."

FROM HIS OFFICE WINDOW Willard Stroud watched the Grand Cherokee come down the main drag, pass the hotel and the line of antique stores, trinket shops, and restaurants that made up the business district of Ossning, turn into the parking area of the city-county building at the end of street. Already the town was half shut down, summer-only places closed, a certainty of winter in the feel of things even though autumn light drenched the street.

In one hand Stroud held a mug of coffee, with the other he absently patted the pocket of his shirt for the package of cigarettes that used to be there. Every morning, drinking his first office coffee, he touched his pocket, finding nothing. Elsie had bought him nicotine gum and nicotine patches, a whole pharmacy of remedies, and they worked— up to a point. Deep down he still craved a smoke. That probably made him, technically speaking, a drug addict.

He could hear Fitzgerald's voice in the outer office, talking with Elsie, passing the time of day. Ordinarily he would let Fitzgerald cool his heels even though the door was open and Elsie knew there was no one with him. You shouldn't be able to waltz right in on the Tamarack County sheriff. There should be some dignity attached to the office. On the other hand, it was a quiet day and the town was half empty and the visitor was someone he was keeping an eye on. Stroud took a last drink of coffee, returned to his desk, called out, "Okay, Elsie."

"I'm not working," Fitzgerald said at once when he entered the office.

"Good," Stroud said.

"Running an errand for a fellow I know."

"Fellow from around here?"

"No," Fitzgerald said but didn't elaborate.

"Care for coffee?" Stroud asked.

Fitzgerald shook his head. "I'm not staying. I'm not working but I know you are." He twisted his head to the side and looked at the framed topographical map of Tamarack County above the filing cabinets. "I remembered it from when I was in before. If it's okay, I'd like to have a close look."

"Help yourself," Stroud said.

Fitzgerald took a slip of paper from his shirt pocket and began studying the map. Stroud could see that what he was looking for was on the far southern edge of the county. He got up from his desk and joined Fitzgerald at the map. "Use some help?" he asked. To his surprise, Fitzgerald nodded. He showed Stroud the slip of paper.

When Stroud first learned that a newspaperman with the *Detroit Free Press* who had won a state lottery was living in the A-frame at Walther Bridge he made a point of looking him up. He wanted to know what was going on. He didn't want to be blindsided by a story appearing one day in the Detroit paper—a story about some goings-on in Tamarack County that he hadn't heard about.

But Fitzgerald told him he wasn't working anymore. He was on indefinite leave of absence from the paper and fishing the Borchard through the year. That wasn't unusual. Dropouts from somewhere, trout bums, were always showing up on the river. What was unusual was that Fitzgerald had stuck it out through a winter, the season that separated men from boys in the north country, and was heading into another. So Stroud had pressed him for a gentleman's agreement: if Fitzgerald went back to work while he was in Ossning he would let the sheriff know in advance. Fitzgerald said he had no trouble with that, and so far he was as good as his word. He hadn't written a line for the Detroit paper.

But Stroud was uneasy. Fitzgerald was friendly and relaxed; people liked him. Elsie, Stroud's wife, did. Elsie thought him good looking in a rumpled sort of way. So, apparently, did Mercy Virdon. She had moved in with him out at Walther Bridge, a fact that was a major contribution to Stroud's uneasiness.

Fitzgerald was now hooked up with the head of the DNR district field office, a thorn in Stroud's side for years, one who made a practice of remaining hazy about the line between her jurisdiction and his. Who knew what Mercy might do—what local scandal she might push Fitzgerald to write up for the Detroit paper? With Mercy there was always some scandal. Maybe he could trust Fitzgerald but he wouldn't put a nickel on Mercy.

There was a name printed on the slip of paper and an address: *Allison Thorne, 62408 Lime Creek Road, Cordlee.* "Know her?" Fitzgerald asked him.

Stroud didn't but he knew the address. With his finger he traced a line on the map from the highway heading west to Traverse City down toward the southern boundary of the

county. "Nothing down there except jack pine. Used to be
some tamarack, how the county got its name, and white
pine. That was before Michigan was logged over."

"A creek?"

"Ditch more like it. Fills in with scum every summer.
The road's name must have been somebody's idea of a
joke. Pea green is more the look." Stroud stepped back
from the map, giving himself a better view of Fitzgerald.
"The fellow you know, he's acquainted with that neck of
the woods?"

Fitzgerald looked back, meeting Stroud's gaze. "Why do
you ask?"

"I wouldn't think anyone you knew would be."

"No lottery winners?"

"Plenty trying to be."

Fitzgerald smiled. "The map's a big help. I see the route
to take."

"You'll need the four-wheeler."

"That bad?"

"Worse."

After Fitzgerald left the office Stroud examined the map
more closely. It was a big county with lots of territory to
cover, much of it difficult terrain. It was a county you could
get lost in—or lose yourself in. Down where Fitzgerald was
going it was easy to fade away into the pine barrens. But
that wasn't what was on his mind. He didn't have anybody
lost. What was on his mind was Fitzgerald. He hadn't hesitated to show Stroud the name and address on the slip of
paper, but otherwise he kept a closed mouth.

Stroud went back to his desk, looked into the empty coffee mug, patted the chest pocket of his shirt. Then he called
out to Elsie, asking if Bonnie Pym had come around yet
with morning sweet rolls from the Six-Grain Bakery.

"NAW," CALVIN TOLD HIM, "never heard the name."

"The address is Cordlee," Fitzgerald said.

"Must be new. I know all the women there."

"What I figured."

"Unless she's over the hill or something."

"Her name's Allison Thorne. That has a young ring to it."

"Then she must be new."

Fitzgerald was willing to let it rest at that, so Calvin left him on the screened-in porch and went back inside the cabin to brew the tea. When Calvin offered him a mug Fitzgerald had said he preferred coffee, so Calvin had told him about an article he read on the benefits of green tea, brewed exactly two minutes. It was what the Chinese drank and they all lived to be octogenarians. "You're a puritan," Fitzgerald said. "No weed, no booze, no coffee. Celibacy next."

"Naw," Calvin told him. "I draw the line before then."

With mugs of tea they sat on the porch and looked out through scrub vegetation at the South Branch, the day warming, sun flashing on the water. Calvin had been thinking about going out and flipping streamers when Fitzgerald pulled up in his vehicle. That was unusual. Fitzgerald didn't ordinarily come around, which was understandable. The dirt road off the highway that led to the cabin was long and rutted, which was the way Calvin liked it, limiting visitors to those with good reason to see him. When he and Fitzgerald got together it was usually at Verlyn Kelso's fly shop—or Calvin stopped at the A-frame at Walther Bridge when they went fishing. They always took his pickup. In Calvin's view Fitzgerald's Grand Cherokee wasn't a proper vehicle for serious fishing. Vehicle like that, you looked like you thought you were in an Orvis ad.

Calvin had to wrench his attention away from the appearance of the river and the possibility of browns moving out of deep cover, stirred by autumn sunlight and the prospect of a good meal before the weather shut down. Fitzgerald was asking if he knew about a group called the Catch and Keep Alliance.

"It's catch and release," Calvin corrected him.

Fitzgerald shook his head. "Catch and Keep. That's what they advocate."

"Here?"

"On the Borchard."

"Naw," Calvin said, "never heard of 'em. You've got people against catch and release, that's so. Figure they ought to be able to keep a fish or two. I agree."

Fitzgerald looked surprised.

"Human nature," Calvin said, "grilling a fish now and then. Besides, catch and release's a scam."

"Try telling Mercy that."

"Mercy believes the DNR propaganda. That's understandable. It's her job. The fact is catch and release doesn't work."

"She's got statistics," Fitzgerald began, but Calvin cut him off.

"I got eyes. I see what happens on float trips—the way people release fish. First of all they play them too long, eight-inch brooks you'd think were monster browns. Then they don't know how to hold them or remove hooks. They put pressure on the gills, force out the hook, draw blood, take pictures, toss the fish in the water. You put a bleeding fish back it ends up dead."

Fitzgerald shrugged. He wasn't convinced.

"I'll tell you something else. The DNR, all the organizations, they aren't serious about catch and release. They were, they'd require barbless hooks."

"Some places do."

"Not the Borchard. It's catch and release but you can use barbs. Ridiculous."

"That's a point," Fitzgerald admitted.

"Then they ought to require everyone have a Ketchum Release on their vest. You got one, you release the fish in the water, never put a finger on it."

"That's another point."

"So there," Calvin said, closing his case.

He and Fitzgerald sat for a while, quiet, drinking two-minute green tea from big mugs, looking out at the river from the porch. Then they began talking about New Zealand, about what the season would be like when Calvin got there, about what bugs would be hatching, about river conditions. Calvin found himself talking with Fitzgerald while one part of his mind, already in New Zealand, was thinking about Patty Dunvoold, his woman down there. Patty was a divorcée with two teenage children and she had no interest in getting married. Having Calvin around half the year, guiding for the angling hotels on the Clutha when he wasn't off fishing for himself, was all she needed.

Maybe it was.

Fitzgerald had put a word in his mind that hadn't been there before: celibacy. Was that what Patty practiced when he was back in Michigan, guiding there? Six months of Calvin, six months of nothing? It didn't seem reasonable.

"Could be you're right," he said to Fitzgerald. "Name like that, Allison, she could be on the young side."

Fitzgerald looked startled by the shift in the conversation.

"You find out," Calvin said, "let me know."

THREE

FROM THE ASPHALT county highway Fitzgerald followed a gravel road deep into the pine barrens, long curls of dust trailing the Cherokee. A few mobile homes were visible, all half hidden in the woods; at each mailbox along the way he pulled to the side, inspecting the numbers. The one he was hunting for, numbers scrawled in faded paint, came at a point where the road abruptly dead-ended into a two-track. An electrical line snaked ahead through the woods.

The route dipped and twisted for another mile or two before he came to a mobile home set on an eroded slash of open ground. Ahead, where the two-track had been, jack pines rose in a solid wall. He switched off the engine but didn't leave the Cherokee. He might have found the place he was looking for but nothing felt right about it. Would a newspaper stringer live back in here? It was a good fifteen miles to a gas-station convenience store. And would she live as dismally as this?

The recluses of the pine barrens tended to have vehicles and parts of vehicles rusting away about them, but Allison Thorne's place was encircled by a small fleet—a yellow school bus, what appeared to be an old military ambulance, several tractors, an assortment of vintage earth-moving machines. The mobile home itself was worn and weathered, flimsy windows sagging in their frames, overhead the canopy of a shingled roof for snow protection. Snow. When Fitzgerald thought of that he wondered how Allison Thorne got out in winter. The county probably plowed only as far as the mailbox.

He considered turning around, letting Phipps do his own

work, heading back to Ossning and some late-afternoon fishing on the Borchard. He could stop at Calvin's place and fish the South Branch. He had a standing invitation from Calvin to use his cabin as an access point. Or he could head over to Kelso's Kabin Kamp on the mainstream and hang around Verlyn's fly shop. There were lots of things he could do—but, doing any of them, he wouldn't understand about Allison Thorne.

She would stick in his mind, planted there by Phipps.

He got out of the Cherokee, made his way across hard-packed dirt. The place was quiet, no children or animals about, but one of the vehicles, a dust-streaked Ford parked at an angle at the mobile home's door, looked like it was serviceable. He noticed then what he hadn't seen from the two-track, a satellite dish set off to the side—an indication, finally, he was at the right place. A stringer for a paper would need to keep up with the area news, such as it was, on the tube.

Steps led to a half-finished wood deck jutting out from the door, salvage lumber stacked on the ground beneath, the boards warped and discolored. Fitzgerald paused at the foot of the steps, thinking it likely he had been seen coming from the two-track, seen crossing the yard. Someone might come to the door—someone, it occurred to him, with an aversion to strangers who could be bill collectors or the government, take your pick.

He waited, shuffling his feet in the dirt, trying to appear harmless. "Hello," he called out when no one appeared at the door. "Anyone home?" When there was no response he called out again. Nothing. The door of the mobile home, he noticed then, wasn't entirely closed. He gave one more try—"Allison Thorne?"—before he took a deep breath and moved up the steps.

In retrospect, it seemed he knew what he would find before he knocked on the door, waited, knocked again, opened the door cautiously, peered inside. In retrospect, he could feel it coming, the sickness rising from his stomach in an acid rush.

In retrospect, he knew from the beginning what Phipps had done to him.

THE WOMAN, her back to him, her hair reddish brown, was bent forward over a small computer table, her face resting just to the side of the keyboard. The computer was on, a screen-saver showing shifting geometric patterns. The woman seemed as if she might have taken a break to rest her eyes—seemed like that except her forehead was pressed flat against the table, both arms dangling to the floor. Fitzgerald started to say something, speak her name again, but stopped before he made a sound. It wasn't reddish brown hair he was looking at. It was blood and gore. The back of the woman's head was nearly gone.

He managed to turn around, stumble back through the door, grasp a railing of the unfinished deck, before his stomach rose into his mouth.

He waited there, wiping himself with a handkerchief, not wanting to go back inside. There was no need. He could drive back the way he came, locate a phone, call the sheriff's office. But there would be a phone inside the mobile home—the quicker way. Phipps had tried to reach Allison Thorne by phone. He had to go back through the door.

He tried not to look at the woman's head, to see everything else. The computer table where she had been working was at the side of a long tunnel of living area off a galley kitchen. From the kitchen a narrow hallway led back to what were probably bedrooms and a bathroom. The living area had a wood-burning stove, a pair of armchairs in front of a TV set, the computer table against a side wall. In contrast to its outside appearance, everything within the mobile home was in an orderly condition.

Everything except the back of the woman's head.

Fitzgerald glanced in her direction, immediately looked away. The woman had been sitting at the switched-on computer when she was battered or shot from behind, her body falling forward, head coming to rest on the table. Given the narrowness of the room, the attack would have come from close behind her. Fired from the kitchen area, a shot would have struck the side of her head, not the back.

He edged his way through to the kitchen, careful to touch nothing. On the Formica counter was an electric coffee-maker, a small amount of coffee in the glass container, a mug nearby, half full. He dipped a finger in the liquid. Stone cold.

He moved back to the living area, avoiding the woman's body, examining the computer table. Would a writer working at a computer return a half-finished mug of coffee to the kitchen? He wouldn't. He saw it then, a matching coffee mug, resting on the carpeted floor just to the side of one of the woman's dangling arms. That mug was also half full. There was little room on the top of the computer table, so after she sipped her coffee the woman must have placed the mug beside her on the floor.

But what did that tell him? That the woman and her killer had drunk coffee together—that the killer, therefore, was someone known to her? Wasn't that the way it was with most killings, carried out by family or acquaintances rather than strangers? Fitzgerald shook his head. What was he trying to do? Who designated him a detective? He had no certainty the dead woman in front of him was Allison Thorne.

FROM THE PHONE on the wall in the kitchen area he made a 911 call, reasonably calm about it, telling the woman on the other end about the situation, giving her the address.

He was told to stay where he was, do nothing, touch nothing. Sheriff's deputies and an ambulance were on the way.

After he replaced the phone Fitzgerald remained in the kitchen, looking along the length of the mobile home into the living area. The killer might have stood here, drinking coffee, looking toward the woman as she sat at the computer table. She hadn't known what was about to happen to her. The killer had drawn some kind of concealed weapon, a handgun most likely, moved behind her, fired at point-blank range. He couldn't have used a rifle or shotgun—couldn't unless he entered the mobile home armed that way and ordered the woman to sit at the computer table, turn on the machine. But that possibility left out of the account the two coffee mugs, the likelihood the woman and the killer had drunk coffee together. Would the killer have ordered that, too?

One thing was certain. The woman was at the computer, working or beginning to, when she was killed.

Fitzgerald went back into the living area, moving around the woman's body, trying not to look. Her forehead had hit the table just to the side of the keyboard. He didn't want to think of that, the front of her head, how it looked. He wanted to concentrate on the computer, a Macintosh, the mouse on a blue pad off to the side, next to that a clear-plastic container of disks placed beside an HP printer. The woman might have been stuck out in the pine barrens in a mobile home but at least she had a phone, a satellite dish, and a computer system. By reaching around her body he could touch the keyboard. He took out his handkerchief, covered his index finger, pressed the space bar.

The screen saver vanished, replaced with an empty screen, an unnamed file of a word-processing program. He knew about that, empty screens. At the last moment of her life the woman had been looking at one. He felt a surge of kinship—at the same time knew the difference, that a bullet had interrupted her flow of words. He closed his eyes for a moment, trying to center his attention. The woman had opened up a new file, meaning to write something, but had been stopped before she entered a word or named the file. Or was it the other way around? Had the killer been going to dictate something to her, waited until she was ready, then pulled the trigger?

Fitzgerald opened his eyes, looked back at the empty screen. There was one thing more.

He covered the mouse with his handkerchief, closed the word-processing program, began searching the computer's hard drive, scanning the names of the files until he came to the one he was looking for: *C/K Alliance.* He opened the file, quickly scrolled through it. There was no question now: the dead woman was the *Free Press* stringer, Allison Thorne.

The story read smoothly, a competent job, but there was no mention of Michigan militia or anti-government groups. The main focus was a meeting with DNR officials that had gotten heated, the catch and keep contingent arguing their position, the DNR defending the policy of catch and release. Two property owners along the river were quoted, while the chief spokesman on the DNR side was the head of the district field office in Ossning, Mercy Virdon. To all appearances, the story was the one Phipps had read and turned down, not the revised story he scheduled for publication.

Fitzgerald closed the file and returned to the hard drive, searching for something more. There were other files that, given the names, might be stories Allison Thorne had intended for the *Free Press* or other publications she was stringing for. There wasn't time to open them, make certain. He went back to the story on the Catch and Keep Alliance, read it again, more carefully this time. He hadn't missed anything. It was able but run-of-the-mill work, publishable but not in the Sunday magazine of a Detroit paper.

He covered his hand with the handkerchief and opened the plastic container of disks beside the computer. He ran through what Allison Thorne had printed on the labels, locating what he was looking for, a disk with the label *C/K Alliance*. He inserted the disk in the computer, brought up a copy of the story he had read on the hard drive. So Allison had made a backup of her story, the usual procedure, but there was nothing more on the disk—and no other disks in the plastic container with material on the Alliance. He might not understand her labeling system—that was a possibility—but all indications were, after a hurried search through the hard drive and backup disks, that Allison hadn't written a word on the revised story.

Fitzgerald kept looking at the backup story on the screen, thinking, knowing he had to act quickly. Stroud's deputies would be on their way to Lime Creek Road; an ambulance was coming. He lifted a sheet of paper from the printer tray, copied down the names of the two property owners mentioned in the story, folded the paper into his pocket. He looked again at the story on the screen, uncertain, trying to make up his mind. Finally he closed the backup story, ejected the disk, replaced the disk in the plastic case. He returned then to the computer's hard drive, reopened the word-processing program, bringing up an empty file. In a few moments the screen saver would fill the screen. Everything would appear just the way it had when he entered the mobile home.

He eased back from the computer table, looking at it, trying to take it all in while avoiding Allison Thorne's body. Her revised story, the one she told Phipps was nearly finished, wasn't the only thing missing. There were no notebooks on the table, no pens or pencils—save for the computer system itself, no working tools of a journalist. The ordinary process was to make hand-written notes, enter the notes in a computer, work the notes around into finished stories.

The notebooks might be kept elsewhere, back in a rear room of the mobile home. Fitzgerald was about to turn, begin moving down the narrow hallway, when, abruptly, he froze. There could be more than notebooks back there. There could be other bodies, an entire family, all massacred.

Or, waiting still, a killer.

He managed to move through the door, reach the edge of the half-finished deck, bend to the hard-packed dirt, before his stomach filled his mouth.

FOUR

MERCY ASKED HIM to spell the surname. Then she told him she had seen it on some paperwork, but it belonged to a male. DNR enforcement people had fined a fellow named Thorne for poaching or lacking a license or fishing out of season.

"Probably all three, as a matter of fact."

"A hell-raiser," Fitzgerald said, "according to Bonnie Pym."

"She'd know."

"But Bonnie didn't know an Allison Thorne."

"Neither do I."

There was silence and Mercy wondered if Fitzgerald was still on the phone line. "You okay?" she asked him.

"Sure," he said, though his voice gave her no assurance.

"Seriously?"

"Sure."

"I should be there."

"I wish you were."

Where she was at the moment was at a public telephone in a student dormitory that Michigan State hadn't filled for the fall term, the pinch-penny DNR rushing in to fill the vacancies. She had anticipated a decent motel, one with long-term suites, but what she got was a student room with four bland walls and metal furnishings. At least the room was a single, but the dorm was mixed-sex, which meant putting something on when she went down the hall to the showers. That the DNR district field officers attending the seminar were housed together made it worse. Those she met on the way were colleagues, males one and all, with whom she had labored to develop a relationship based on professional competence. Having them eye her in a different light as she passed by in robe and shower clogs was downright maddening.

A weekend was coming up, and on weekends she drove back to Ossning. She could make a long weekend, cutting out early, probably causing little notice. Besides, the seminar had become a drag—the latest on stream management, with MSU experts droning on, so impressed with how much they knew you wanted to gag. She had learned a few things, she had to admit—but only a few. The bottom line these days was to leave streams alone, let nature heal itself. The more you tinkered, the worse the results. With the really big problem, acid rain choking everything, there wasn't much to be done short of massive global change.

But if she went back early she might give Fitzgerald the wrong impression. He would do it for her. He wouldn't hesitate. But on her side she was trying to maintain a measure of distance, letting him know there were limits to living together, that she wasn't there for his every need. She wasn't a wife. He had gone through a bad experience, discovering the dead woman that way, but now it was over. Willard Stroud had taken charge. All Mercy could do now was hold Fitzgerald's hand, give him comfort. Like a wife.

"This Phipps," she said to him, "who'd you say he was?"

Fitzgerald told her again and this time she listened, concentrating. When he was done she said, "So why didn't you tell him to find Allison Thorne himself?"

"I should have."

"He interrupted your work on the novel."

"In a way. The reason I went along—it had something to do with what Allison was working on, the Catch and Keep Alliance. It caught my attention."

Mercy said, "You didn't tell me about that. What's that got to do with anything?"

Fitzgerald explained, telling her about the article for the *Free Press* that made a connection between the local organization and some Michigan militia group. Phipps had gone ahead and scheduled the article for publication in the paper's Sunday magazine. "I asked Calvin about the local group," Fitzgerald added. "He'd never heard of it."

"Of course not. Calvin lives in a cocoon. He guides, he fishes—that's it. Then he goes to New Zealand half the year and does the same thing. Calvin couldn't tell you the name of another soul on the South Branch, not that there is one within a mile."

"But you know about them."

Mercy couldn't keep the irritation out of her voice. "The people who want to keep fish? It's my business to know."

"I should have called you," Fitzgerald said, "before I went looking for Allison."

"That's true." Then she softened and said, "I would've been in the seminar anyway. You wouldn't have gotten me."

MERCY TOLD HIM what she knew about the background of the Catch and Keep Alliance, which in fact wasn't a great deal. Getting flies only, catch and release water on a lengthy stretch of the Borchard's mainstream and smaller portions of the North Branch and South Branch had been a long, acrimonious battle. The DNR and most of the conservation groups had been pitted against a vocal group of property owners on the river and Chamber of Commerce types in Ossning.

"The Chamber thought the regulations would drive away bait fishermen, along with the money they spent in town. We had studies showing fly fishermen actually spend more—and more of them would fish the river if we had a no-kill regulation. But the Chamber wasn't convinced. For their part, the property owners thought their God-given rights as American citizens and Tamarack County taxpayers included eating fish if they damned-well wanted to.''

Fitzgerald said, ''Calvin agrees with them. He thinks it's natural.''

''You know something? Calvin's got some right-wing tendencies. Don't let his ponytail fool you.''

''He's got opinions,'' Fitzgerald admitted.

''Half of them wrong. Did he tell you catch and release doesn't work?''

''He mentioned it.''

''I've sent him studies but he's so stubborn it doesn't make any difference. One they did out in Yellowstone shows trout are caught and released an average of eleven times apiece during a season. Some die, sure, but most live again to be caught another day. The health of every fishery improves with catch and release.''

''He thinks catch and release doesn't make sense without requiring barbless hooks.''

Mercy shook her head. ''I'm for barbless. Who isn't? But there's some research—controversial, it's true—that shows it may not be so important. Fish are released in about the same amount of time regardless of the hook.''

She knew she was on her soap box, rattling on. But Calvin was a sore subject. He probably wouldn't irritate her if she didn't like him so much—and, after her marriage to Verlyn Kelso fell apart, they had been a pair for a while. That was an interlude in her life she would just as soon forget. Only one good thing had come from it: Calvin had taught her a few things about tying tiny flies, midges and the like. When it came to tying, Calvin was a genius.

''Eventually we won the battle but there was leftover bitterness. And we made our point—the river's in better shape because of catch and release. I know, Calvin doesn't believe it. But Calvin's wrong. Anyway, there's this bitterness and every now and then there's an effort to reverse the regulations. It's America, after all—the way the country works, people getting together, forming organizations, lobbying for something or other. That's what this latest group is all about. They've had a few meetings, produced some literature they stick in mailboxes. I went to one meeting at the VFW, invited, and got myself roundly chewed out.''

''I know,'' Fitzgerald said.

''How?''

''From Allison's story. It was on the hard drive.''

''What hard drive?''

''In the mobile home. I went into her computer, opened the file. You're mentioned.''

''You read the story *there?*''

''The main thing in it was the meeting the Alliance members had with you. You were quoted a few times.''

''Good Lord. I remember Gus Thayer at the meeting, covering it for the *Call,* but I don't remember anyone else. Allison Thorne didn't speak to me afterward.''

''She wasn't interested in you.'' Then Fitzgerald asked, ''The Alliance members, they're all property owners on the river?''

''As far as I know. The Chamber has dropped out. But I've never heard talk about a connection with any militia outfit. That's wild.''

''But it's possible?''

''Well, sure. I suppose so.''

There was a pause on the other end of the line before Fitzgerald said, ''Allison told Phipps she had evidence.''

''And you think that's what got her killed?''

BACK IN HER ROOM, four bland walls and metal furnishings, Mercy propped pillows on the bed and settled in with a folder of journal articles to read for the seminar. But not just yet. Angling her head toward the window she could see the upper branches of a sugar maple, the leaves starting to turn. One thing to say for MSU—the campus was a dream this time of year. In Ossning there weren't many maples, but those there were would be full crimson now among the pines.

Which brought her back to the phone conversation with Fitzgerald.

Fooling with Allison Thorne's computer had been stupid. Willard Stroud would have his hide if he found out. Fitzgerald said he was careful not to leave fingerprints, but in a situation like that, dead body right beside you, how could you be absolutely certain? And the story he found hadn't been worth the risk. It hadn't said a word about a link between the Catch and Keep Alliance and any militia group. It seemed to be the story the *Free Press* had turned down, not a new story Allison Thorne was working on that Phipps had slated for publication.

Fitzgerald said three names were mentioned, hers opposed to ending the no-kill regulation, two property owners in favor. He asked if she knew the people and she told him of course she did. They were all at the meeting together; besides, it was her business to know. But based on what she knew they were harmless—people with time on their hands and too much money. You didn't live on the mainstream of the Borchard these days without money.

"Meaning me?" Fitzgerald had asked.

"If the shoe fits."

"Anyway, I want to do some checking around. I feel I owe it to the paper. One of its stringers was murdered—maybe murdered in the line of duty. The paper can't ignore that."

Mercy said, "Fine. But you're on leave of absence, remember? If the *Free Press* wants to investigate the murder, let them send someone to Ossning. Let them send Phipps. He isn't working on a novel.''

''You've got a point,'' Fitzgerald said, though she knew he didn't think so. She caught the tone in his voice, thick with false understanding, the tone a man uses when he plans to ignore all the perfectly sensible things you have just said.

Mercy began reading one of the seminar articles—about the construction and maintenance of sand traps on small streams—and got no further than the tedious opening page before she was back thinking about Fitzgerald. He was in his second year of living on the Borchard but he didn't know the territory. Ossning was an in-grown place with old families and old feuds and lots of things better left alone. She had lived in the town her entire life and still wasn't always certain of her footing. If Fitzgerald started his own investigation of Allison Thorne's murder you couldn't tell what he might stumble into. There was no good reason to think militia types were involved, but if they were—if Allison Thorne had turned up some real evidence—he could find himself in serious trouble. Remember what happened out in Oklahoma City. Mercy had read somewhere that, contrary to all reason, the underground anti-government movement in the country had become even stronger following that mad devastation.

She began packing then, taking her time about it, not tossing things in her duffel bag. She even put the folder of seminar readings in the bag. There didn't have to be an appearance of furious haste in the way she was acting.

Like a wife.

FIVE

WILLARD STROUD put him in the small windowless room he used for interviews. He wasn't conducting a formal interview but he wanted Fitzgerald to feel it wasn't a casual conversation, either. He needed some answers. To soften things he had Elsie bring them each mugs of coffee. Fitzgerald still looked like he needed that.

Zack Cox, the deputy who arrived first at Lime Creek Road, had found him sitting in his vehicle, ashen-faced and shaky. When Stroud appeared he got a quick statement from Fitzgerald, then told him to go home, get cleaned up, come into the city-county building when he felt up to it. He hadn't wanted a newspaperman around while the county medical examiner, Slocum Byrd, did a preliminary analysis of the body and the mobile home was searched.

"Feeling better?" he asked him now.

Fitzgerald nodded and managed a weak smile.

"Good," Stroud said. "Then clear up something for me. You came in this morning, looked up an address out south in the county. Then you went down there, found a dead woman, and it so happens she worked for the Detroit paper you work for. That's a coincidence and I'm not comfortable with coincidences."

"Neither am I," Fitzgerald said.

"Then maybe you ought to explain."

Stroud sipped his coffee, patted his breast pocket, sipped more coffee. Fitzgerald didn't answer him right away. It was as if he was considering his reply—or getting his story straight.

"Look," Fitzgerald said finally, "what I told you this

morning, that was the whole thing. I wasn't working for
the paper—and neither, to be technical about it, was Allison
Thorne. She was a stringer, paid space-rate if anything she
wrote was printed. I went out to see her as a favor for a
fellow I know on the paper. He called this morning before
I came in here.''

''What's his name?''

Fitzgerald told him and Stroud wrote the name down. He
wanted to give the impression he meant to check. ''A favor—that sounds like working.''

''I wasn't writing for the paper, that's what I meant. I
told you I'd let you know if I started doing that again. So
I didn't say anything when I came in here. There was nothing to say.''

''You could have told me about the story the woman
was writing.''

''It was about a group of people on the river calling
themselves the Catch and Keep Alliance. That's all I knew.
Detroit didn't want me involved in the story. They just
wanted to find out why they couldn't contact her.''

''And you found out.''

Stroud pushed his chair back from the table. Putting faith
in a newspaperman was a mistake—they would smile at
you while they slipped a knife in your back. But the fact
was, he believed Fitzgerald—believed he would keep his
word. A second fact was he needed Fitzgerald on his side,
cooperating. Fitzgerald was the one who had come upon
the murder scene. Stroud needed what he had seen, what
he remembered, all the details.

''All right. Go through it again. Start from when you left
here.''

Fitzgerald repeated the story he had given on Lime Creek
Road. Stroud stopped him at points, getting more detail,
but the story was the same. The door of the mobile home
had been open—that was why Fitzgerald had gone in. Oth-

erwise he would have kept calling out Allison Thorne's name, and if there was no response, and there wouldn't have been, he would have left. And the computer was switched on. Allison Thorne had been sitting in front of it when she was shot.

"She must have been working," Fitzgerald said.

"Nothing there," Stroud said. "She'd opened a word-processing program but the file was empty."

"So she was just starting to work. Or maybe the killer told her to write something, then shot her before she could."

"That doesn't make sense."

"It doesn't," Fitzgerald agreed.

WHEN THERE WAS a knock on the interview room door Stroud got up and spoke with Elsie in the hallway. She said there was a call for him. He went back to his office, closed the door, and talked to the medical examiner. Slocum Byrd had the time of death.

"A good forty-eight hours before she was found, Willard."

"And there's no question she was shot? Nothing else?"

"Nope. One bullet, back of the head. Slick as a whistle."

Stroud closed his eyes. Slocum had a gift for tasteless phrasing, one shared with every medical examiner he had known. Did the work do it or were they born that way? One of life's minor mysteries.

"Another thing you should know. She was pregnant, right near the end of the first trimester."

"God help us," Stroud said. He kept his eyes closed and leaned back in his chair. He would never understand that, either. Life was all we had and we wasted it right and left. Then he pulled himself upright. He had another wasted life on his hands now—and a hunch who had done the wasting. Or, more accurately, why.

"Give me your opinion," he said when he returned to Fitzgerald in the interview room. "Allison Thorne was shot in the back of the head, the bullet exiting through the front. Her head, sitting there at the table, was exactly in line with the computer monitor. You'd expect the bullet to hit it. Instead it went through the wall just off to the side. Flimsy things, mobile homes. Anyway, from the hole we can figure pretty much where the killer stood. Not directly behind her. There was a slight angle, enough so the bullet exited above her right eye, missed the monitor by a fraction, went through the wall."

"I didn't know that," Fitzgerald said.

"You wouldn't, not the way her face was down on the table." Stroud paused, looking at Fitzgerald, going slow. "So the killer was handy with a gun. Or lucky. But let's say he was handy and he wanted to kill the woman but he didn't want to shatter the monitor. So he took his time. The woman was sitting at the computer, getting ready to do something, behind her he's setting up the angle. All very calculated. Up here, we don't get killings like that very often. We get crimes of passion, people all heated up, pulling a gun or knife. They leave a big mess. This killing wasn't like that."

"No."

"So how do we figure a killing like this one? Very careful, calculated."

"Fingerprints?"

"Nothing good enough."

"And no other evidence?"

"Like I say, a very careful killing. Who'd do it that way?"

"I think you're going to tell me," Fitzgerald said.

Stroud allowed himself a smile. Then he got up, went to the door, called to Elsie to bring him the fax sheet that had come in from Lansing on Raymond Alvin Thorne.

"WHAT IT BOILS DOWN TO is he's done about everything short of murder. Began when he was twelve—stole a car and wrecked it over in Kinnich, went on from there. Surprising thing is he's only spent three years total in Jackson. Lucky guy like that ought to play the lottery."

"I take it," Fitzgerald said, "he's Allison's husband."

Stroud kept looking at the fax sheet. "I've got his birth date here. Ray Thorne's forty-seven. How old would you say the woman was?"

Fitzgerald shook his head.

"Late twenties, according to Slocum Byrd. Incidentally, she was pregnant, maybe three months along."

"That's awful," Fitzgerald said.

"Ray might be her husband, but I got a feeling he wasn't. Elsie checked and there's no record of a marriage in Tamarack County. That doesn't mean much. They could have been married anywhere. But my feeling is they were only living together out there on Lime Creek Road."

"She was using his name."

"True," Stroud said, "but maybe she just liked it better."

"Any background information on her yet?"

"We're working on it. Trying to locate next of kin. Woman that young, there should be parents living."

"I don't envy you having to tell them."

"Never gets easier," Stroud said.

They sat there, sipping what was left of the coffee, not looking at one another, letting time pass. It was Fitzgerald who broke the quiet. "So you're looking at Ray Thorne as her killer?"

"A police record, prison time—the arrow points his way. And the fact we haven't found him yet. The state police are hunting for the vehicle he drives—blue Ford Econoline van. But there's something that doesn't figure: Why would he want to kill a young woman like that?"

"Because she was pregnant?"

"Maybe. But that early along he might not have known she was. If he did, and they didn't want a child, they could have done something—got an abortion over in Traverse City. There was no reason to kill Allison because she was pregnant."

"Except if it just irritated him. She wasn't supposed to get pregnant but she did."

"Then he would have killed her in anger. He wouldn't have been concerned about tearing up the computer system. You look at his record you don't get the impression Ray Thorne's a computer type. And why kill her in the mobile home at all? He wanted to kill her, he's the type would shoot her out in the woods, bury the body, nobody would ever know. If he was questioned he'd say she took off for another man."

Fitzgerald said, "So if Ray Thorne isn't the one, who is?"

"You said you didn't go past the kitchen of the mobile home."

Fitzgerald nodded.

"You did, you wouldn't have found anything. Two bedrooms, bathroom, everything spic and span. I got a notion Ray didn't spend a lot of time at home—or else Allison was always picking up after him. It was her place, that mobile home."

"Meaning?"

"Ray was occupied elsewhere."

"He has a good-sized junkyard outside."

"So does everyone living down there."

"Job?"

"I'd be surprised."

Fitzgerald waited.

"Just a feeling," Stroud said. "Whatever Ray was up to, that's what did in Allison."

SIX

A PART OF HIM wanted to head back to the A-frame, have a drink, crawl into bed, blot out the day. But another part wasn't up to an empty house, a vacant bed, the deep quiet of the woods. The end of Allison Thorne's life would cause him, in the dark night of the soul somewhere between drink and sleep, to begin a consideration of last things. He wasn't up to that, either.

Fitzgerald parked the Cherokee in front of the Borchard Hotel and went inside. The barroom off the lobby was dark and empty, the half-priced drinks before dinner still an hour away. The bartender, Sandy, looked his way when he came in, but she didn't come right over when he took one of the high, padded stools at the bar. Sandy had a gift for reading moods. She could tell he needed space as much as a drink.

All the same, she was bubbling over with questions. News of the murder of Allison Thorne would have run through Ossning by now, and the barroom of the hotel was one of the centers for dispensing the latest information. Sandy's job bore some similarity to that of a news reader on CNN. At the moment she couldn't wait to have her script updated.

"Beer?" she asked him finally.

"Whiskey."

"No ice, right?"

When Sandy came back with the drink she took up a position in front of him, a hip thrust to one side, a hand absently running through frizzy brown hair. She was trying hard to look casual. "Phil told me," she said. When Fitzgerald looked blank she added, "One of the ambulance guys."

Fitzgerald asked, "Did you know Allison Thorne?"

"Nobody did. But I knew Ray, all right. Complete loser."

"Seems to be the consensus."

"He never came in here. Didn't have the nerve." Sandy leaned forward and braced a hand against the bar. "He do it?"

"I don't know."

"He probably did. Guys like that, they snap, you don't want to be in the way. You were lucky he wasn't still around."

"I suppose," Fitzgerald said. He was going to add that he didn't feel particularly lucky when Sandy looked up, toward the entrance door, then leaned close across the bar.

"Your luck just changed," she whispered.

IT TOOK THE EDITOR, publisher, and sole reporter of the *Ossning Call* a while to adjust to the darkness and detect Fitzgerald at the bar. Then he came right over from the entrance. Gus Thayer didn't have a gift for sensing moods.

"Called your place and left a message. Stroud said you'd gone home. Then I spotted the vehicle parked out front." Gus told Sandy to pull him a beer while he worked a spiral notebook out of his hip pocket, dropped it on the bar, flipped to a fresh page. "I could use a quote or two."

"Afraid the sheriff's your man," Fitzgerald told him.

"Look of the murder scene, that sort of thing. I filed a couple 'graphs with the AP. What I need is for the *Call.* Page one."

"Sorry."

Gus squinted at him through a pair of black-rimmed glasses beneath crewcut hair that looked like a bristling field of gray spikes. Fitzgerald read the look. *What the hell,* it said. *We're in the same business. You scratch my back, I'll scratch yours.* The problem with the look was that Gus Thayer had nothing Fitzgerald needed.

When he moved north from Detroit, Gus had wanted to do a feature story for the *Call,* the point being that after Fitzgerald won a state lottery he hadn't gone off to Florida and bought a condo and cruiser but settled on the Borchard River at Walther Bridge and became a member of the Ossning community. Gus said Ossning needed all the good news it could get. Fitzgerald said that was fine but he didn't care for the publicity, thanks all the same. Gus was miffed over the lack of cooperation but had written a story anyway, minus quotes from Fitzgerald, and continued to treat him as if they shared a bond. They were fellow journalists, living on the edge.

"Off the record then," Gus said, and closed the spiral notebook. "My theory is the husband drilled her."

Against his better judgment Fitzgerald said, "Oh?"

"Up here, a wife pulls the trigger, she drills the guy a dozen times while he's sacked out. Husbands don't waste the ammo. One shot, they get in the pickup, hightail it for Canada."

"Interesting," Fitzgerald said.

"On the other hand, what I hear is there's no evidence of a fight. Husband gets rid of his wife, there's usually a blow-up first—things thrown around, busted up. Maybe she's coming at him with a blade, that's why he drills her. So that's a problem, lack of a mess. Don't suppose you'd care to confirm or deny."

"No," Fitzgerald said.

Gus took a long drink of beer, wiped foam from his lips with the back of a hand, tried a different tack. "Let's see if I got the sequence right. Off the record still. You went to her place because she was stringing for the *Free Press.*

About a story—something she was doing but hadn't finished. You wanted to find out why."

"Stroud told you this?" Fitzgerald asked.

"But he didn't say about the story—what it was."

Fitzgerald shrugged. "The story doesn't matter if the killing was the result of a domestic dispute."

"True," Gus agreed, "but makes you think. Journalist working on a story gets drilled—" He took another swallow of beer and squinted at Fitzgerald from behind the black-rimmed glasses. "She tried to get on with the *Call.*"

"Oh?"

"She was new up here, trying to put together a bunch of papers, stringing for them. She wanted to send in her résumé and I said okay, but we couldn't pay. She said that wasn't the kind of stringer she wanted to be. The reason I remember is her name. Women up here don't have names like Allison."

"When was this?" Fitzgerald asked.

"Six months ago, give or take. The last name didn't ring a bell at the time. Now it does. Ray Thorne made the paper a few times."

"Anything serious?"

"Enough to get him a ticket to Jackson. But I got to look up the details." Hope rose in Gus' eyes. "You'd be interested?"

"No," Fitzgerald said.

"THAT WAS QUICK," Sandy said after Gus Thayer left.

"I disappointed him."

"Don't think you've seen the last of him. My ex, Rollie Wink, was killed in an accident out at the Weyerhaeuser plant and there was a big funeral and all. Gus moved right in with us, made himself part of the family. We kept throwing him out and he kept turning up. He wanted to know if we were going to sue because of the accident. Rollie wasn't even in the ground yet."

"I'm sorry," Fitzgerald said. "I didn't know."

Sandy shrugged. "It was a while ago. Then it turns out Rollie had an alcohol level three times the legal limit when he's killed. He had this habit, drinking his lunch. Anyway, Gus gets hold of the story and puts it on the front page. Rollie's Uncle Earl was so mad he went looking for Gus with a shotgun. Willard Stroud locked up Earl for a couple days, cooling him off."

"Tough times," Fitzgerald said.

"Aren't they all?" Then Sandy asked if he wanted another drink.

"Think I'd better be going."

"Crappy day, huh?"

Fitzgerald said, "I've had better."

HE STILL DIDN'T FEEL like going home. He took the long route, driving the South Downriver Road out of Ossning. When he came to the gravel road leading to the campground at Danish Landing he turned off and drove down to the river. The DNR had stabilized the landing with wood pilings that kept silt from washing into the river, the river spreading out beyond and flowing in a straight line for fifty yards or so before turning sharp right below the high banks of the campground. Small trout dimpled the surface in the slow water across from the landing, sun still reaching it.

When he first came to the Borchard on weekends, driving up from Detroit after work on Friday, the landing was where he fished. He didn't know any other place. He pitched a tent in the campground, put on waders, fished the entire time, stopping only for a few hours of sleep. What he ate came from cans. He got to know every holding place on the stretch of water from the landing to a green-painted summer cabin a couple-hundred river yards downstream.

Nobody ever seemed to use the cabin, so he got out of the river there and walked back to the campground along a trail through the pines. At the tent he would open a can of sardines, sip some whiskey, then go back to the landing and start fishing downstream again.

The only fly he used in those days was an Adams or, no fish feeding, a Woolly Bugger. He never kept any fish. When he got back to Detroit late Sunday night his wife would ask where the fish were and he would explain again that he released those he caught. It was a matter of aesthetics: trout were too beautiful to kill. She would look at him, head cocked to the side, but wouldn't ask him to explain. They were at a point in their marriage where they had given up explaining. If he had, he would have quoted Thoreau on brook trout he caught in a remote stream in Maine: *these bright fluviatile flowers, seen of Indians only, made beautiful, the Lord only knows why, to swim there!* Before he finished, his wife's eyes would have drifted away. They were at a point in their marriage where they had given up listening, too.

He met Calvin McCann at Danish Landing one evening. It was getting toward dark and Calvin was canoeing the stretch of river in an Old Town, checking on a spinner fall of brown drakes. Fitzgerald was drifting an Adams along a wood pile at a place where the river narrowed, so Calvin held the canoe above him.

When Fitzgerald had fished through, Calvin paddled up to him, holding the canoe against a downed cedar. "You want to give the fly a little action," he said. "Skitter it. This time of day, browns get aggressive. They want to smack something. You don't mind my saying, something better than a ratty Adams."

Calvin took a fly box out of his vest, opened it to the biggest assortment of dry flies Fitzgerald had ever seen, and handed him one. "Fly like this, some white hackle, you see it on the water. It gets pitch dark, put on a Muddler, dope it up with flotant so it stays in the film, fish it fast. Browns come out of their spots to take it.'' Then he looked at Fitzgerald, gray ponytail dangling beneath a Western Stetson. ''You got a Muddler?''

Later, after Fitzgerald had gotten to know him, Calvin maintained Fitzgerald had it wrong. They hadn't met for the first time on the river near Danish Landing but in Verlyn Kelso's fly shop at the Kabin Kamp. ''Take some vitamin E,'' Calvin suggested. ''Improves the memory.''

THREE MESSAGES were on the answering machine, all from Phipps, all saying the same thing. ''Call me, goddamnit!''

In the kitchen Fitzgerald poured a glass of whiskey, added a splash of water, took the drink to the living room and stood at the glass-walled front, looking down through the cedars at the Borchard. Night was closing in, shutting down the view. Before he sat down in an armchair beside the phone and dialed Phipps' number he put Christy Moore on the CD player and turned on every light in the room.

''About time. We got an AP story,'' Phipps said. ''That's how we heard.''

Fitzgerald said he had been in the Tamarack County sheriff's office. There hadn't been any time to call. Besides, he didn't have anything to add. And besides that he gave the sheriff his word he wouldn't get involved in the story.

''You kidding me? The AP said you found her. You've got all the scoop.''

''Sorry. You need more, send somebody up.''

While Phipps fumed Fitzgerald held the phone away from his ear and sipped whiskey. ''Okay,'' he heard Phipps say, ''tell me this. You turn up her story?''

''No.''

''Notes?''

''No.''

"You checked her computer?"

"That's tampering with a crime scene."

"You're a reporter."

"On leave."

"Okay, reporter on leave, what do you think of this? Allison Thorne was killed because of a story she was doing for the *Free Press*. You got it? That's page one across the country."

"Don't bet on it," Fitzgerald said. "You said the story was about people living on the river wanting to eat a few fish. They were interested in the publicity. Why would they kill the reporter?"

"I said she'd turned up a connection with some militia crazies. They're paranoid, want a low profile. So they took out Allison."

"That's how you keep a low profile?"

Phipps paused, thinking it over. "So who did it then?"

"The local bet is the husband. A domestic squabble of some sort. Apparently he isn't a nice fellow."

"Yeah?" Phipps said. "Then how'd Allison get hooked up with him?"

"Things happen."

"Brilliant. Now let me give you some facts. The AP story comes through, I can't reach you, so I pulled Allison's résumé out of the file. She gets a degree in English at Ann Arbor, right away gets on with the *Grand Rapids Post*, writing features and handling the education beat. She's making a name for herself when, like that, she up and quits. Next thing she's living in the north, using the name Allison Thorne, shopping around for work as a stringer. Her name before she got married was Wardlow."

"You're positive she was married?"

"Résumé says so."

"Anything else?"

"You're interested?"

"No."

There was a heavy-breathing pause on the other end of the line before Phipps said, "So the sheriff up there, he's after the husband?"

"Better ask him."

Another pause. More heavy breathing. Then Phipps said sourly, "If you gave me his goddamn phone number would it break your word?"

FITZGERALD WAS ON his second drink when he heard car tires on the crushed rock of the driveway. His fear was instant, thrust back inside the mobile home, aware of the long hallway leading to the rear. He thought to switch off the lamp beside his chair, immediately realized it would do no good since all the other lights in the room were on. Christy's voice filled the space. He started to get up, moving at least, when he heard a car door shut—and recognized the sound.

And felt his heart lift with joy.

SEVEN

"LET'S TALK ABOUT the two names in Allison's story," Fitzgerald said. "See where we are."

"Now?"

"Something else in mind?"

"In mind," Mercy said. "The rest of me needs a break."

He had made coffee and brought two mugs to the bedroom. They were propped up with pillows, a ladder of light traced across their faces from where sun pierced the venetian blinds. It looked like a perfect fall day outside, Fitzgerald had told her. A day for tossing bright streamers up against log jams. A day for floating the river. A day for packing a lunch and hiking to a beaver pond in the jack pines.

"Now?" Mercy asked him, and Fitzgerald said, "Afterward." Then he brought up the names.

"Nunemaker," Mercy said. "Ring a bell?"

Fitzgerald shook his head.

"You haven't lived in Ossning all your life, that's why. Cameron Nunemaker made flyrods, split-bamboo beauties, real works of art. At first he made them just for friends, then he started a small business that turned out to be surprisingly successful. Only a few people around Ossning could afford a custom-made Nunemaker rod but he had customers in Detroit, Chicago, out west, even. Every rod bore Cam's signature and the date it was made. Eventually they became collector items with hefty price tags. When Cam died, his wife, Sarah, stayed on in their place on the mainstream. She's in her seventies now, still bird hunts and fly fishes, using Cam's old equipment."

"And she doesn't believe in catch and release?"

"Cam was dead before it went into effect. He was ahead of his time as far as conservation went but he liked to keep a fish now and then. Sarah lives in a time warp. Whatever he did, she does."

"Sounds like a loving wife."

"Or a sappy one. Anyway, we leave her alone. Sarah's a local institution."

"Harmless?"

"In her seventies? She's in great shape, though, for a woman that age—and smart as a whip. She produced a catalogue for Cam's rods, using one of those computer publishing programs. She still does things like that, full color, very professional looking. Anyone in town needs something like that, they go to Sarah. Except for expenses she won't take a cent. Another thing—Sarah's lonely out there on the river. I'd guess that's the main reason she got revved up over the catch and keep business. It wasn't only because of Cam. It was having meetings, people around."

"She started everything, you mean?"

"I think so. But she's not the one who makes the most noise."

"The other name?"

"Mysterious Max," Mercy said.

FITZGERALD MADE PANCAKES with sliced bananas in the batter and they ate in the kitchen, sunlight flooding the trestle table. Afterward he suggested they forget about Max Ringwald and go back to bed, but Mercy said no, if they did they would be there the rest of the day. Fitzgerald said he could live with that but Mercy refilled the two coffee mugs and carried them to the living room and Fitzgerald followed. They sat together on a couch in front of the stone fireplace, sunlight in pools around them on the plank floor.

"To be honest," Mercy said, "I'm not exactly neutral about Max. We've gone a few rounds together."

"Tell me," Fitzgerald said.

"He's been in the office about the Borchard's designation under the Wild and Scenic Rivers Act, what property owners can and can't do, that sort of thing. He's actually read the act, which is pretty rare for someone up here, but he can never spare any time for chit-chat. He gives the impression he wants information but doesn't want to talk to you to get it. You know what I mean?"

"Fisherman?"

"That's why most people live on the river. I've never actually seen him out but I know he buys flies at Verlyn's shop."

"He's new up here?"

"Retired military officer—light colonel, I think. Then he did something for the state down in Lansing, something with the national guard. After that he moved up to Midland with Dow Chemical, same sort of work involving security. Then he turns up here, retired apparently, and buys a big clapboard place that was a private fishing club back in the 'twenties and 'thirties. The house had gone to rack and ruin and he fixed it up. You've fished past it—lots of white wood and black shutters, lawn in front, smooth as a golf green. It's about a mile downstream from the second Trout Unlimited access, north side of the river."

"I think I remember it," Fitzgerald said.

"His nearest neighbor on the river is Sarah Nunemaker. Not that they're close. Sarah's place is a half-mile or so upriver, north side. Anyway, money was apparently no object in fixing up the old club. Then Max started buying up adjacent property and stringing barbed wire in the woods to mark off boundary lines. People around town weren't used to that, running into wire when they were out picking morels or hunting. There was some grumbling—and more.

Max installed a gate at the entrance to the road into his place, big electronic affair, which was like painting a bull's-eye out there. Kids drove by and shot up the thing. Max tried moving the gate farther in on his road but the same thing happened. Finally he got the message and gave up. People didn't want to drive down his road, they just didn't like being told they couldn't.

"I got involved with Max another way. Besides the barbed wire, he marked off his property with No Trespassing signs, nailing them to the pines every dozen feet or so. Visual pollution, though he was within his rights. Then he started wallpapering the river bank with No Trespassing signs, including property that wasn't his but belonged to the state. So I had to go out, tell him to take the signs down.

"Max said canoeists couldn't tell the difference between what was state and what was private. They threw beer cans in the woods, defecated there, did everything else imaginable and the authorities—meaning me—didn't lift a finger. So he'd taken matters in his own hands. I told him I sympathized with him, which I did. Canoeists can be slobs. So can fishermen, for that matter. But that's what you have to put up with if you live on the river, together with the fact you can't put signs on property that doesn't belong to you. Anyway, Max said, 'Try and stop me,' and I said, 'Bet on it.'"

"And?" Fitzgerald asked.

"Every month or so I send someone out, he canoes the river, takes down the signs. Couple days later they're up again."

"Can't you get an injunction or something?"

"That's a lot of fuss. It seemed easiest to try to outlast him. But I'm beginning to wonder. Max is a tough customer."

"I know." When Mercy looked at him Fitzgerald said,

"He called up the paper, complaining about Allison. Said she was pushing him too hard about the article she was writing."

"How do you know that?"

"Phipps told me. It doesn't mean much. People complain to the paper all the time. They like their names in print but don't want their privacy invaded. The question is whether Max Ringwald was irritated because he had something to hide."

"Involvement with militia types? Hard to imagine. Mysterious Max keeps to himself."

"So do militia types."

"You know what I mean. Incidentally, he's no spring chicken. Late sixties, I suppose."

"Wife?"

"You'd hardly know it. She's seen around town now and then, getting groceries. But as far as I know she doesn't have any friends, doesn't do anything. She's a type you see up here now and then—virtual recluses. Husbands buy remote places on the river, plunk the wives down in them, there they stay. Why do they put up with it? Don't tell me it's because they're loving wives."

"Wouldn't think of it."

"Lucille," Mercy said. "That's the poor woman's name."

THE POOLS OF SUNLIGHT had shifted, moving toward the glass front of the A-frame. They moved with them, trailing warmth.

"You're cutting class," Fitzgerald asked, "because of me?"

"Who else?"

"Won't they give you demerits or something?"

"Probably. Listen, Fitzgerald," Mercy said, "keep out of this. It's none of your business."

"It feels like it is. I'd never seen what a bullet does to the back of a head. I want to know who pulled the trigger."

"Stroud will find out."

Fitzgerald shrugged. "Maybe that's why I didn't tell him about Allison's revised story. I want to find out for myself."

Mercy said, "Say that again."

"I told him about the original story on the Catch and Keep Alliance. I didn't tell him anything about the new one on a militia connection."

"That's withholding evidence. Good Lord, Fitzgerald."

"Not really. I didn't find any revised story on her computer. No notes, nothing."

"You think that matters? You should have told Stroud everything Phipps told you."

"Agreed," Fitzgerald said. "But I'll tell you something else. I came within a hair of erasing Allison's story—so Stroud wouldn't find it. I copied down the two names, Sarah Nunemaker and Max Ringwald, and I was just about to—"

"Good Lord."

"But I didn't. The story's there, on the hard drive and a backup disk. Stroud can find it if he looks. The murder scene—I left it just the way it was."

"Except for the little matter of entering Allison's computer, copying down names, almost erasing her story, then not telling Stroud about the militia business. Except for that."

"I shouldn't have told you. There's no reason for you to be involved."

"A little late in the day for that," Mercy sighed.

"Go back to Michigan State. Finish the seminar."

"And leave you alone with this? Look what you've done already. No way."

Fitzgerald smiled at her. "Then explain this: Phipps told

me he checked Allison's résumé. She has a promising career going, chucks it all, comes up here to live with an older man with a prison record in a mobile home back in the pine barrens. Why?''

"That's no mystery. Bright, educated, dutiful young woman suddenly feels she's missing something in life. Not marriage—she might have that already. What she's missing is romance. Any idea what that means to a woman?''

"I think you're going to tell me.''

"Getting mixed up with a man she shouldn't, a type she's always been denied.''

"And for Allison that was Ray Thorne?''

"So it seems.''

"How would they even meet?''

"Some beer joint somewhere. Allison went slumming. That's usually how it happens.''

"Tell me something else,'' Fitzgerald said, smiling at her again. "Does the need for romance afflict only young women?''

"Very funny. Just leave it that I understand the Allison Thornes of the world. It's the Lucille Ringwalds I don't get.''

"Loving wives.''

"Sappy wives.''

Fitzgerald finished his coffee and said, "Let's take a quick nap before we set out. We've got a big day ahead.''

"I suppose,'' Mercy said. "But why quick?''

LATER, FITZGERALD asked, "So how do we go about it?''

"Talking to them? I don't see any reason to bother Sarah. With Mysterious Max we just drive up, knock on his door. The worst he can do is shoot us.''

"Very funny. What I'm wondering is whether I should go alone. You've had trouble with him.''

"True. But at least he knows me. He might have heard

about you, lottery winner and all, but he might not know your face. I might be able to get us a foot in the door.''

"I'll tell him I'm with the *Free Press*," Fitzgerald said, "taking over for Allison, finishing up her work. I'm going to get the catch and keep story in the paper."

"Sounds as good as anything."

"Let's go out and fling some streamers first. Then a picnic."

"Actually," Mercy said, "I was thinking about another nap."

EIGHT

THAT WAS IT—*Ray* Thorne.

Now, the name recalled, there was something else Bonnie Pym couldn't put her finger on. Where, recently, had she seen him? She could picture his face—dark skin, scar along one cheek, ice-gray eyes—but couldn't make out the background. She knew it was somewhere.

After a while she gave up and let her subconscious work on the problem.

The answer came while she was home, half-watching an old Doris Day movie on the tube, bare feet up on the coffee table, sipping a beer. She checked the time: nearly ten o'clock. She threw on jeans, a fresh blouse, worked with her hair, and put on earrings, a pair she didn't think he had seen before.

The drive from Ossning along the North Downriver Road to Walther Bridge took fifteen minutes. She knew she was driving faster than she should, but the information burned inside her like a hot coin. This time of night deer bolted from the woods, you couldn't stop in time, you ended up with a totaled car or worse. She kept putting deer whistles on the front bumper and they kept falling off. What you needed in the north woods at night was one of those Army vehicles, a Hummer.

Going down the narrow lane of crushed rock that led to the A-frame she took it slow even though she could feel anticipation building in her chest. Then came the letdown. Parked under the yard light beside Fitzgerald's Grand Cherokee was Mercy Virdon's DNR Suburban. Bonnie ran through the days of the week in her mind. Mercy drove back from Michigan State on Friday nights, yet this was Thursday and here she was. For some reason Mercy had come back a day sooner and Bonnie could guess the reason.

There wasn't a light showing in the A-frame.

BONNIE KEPT what she remembered locked inside her until the next morning. Fitzgerald wouldn't be stopping by the Six-Grain Bakery, not with Mercy back in town, so she decided to get what use she could from the information. At mid-morning she left the bakery in the charge of a high-school girl on a work-release program and drove a box of sweet rolls to the city-county building.

She usually let the girls she had gone to school with who were imprisoned as secretaries in the building have first pick of the rolls, stopping last at the sheriff's office. This morning, unable to wait that long, she went there first. She shot the breeze with Elsie, the sheriff's wife, while Elsie picked out the rolls she wanted and arranged them on a glass plate. When he heard her voice Willard Stroud called out from his office and told her to come in and tell him the gossip. He always said the same thing.

"Like this pair?" she said when she was inside the office and out of Elsie's line of vision. She turned from side to side, giving Stroud a good look. The earrings were the same pair she had put on the night before for Fitzgerald.

"They're you."

"You always say that."

"It's always true."

"Mind if I sit down?"

She saw Stroud's eyebrows edge up. The ritual of their morning conversation didn't include Bonnie taking the chair across from the sheriff. She knew where to draw the line when she entered the offices of the city-county building, which was before she was tempted to sit down and cross her legs with a switching sound of her pantyhose and lean forward in earnest conversation. But this morning was different. She had important information, and the sheriff was the one to hear it.

"You found him yet, Ray Thorne? I know," Bonnie added hurriedly, "none of my beeswax. I just thought you might have and so you'd know already."

"Know what?"

"For a while I couldn't remember his first name. Then I couldn't remember where I'd seen him. Recently, I mean."

Stroud got up, walked around the desk, closed the office door. Bonnie could imagine what might be going through Elsie's head. She made a mental note that, on the way out of the office, she would say something to Elsie, letting her know nothing had taken place inside the office other than a serious conversation. Not that Bonnie would mind if more had. She had never understood what a big healthy man like Stroud saw in a dried-up prune like Elsie.

"How recently?" Stroud asked when he came back to his desk.

"Couple weeks ago, give or take."

"And?"

"It was out at the Keg O'Nails. I was with someone and Ray Thorne came in and started talking with Deke Musso. It was sort of quiet in the place—"

"Unusual," Stroud said.

"—you could hear what they were saying. It was about booze."

"Not unusual," Stroud said, "given Deke sells it."

"But that's the thing."

"What is?"

"Ray Thorne wasn't buying. He was selling."

Stroud's eyes narrowed. Bonnie had never felt him looking at her with quite such intensity. "I mean, I think he was. I wasn't exactly listening. It was just something I over-heard.''

"Go on."

"Deke was shaking his head but Ray Thorne kept push-ing him—you know, with what he said. There was talk about money—I remember that. And brands—Jack Daniel's, that sort of thing.''

"It was liquor they were talking about, not beer?"

"Yes."

"And it was the manager Ray was talking to?"

A sour look twisted Bonnie's face. "It was Deke, all right."

"Not one of your friends?"

"That jerk? There was any other place, I wouldn't set foot in the Keg.''

"All right. The person you were with," Stroud said, "he can verify this?''

"I figured you'd ask."

"Well?"

"I was feeling blue that night. Nothing to look forward to but another day of work. It's the middle of the week and you're not sure you can last to the weekend. You ever feel that way?''

"No."

"Anyway, there wasn't another person. I went out alone, seeing what might happen. I was sitting at the bar—that's how I overheard the conversation." Stroud lifted his eye-brows again, as if he was suddenly seeing her in a new light. Bonnie shifted in her chair. "I don't hang out there, that's what you think. And I don't run around by my lone-some.''

"Wouldn't think you'd have to," Stroud said, a slight smile on his face.

Bonnie brightened. "You got that right, sugar."

"One other thing," Stroud said. "How do you happen to know Ray Thorne?"

"I just do. You see him around."

"Nothing more?"

"Personal, you mean?" Bonnie shook her head. "You just know about some guys. Pure misery."

"Like Deke Musso?"

"Two of a kind," Bonnie said.

AFTER BONNIE PYM left his office Stroud stayed at his desk, nibbling on one of the sweet rolls Elsie brought him. He knew what the next step should be. He should send a deputy out to the Keg O'Nails, have him talk to Deke, find out who else was in the place that night—someone who could confirm what Bonnie had overheard.

There was no guarantee Bonnie had things straight. Stroud liked to tell her, only half teasing, that the earrings put a lot of weight on her brain. Her story needed to be checked out.

Which was easier said than done. Regular customers of places like the Keg O'Nails suffered memory loss when the sheriff's office asked questions. It was a matter of self interest. Someday the sheriff's office could be asking questions about them. In Ray Thorne's case memory loss would be intensified since it would be all over the county by now that he was wanted for killing his wife. No barfly would want to be known as the one who fingered him, guilty though he might be. As for Bonnie's story about Ray Thorne trying to sell liquor, it was unlikely Deke Musso would recall that, either. The north woods believed in free enterprise. Laws limiting it were the sheriff's problem. Without a nudge in the right direction, it would be a waste of time talking with Deke.

Stroud was nibbling more of the sweet roll and pondering

the amount of nudge it would take when Elsie called from the outer office to tell him that Fitzgerald was on line one.

"What about?" Stroud called back.

"Didn't say."

"I keep telling you. You're supposed to ask." Then he picked up the phone and said, "Stroud here."

"The *Free Press* has Allison Thorne's résumé on file. She sent it in when she was trying to get freelance work. It says her maiden name was Wardlow and she worked for the Grand Rapids paper before she came up here."

"You just happened to learn this?" Stroud asked after a moment's pause.

"The fellow I told you about on the *Free Press* called me. I thought it might help in locating her family."

"He say anything else?"

"Only that the résumé indicates she was married to Ray Thorne."

Stroud was figuring how he would thank Fitzgerald for the information, thank him in a way that didn't sound overly grateful, when Elsie called out that Mercy Virdon was on another line.

"What about?" Stroud called back.

"I asked," Elsie said, "all she said was trouble."

Stroud put Fitzgerald on hold and punched another button on the phone. "Get out to Lost Finger Lake," Mercy said at once, "the old cabins there. And send an ambulance. Not that it'll do any good."

NINE

STROUD EXAMINED the county map above the file cabinets after he told Elsie to call for an ambulance and alert any patrol car in the area. Then he left the city-county building himself. He knew where he was headed but had wanted to double-check the most direct route from Ossning. He hadn't been to Lost Finger Lake in years.

The lake was small, private, set deep in the jack pines. Stroud's understanding was that the property had been owned since the early 1900s by a group from Grand Rapids who fished the lake for bluegills and crappies. Tamarack County was trout country, fly fishermen coming from near and far to cast for browns, rainbows, and brookies in the Borchard River. Fishing for bluegills and crappies on a small lake was so odd it escaped attention.

The Grand Rapids group lived a quiet life when they were in residence in cabins beside the lake. And no one from town was tempted to hike in and poach on their fish, or hike in and party in their cabins over the winter. There had been no reason for the sheriff's office to keep a close eye on the property.

The long two-track road in from the county highway was heavily overgrown, indicating it had seen little recent use. For all Stroud knew, membership in the fishing group had dwindled, maybe to nothing. That was the fate of most of the clubs that had once been common along the Borchard, membership falling off to a point where taxes could no longer be paid and the properties were sold. People seemed less clubable than in the past—or was it that, awash now with money, they could go it alone, not needing to share the expense of river property with others?

Stroud was thinking about that when the road dipped from the tunnel of pines and opened on a vista of meadow, the lake in the center of it, a narrow body of blue water fringed with brown reeds. Even if it held no trout, the lake was more inviting than he remembered. Along one side a drooping electrical line extended to a half-dozen cabins set in a tight row just in front of a wall of pine, plain log places black with age, overtaken with weeds. Apparently the cabins saw no more use than the road.

A patrol car had arrived ahead of him, parked at an angle beside one of the cabins. Next to it, Stroud noted with sudden irritation, was a DNR Suburban. Mercy Virdon had phoned in the report but he hadn't expected her to be present. She had no need to be. He would let Mercy know that in no uncertain terms.

But when he drew close to the two vehicles he could see a third, parked on the other side of the cabin and out of view from the head of the lake, a blue Econoline van. The DNR abruptly vanished from his mind.

ZACK COX CAME AROUND the cabin before Stroud could get out of his car. "Ray Thorne?" he asked his deputy.

"Hard to tell."

"And?"

"Smack in the back of the head."

Stroud felt his eyes close involuntarily, then snap back open. "All right. Let's have a look."

He followed Zack around the cabin to the blue Econoline. Both its front doors were open, Mercy standing beside the one on the driver's side with another DNR type, both of them in green and khaki outfits, both peering inside the vehicle. Stroud glanced at them but said nothing. "The license number," Zack said, "it checks out." But he didn't pause at the van. He moved on to the second cabin in line, Stroud following.

The body lay face down beside a scarred, wooden table in the center of the main room. Stroud knelt down, examined the head long enough to verify what Zack had said. What could be seen of the man's hair held his attention, a thinning mixture of gray and black hanging low on the back of his neck, the hair of a man heading into middle age. The contrast with the still-youthful appearance of Allison Thorne was striking, save for the terrible similarity of blood and matter thrust together in a darkly clotted mass.

An old-fashioned metal cup rested on its side beside the body. Stroud took a ballpoint pen from his shirt pocket and lifted the cup by the handle, smelled inside. Detected nothing. If there had been liquid in the cup when the body fell to the floor the contents had evaporated. He replaced the cup and stood up.

A wooden chair was pulled away from the table at a slight angle, a second metal cup upright on the table in front of it. Directly across the table another chair was pulled away at an angle—the chair the dead man may have been sitting in when he crumpled to the floor, the cup falling with him. His back would have been to the lone window in the room, light coming from that direction. He may have been sitting at the table with the killer, the two of them drinking something from the metal cups, when the killer moved behind him, fired from close range. Stroud made a mental note to have the wall opposite the window checked for a bullet lodged in the logs.

He turned then, making a slow circle, taking in the rest of the room. It was bare bones: old cast-off furniture and lamps, no rugs, a basic kitchen with a small refrigerator and propane stove beside a rusting sink beneath the window, the wood table and chairs. As he looked, a conclusion bore in upon him: Ray Thorne, if that's who the dead man was, hadn't killed his wife. He himself had been killed, and in the same manner. The metal cups even duplicated the coffee mugs in the mobile home, the killer so methodical he repeated everything—everything except, this time, drinking coffee with the victim. Was that significant? Stroud looked again at the stove in the kitchen area. No pot on it, and none in the sink waiting to be cleaned.

He turned then, realizing that Zack was trying to get his attention. Zack kept dipping his head toward the cabin's other room. "Guess what?"

"In there?"

"Better see for yourself."

Two single metal beds and a chest of drawers had been pushed together against one wall, leaving the rest of the room open for storage. Stroud whistled into the silence. What the room stored were cases of liquor, stacked from floor to ceiling, a miniature warehouse. He ran his eye down the boxes: whiskey, gin, vodka, stacked together according to type and brand. He kept looking at the boxes, doing a quick count of the number, then turned back through the doorway into the cabin's main room, examining it again.

"How about that?" Zack said.

Stroud nodded. He wanted to concentrate on the room, verifying his first impression. If you excluded the body on the floor and the fallen cup, everything about the cabin was neat and orderly. The structure itself was primitive, the furnishings decrepit—that was different. The mobile home was modern in comparison, but the careful housekeeping—there was where the similarity was.

He was about to ask if Zack had noticed the same thing when he heard the siren. From the cabin door he saw the ambulance emerge from the pines and descend to the lake, lights blinking, siren blaring.

"Them cowboys got no sense," Zack said. "Half the town will trail along. Nothing better to do."

"Get on the radio," Stroud told him. "I want a patrol car blocking the road. Totally blocked. Only Slocum Byrd gets through."

"Gus Thayer will have heard on his police radio."

Stroud shook his head. "I'll give him a statement when there's something to say. Otherwise I don't want any press people hanging around." Then he said to Zack, "What the hell's Mercy doing here?"

"She was here when I came. I don't know why."

"She see the booze?"

"She was standing outside the cabin when I came. She just pointed inside."

"Who's the fellow with her?"

"She didn't say."

Stroud looked at him. "You didn't learn a lot, did you? Okay, get on the radio. Then tell the ambulance boys there's nothing to do until Slocum arrives. And get the place dusted for prints before they start poking around."

When Stroud went around the cabin to where the blue Econoline was parked Mercy and the DNR fellow were standing beside it, waiting for him. Mercy inclined her head toward the van and said, "We didn't touch anything."

"Wouldn't think you would."

"It seemed funny, doors wide open. It was what we first noticed—before we saw inside the cabin." Mercy paused, looking at Stroud sheepishly. He couldn't remember seeing that expression on her face before. "I should have said. This is Ted Tinnery from the Traverse City field office."

"And?"

Mercy said, "About Ted or the van?"

"Goddamnit, I want to know what's going on. You called the office, said to get out here, remember? Zack gets here, there's the two of you waiting. That's what I want explained."

"It's not so complicated," Mercy said.

"I'm all ears."

"Ted's a fishery biologist. He was supposed to check out the lake, do some preliminary work on it. He's got a report to write for Lansing. Anyway, he stopped by our office before he came out. He thought I wasn't in Ossning, that I was downstate for a seminar, but it so happens I was in, so I decided to come out with him. The Ossning office will have charge of the development and I wanted to get a first-hand look. I've never been out here before."

Stroud held up a hand. "Wait a second. Why aren't you downstate?"

"Personal reasons."

"And what's the business about development?"

"It's a long story. What it comes down to is the property has been given to the state. The fishing group—I don't know, they just weren't interested anymore. Lawyers have been working on the transfer for years—a legal tangle of some sort. The transfer became final a month or so ago. We're standing on state property and the DNR's in charge."

"Meaning you?"

A grin edged onto Mercy's face.

"You might have let me know." Then Stroud said, "But that doesn't explain about the development."

"Just future plans for the property. I can fill you in later. Nothing's definite yet."

"All right. You came out here to see what the place was like. Then what?"

"Ted and I pulled in and we saw the van like this, doors open. We thought people were in one of the cabins, which they shouldn't have been. On the other hand, they might be people from the fishing group, people who didn't know the transfer had gone through. So Ted and I went to check the cabins. They were all shut up but for the one, and its front door was open.''

"You went in?"

"Looked in. It seemed pretty clear he was dead. Ted stayed there, by the door, and I went back and called you on the car phone."

Stroud turned slightly so he was looking beyond Mercy and Ted Tinnery, looking out at the sliver of lake basking in sunlight. Now, a body in one of the cabins, it didn't appear so inviting. He turned back to Mercy and asked if there was any other road into the property.

"Our maps don't show any. The property's pretty remote."

"We'll check it out. Now tell me about the van. What's so interesting inside?"

"See for yourself," Mercy said.

There was nothing out of the ordinary about the front of the vehicle, beyond the fact that several empty beer cans littered the floor between the two seats. What one would expect from the likes of Ray Thorne, Stroud was thinking, when he twisted his head to look into the rear. Both rows of seats had been removed to make room for stacked cases of liquor. Despite himself, he whistled into the cavity.

"Big boozer," Mercy said from behind him, "or a heap of friends."

"CAN'T TELL ANYTHING for certain," Slocum Byrd told Stroud. "A guess is he's been dead maybe three days."

"So he could have died about the same time as Allison. We just found him later."

Slocum shrugged.

"Can you tell who died first?"

Slocum shrugged again. "He's the husband?"

"It's possible. See if there's any identification. And see

what you can do with the timing of death.'' Stroud turned
away and went back inside the cabin. He wanted one more
look at the body before the medical examiner went to work.

Nothing caught his eye that he hadn't noticed before—
nothing except that the man's face, insofar as he could see
it pressed against the floor, appeared almost peaceful in
repose. There was no suggestion of frenzy, of a painful
death. No doubt that was too much to read into the rigid
form beneath him. Still, Stroud had a distinct feeling that
the victim had been sitting at the table, suspecting nothing,
when he was shot. Very likely he was dead before his body
hit the floor.

The killing had been efficient, circumscribed, carried out
with no resistance—to all appearances, identical to the killing in the mobile home on Lime Creek Road. Neither were
typical Tamarack County murders. He was all the more
certain of it. Both had the look—

Stroud shook his head slowly, resisting the word that
kept insisting itself in his mind.

The look of executions.

TEN

"THE GRAND RAPIDS FOLKS at Lost Finger Lake," Mercy explained, "called themselves the Loyal Union of Michigan Panatics. Get it? LUMPS. Too cute for my taste."

"Fly fishermen?" Fitzgerald asked her.

"Actually, Ted knows more than I do."

"Only a little," Ted Tinnery said. He was settled beside Mercy, drink in hand, in one of the canvas sling chairs on the deck of the A-frame. Fitzgerald stood at the railing. Beyond them, late-afternoon shade gave way to intense sunlight on the river below. "They were into fly fishing, tying their own flies, all that. But apparently they only went after panfish. Didn't care a whit about trout."

"Doesn't make much sense," Fitzgerald said, "coming up here for that sort of fishing. It's probably as good around Grand Rapids."

Ted Tinnery shrugged. "The ambiance possibly. The north woods. The privacy the property gave them. Who knows?"

"But Fitzgerald's got a point," Mercy said. "You wonder. Did they haul themselves up here to fish or were they fanatic about something else?"

"Play poker and drink whiskey," Fitzgerald said.

"Anyway, they ran out of interest or energy or something."

"Probably not panfish," Ted Tinnery said. "Lake's probably overrun with them."

"They wanted out," Mercy said, "but you can't just give something to the state. There's all sorts of legal hoops you have to jump through. Just now it's settled—and it's our baby.''

"And you've got plans," Fitzgerald said.

"Ted has."

"We've got to run tests on the lake," Ted Tinnery said, "study the water quality and temperature swings, see what the food chain amounts to. But from other lakes this size in the area we've got a pretty good idea already. We might be able to develop a nice little bass fishery here."

Mercy said, "The idea would be to take down the cabins and close the road, make it hike-in wilderness fishing. No boats, only float tubes, flies, catch and release, and restricted times. The lake wouldn't be open until after the spawning season. You could fish the Borchard for trout in the morning, then, canoe traffic building up, hike in to Lost Finger in the afternoon and cast for bass, then head back to the Borchard for an evening hatch."

"Paradise," Fitzgerald said.

"Except the murder changes the timetable. Ted wanted to begin testing this fall. That's why he came over today, to see what was needed, get organized. Now Stroud has closed off the property for the time being. We could probably overrule him, at least to the extent of starting tests on the lake, but it isn't worth the hassle. It's a good-sized property to police. We'll need Stroud's cooperation in the future."

"The dead man," Ted Tinnery said to Fitzgerald, "Mercy said you found his wife murdered in a mobile home."

"We think they were married. And the dead man may be Ray Thorne."

"But you discovered the woman's body."

Fitzgerald nodded.

"Just the day before."

Fitzgerald nodded again.

"Believe me, I know how you felt. The man in the cabin was the worst I've seen. When Mercy went to use the car phone I couldn't keep looking at him. I thought I'd lose my stomach."

Mercy said hurriedly, "Tell you what. Let's have another drink, then go into town and grab a bite to eat before Ted heads home. The hotel has decent food, assuming you like steak or walleye."

"Both," Ted Tinnery said.

AFTER DINNER Mercy and Fitzgerald walked Ted Tinnery to his car, then went back inside the hotel and took the high, padded stools at the bar.

Sandy asked what they wanted to drink, and Fitzgerald said they didn't want anything for the moment, they just wanted to sit for a while and hear Nils play the accordion. "Hey," Sandy said, "feel free."

"How'd you know?" Fitzgerald asked when Sandy left them.

"That you lost your stomach after you found Allison? You went white as a sheet when Ted said he nearly did at the cabin. I thought you'd throw up again."

"Women handle blood better than men. Isn't that the view?"

"Don't kid yourself. When I saw Ray I wasn't sure I could make it from the cabin door to the car phone."

Fitzgerald said, "Let's change the subject. Tell me about Ted."

"What about him?"

"Not bad looking."

"You know something? Ted's done all the course work for a doctorate in biology. He understands everything about lakes and rivers—beyond that, he really cares. But he doesn't fish. All that knowledge and he doesn't have the slightest interest in wetting a line. Can you imagine?"

"No."

"The fact is I can't figure him out."

"And you can me."

"With the wind in the right direction."

Fitzgerald said, "And look what it got you. You came back for me and walked in on another murder. Love hurts, to coin a phrase."

"Not so much as its absence, to coin another." Then Mercy said, "This is getting dopey. Let's listen to Nils."

Perched on the edge of a stool at the front of the dining room, Nils was playing "Trail of the Lonesome Pine," eyes closed, absorbed in the music. Overhead light gleamed from his oiled hair, full and jet black despite his age, and the ancient gray suit he invariably wore when he played for the customers in the hotel dining room. The diners studiously avoided looking his way. Everyone knew Nils, but it wasn't the custom in the north woods to acknowledge in public a man working for his keep—an evening meal together with schooners of beer for Nils and his girlfriend, Wilma, at the bar. No one clapped when he finished a song, and Nils himself only adjusted the weight of the accordion before launching into another.

"He's good tonight," Fitzgerald said.

"You can tell?"

"I think I'm developing an ear. You hear enough, you can detect the subtleties. Listen."

Mercy waited through "My Blue Heaven" before she said, "I like Nils. I'm still working on accordion music."

Fitzgerald smiled at her. "Back home," he said, "Ted Tinnery didn't mention what you told me about seeing liquor in the van."

"It doesn't mean anything. Stroud's got him sworn to secrecy. He doesn't want the story circulating until he knows what Ray Thorne was up to."

"If it really was Ray Thorne."

"Right."

"So what do you make of it?"

"He was loading liquor from the van to the cabin or vice versa. Either way you've got to figure he was bootlegging. Michigan's liquor is taxed to the teeth. He was probably buying it across the border, peddling it down here."

"Stroud didn't say anything about liquor in the mobile home. He said it was as neat as a pin. What I saw certainly was."

"Assuming Stroud was telling you all he knows."

"Assuming that," Fitzgerald agreed.

"What it looks like is Ray Thorne was using the lake cabin as his warehouse. He must have known the Panatics weren't using the place anymore, that no one went in there. He had a nice setup."

"Until somebody else learned about it."

"And went in there," Mercy said, "and put a bullet in the back of his head."

"Which proves he didn't kill Allison. It's not a murder-suicide, anything like that."

"No. But he could have killed Allison, then someone killed him. Killed him *for* killing Allison."

"Let's not get too complicated. Let's stick with the idea that Allison and Ray Thorne were both murdered—and by the same person."

Mercy said, "Wait a minute. Why are we concerned at all? It's not our problem."

"I think it is. I found Allison and you found Ray. She was doing work for my paper and he was killed on state property that your office will manage. We're involved."

"Try telling that to Stroud."

"If I need to. So the question is," Fitzgerald said, "why? Why were both of them killed?"

"Something to do with the liquor, I'd bet."

"So would Stroud."

"He gets things right now and then."

Fitzgerald nodded. "Who might know about the liquor if Ray Thorne was peddling it around Ossning?"

"Sandy?"

"I stopped in here yesterday after I left Stroud's office. All Sandy knew was that Ray Thorne was a bad apple."

"Bonnie Pym?"

"Someone closer."

"Of course," Mercy said. "Nils."

AFTER NILS FINISHED his set and sat at the bar with Wilma, and Sandy pulled two schooners of beer, Fitzgerald and Mercy moved down the length of polished wood and took stools beside them. Fitzgerald asked if they had heard about the two murders in the county.

"You'd have to be dead cold yourself," Nils said, "otherwise."

Wilma wiped a line of foam from her fiery lipstick and said, "A young fellow and his wife, Sandy said. Both shot dead."

"It's not positive," Mercy said, "that they were married."

"He wasn't no young buck, neither," Nils said.

"You knew him?" Fitzgerald asked. "Ray Thorne?"

"Naw."

Fitzgerald glanced at Mercy, read her eyes, looked back at Nils. What Mercy was telling him Fitzgerald already knew. Old Finns who lived back in the woods weren't inclined to do a lot of talking, especially if the talk had any connection with the law. They were anarchists by nature, believing the only good laws were those easily evaded. Whatever Nils knew about Ray Thorne would have to be pried out of him, piece by piece.

"You just happened to know he wasn't young?" Fitzgerald asked.

Nils shrugged.

Mercy said, "If you needed booze in the county, I heard Ray Thorne was the man to see." When neither Nils nor Wilma responded, Mercy went on, "Or maybe you didn't exactly need the booze, you just didn't want to pay the bandits in Lansing their tax. You can understand why people get their backs up. I suppose Ray Thorne smuggled it across from Canada, tax free."

"Naw," Nils said.

"He wasn't the man to see?"

"You get caught up north, Canucks toss you in the tank for good."

"They throw away the key," Wilma said, underscoring the point.

"So Ray Thorne didn't smuggle the booze from Canada?"

"Why'd he need to? Down south, you pay the bastards the tax, you still come out ahead."

"Compared to Michigan."

Nils nodded.

Fitzgerald said, "So he'd drive down south, Indiana or somewhere, fill up his van, come back here and sell around the county. He probably called on a regular round of customers."

"Naw. They come to him."

"But how would they know he had booze for sale?"

Nils and Wilma looked at Fitzgerald, then at Mercy, as if both were sunk in invincible ignorance. Finally Wilma said, "They read the *Call*."

"Afraid I'm not following," Mercy said. "There was something in the paper?"

"When he had something," Wilma said.

"Of course."

"He put in one of the little notices."

"Classified ad?"

"Under Firewood for Sale. Always said the same—top quality, low price. Gave a number you could call up on the telephone. Everybody knew."

"Good Lord," Mercy said.

"You're looking at two people who didn't know," Fitzgerald said. "And you can be certain Willard Stroud didn't. But let's stay on track. After someone called Ray Thorne and told him what they wanted, then what?"

"What you think?" Nils said. "He brought the stuff and they paid."

"Cash?"

"I wouldn't guess he'd take VISA," Mercy said. "On the other hand, I wouldn't have guessed he was advertising bootleg liquor in the town rag."

Fitzgerald said, "So when he sold out a supply, he went back south, filled up his van, started in again. Is that how it worked?"

Nils shrugged, his interest in the subject waning.

"One more thing," Fitzgerald said hurriedly. "How often did Ray Thorne have a notice in the *Call?* Every month?"

"Naw."

"Not that often?"

Wilma looked at Nils and said, "He don't keep up with much."

"Then how often?"

"Every month it used to be."

"But it's been more often, you mean, recently?"

"He don't miss a single week," Wilma said, "now."

"STROUD'S GOING TO bust a gut when he learns," Mercy said on the drive back to Walther Bridge.

"Maybe not."

"You don't know him the way I do."

Fitzgerald said, "He has the idea that what Ray Thorne

was involved in caused Allison's death. In other words, Ray was the main victim, the primary one. This adds weight to the idea, especially if Wilma's right and Ray had stepped up his operation. There might be some big players around in bootlegging, even up here. Maybe they were willing to tolerate Ray up to a point—and he crossed the point. So they sent a message."

"By killing him? That's a strong message. But why kill Allison, too?"

"Wilma said the ads in the *Call* gave a phone number. We'll have to check, but let's say it's the phone in the mobile home. That means Allison was in on the operation."

"Ray had a phone in the blue van. Ted and I saw it."

"It probably doesn't matter. The killer would think it unlikely that Ray's wife was completely in the dark about the bootlegging operation. So she was killed, too."

"But Allison was trying to catch on as a newspaper..."

"Stringer."

"So why do that if she and Ray were into bootlegging?"

"I don't know. Maybe it was a cover. Nobody would suspect her of anything if she was an upright journalist."

"Or maybe she was trying to get space for herself, keep some distance from what Ray was up to."

"Maybe. But it doesn't matter now," Fitzgerald said. "They're both gone. What matters is who killed them."

Mercy looked ahead into the tunnel of light along the deserted highway. On either side dark seas of jack pine stretched to unseen horizons. Above, stars streaked a black sky. She shivered and said, "I just realized something. You said Allison worked in Grand Rapids—where the Panatics were from. She could have known about them, known about the property up here, known it wasn't being used. There's a tie-in." Then she said, "This is getting too much. When we get home let's call Stroud, tell him what we know about the bootlegging. If that's behind the murders, we've got no business being involved. It's too dangerous.''

"Agreed."

"Oh, no," Mercy said. "I know that tone. You don't agree at all."

"The two names in Allison's story—I want to check them out, that's all."

"But why?"

"For Allison's sake, I suppose. If she was into bootlegging with Ray, then it's Stroud's business. But if she was trying to develop a story and that's what got her killed—"

"Then it's your business?" Mercy turned, seeing Fitzgerald's profile in the green glow of the dashboard, the set of his chin. She sighed and said, "I'll phone Stroud first thing in the morning."

"Rather I did?"

"No," Mercy said, and sighed again. "He's used to getting bad news from me."

ELEVEN

WHAT WAS HIS next move?

Until now it had been a snap—taking a couple days off from the paper, driving up from Detroit, locating Ossning, checking into the Wolverine Motel on the edge of town. There was no point, Phipps had decided, phoning up the local sheriff. All he would get was a runaround. He had to go up there, north woods, poke around himself. Now, standing in the middle of a white-walled room, overnight bag tossed on the bed, he had the sinking feeling he'd made a mistake.

It wasn't that he was suddenly uncertain about the story. The murder of Allison Thorne, getting to the bottom of it, could resurrect a career, his, that needed a big-time jolt to get back on track. The problem was he was rusty as a reporter. His bottom had been molded so long to an editor's chair he wasn't up on the tricks of the trade.

He sat on the edge of the bed, peeled the wrapper from a cigar, fingered the lighter in his trouser pocket. The desk clerk, a hollow-cheeked senior citizen, had informed him that all the rooms in the Wolverine Motel were no-smoking rooms. *"All?"* Phipps had asked, astonished that the reach of the culture police extended even to the north woods.

"You need a smoke," the desk clerk suggested, "a plastic chair's outside your door."

"How about in winter?" Phipps inquired.

The clerk shrugged. "It's fall now."

Instantly it was evident to Phipps why men joined militia outfits. Out in the pines they could shoot guns, smoke their heads off, scheme to rid the country of old fools like the desk clerk.

He fixed the unlit cigar in the corner of his mouth, opened his bag, withdrew a bottle of whiskey. The culture police hadn't yet figured a way to outlaw a late-morning relaxer. In the bathroom he filled a plastic cup, then returned to the bed and stretched out, his back against the headboard. What he needed, in addition to a drink, was time to think. It would come to him—his next move.

The obvious one was to get in touch with Fitzgerald, see if he could wring some cooperation out of him. The hitch was a lack of leverage. Fitzgerald had won a lottery and was on leave from the paper and writing a novel, so Phipps couldn't dangle the prospect of money in front of him or fifteen minutes of fame as a journalist. Yet that wasn't the real hitch. If Fitzgerald cooperated on the story he might end up running away with it, leaving Phipps with crumbs. He would lay odds Fitzgerald wouldn't get to first base with the novel, but the sonofabitch could write a sweet news story.

So forget Fitzgerald.

And try leaning on another journalist.

The thought was so good Phipps spilled part of his drink in his haste to get to the phone beside the bed. "Listen," he asked the desk clerk, "you got a paper in town?"

"Paper?"

"Local bugle. Town rag."

"The *Call*."

"It's where—its office, I mean."

"Downtown."

"And that is?"

"Only way there is," the desk clerk said. "Straight ahead."

"ABOUT THE MURDER, right?" Gus Thayer asked after Phipps introduced himself and handed over one of his *Free*

Press business cards. The editor-publisher of the *Ossning Call* had looked closely at the Gothic lettering, obviously impressed. Phipps waited, letting the realization sink in that Gus Thayer was dealing with a metropolitan journalist, before he began revealing his hand.

"Right," Phipps said.

"First or second?"

Gus Thayer's eyes behind thick black-rimmed glasses didn't seem to blink. They stared back—big, bright, innocent. Or maybe, it occurred to Phipps, a little wacky. He had never understood the romance some of his colleagues had with the idea of running a small-town weekly—owner, editor, reporter, a wise old curmudgeon who functioned as the moral and mental compass of the community. He knew intuitively what the reality would be. Like this—a cramped little shop on the main drag of a godforsaken town, the place musty with the smell of old newsprint, working twelve-hour days to write up the school board and the gardening club and the Boy Scouts, having advertising pulled when you carried a story about a local businessman picked up for DUI. He knew intuitively how you would end up—poor, beaten down, a little wacky.

"Mind if I light up?" Phipps asked. From his shirt pocket he took the cigar, the one he had unwrapped at the Wolverine Motel, and applied his lighter. "Now what are we talking about, Gus?"

"You don't know?"

"Try me."

"They found Allison Thorne's husband out at a lake. Shot dead. Same way, too—drilled in the back of the head. One bullet each. I got that, how they were killed, from one of the ambulance boys. Got the name, too—Ray Thorne. The medical examiner found identification in his wallet. The sheriff's keeping a lid on everything."

"Hold on," Phipps said. "Which one was killed first?"

Gus Thayer shook his head. "I haven't got that yet. The way I had it figured, Ray was the one drilled his wife. But he couldn't have. What I figure now is they were killed about the same time by the same person. Somebody who knows guns and doesn't waste ammo."

"Like who?"

"No idea."

Phipps examined Gus closely. Buzz-cut gray hair to go along with the big black-rimmed glasses and innocent eyes—more evidence he was a little wacky? Or was it a cover, the guy shrewd in a small-town hick sort of way, knowing more than he was saying? Phipps decided he would pass along a little of his own dope, see what might develop. He began telling Gus about the story Allison Thorne had been working on for the *Free Press*, keeping just to the group that wanted to reverse the catch and release regulation on the Borchard River.

Gus looked puzzled. "The *Free Press* was interested?"

"We shouldn't have been?"

"I wrote that up for the *Call*, the meetings they had. Three or four 'graphs."

"It was local stuff, you're telling me?"

"Yeah."

"Allison didn't think so."

That got Gus' attention. Behind the big glasses his eyes snapped up and down like they were on rollers. Phipps said, "This place where the husband got it—a lake, you said?"

It took Gus a moment to adjust to the shift in the conversation. "Yeah, small lake, private. Back in the pines. There's sort of a compound there. Nobody knows much about it."

"So what was the husband doing there?"

Gus' eyes blinked again. He looked, it occurred to Phipps, like a hound dog beginning to sniff out a scent.

"I'm going to tell you something, Gus, off the record. One journalist to another. The story Allison was working on—what it was really about was some militia outfit. They're mixed up with the group on the river. I don't know how—maybe funding them, maybe more. Maybe the catch and release stuff—"

"Catch and keep," Gus corrected him.

"—maybe it was only the tip of the thing. You know, part of a move by the militia to get involved in local issues. Get some credibility or something. I don't know—but Allison did. She was talking to her sources, working up the story. My guess, that's why she was killed—she knew too much. The militia outfit silenced her."

Phipps sat back, reading the reaction in Gus' eyes. Wacky or shrewd, Gus recognized a potential story when it was dropped in his lap, a potential knockout story. A story like this, militia activity that resulted in the murder of a journalist and her husband, would be picked up around the country. Gus might move up and out from a place like Ossning, on his way to the real world. Phipps sucked on his cigar and watched ambition simmer in Gus' eyes.

"This lake," he said, fanning the flames, "private, nobody knows about it, a compound. Sounds like a place a militia outfit could hang out, have maneuvers, shoot up things. You think so?"

"Yeah."

"Could be that's why the husband was out there—looking it over for Allison, seeing what the outfit was up to. Maybe more, like trying to infiltrate the group, work from inside."

"Yeah."

"He made some mistake, they uncovered him, took him out."

"Yeah."

"But you never heard about militia out there?"

Gus shook his head. "But it's possible. You could do a lot of training, a place like that, and nobody would know."

"So what do you think? Could we go out, have a look, see for ourselves?"

"The road's closed off."

"Meaning what?"

"Sheriff's orders. He keeps a deputy stationed out there. On the lake, the cabin where Ray Thorne was killed, the sheriff's got it cordoned off."

"A deputy's there all the time?"

"They keep changing off."

"There's another way?"

Gus beamed. "Up here there's always one."

"So let's do it."

"I'd have to check a map. But how I see it, we could put in a canoe at the Trout Unlimited access, paddle down-river, go overland from there."

"What kind of hike we talking about, Gus?"

"I'd have to check a map—"

"You already said that."

"—but maybe four, five miles."

Phipps rolled the cigar around in his mouth, settled it in a corner. Did he really want to put himself in the hands of a guy who might be a little wacky? The story that might result, on the other hand, could be a whopper. Phipps could see it scrolling down on his computer screen: first-person account of a *Free Press* editor going overland through forest to discover the base camp of a militia outfit, thereby unraveling the murder of a young reporter and her husband. You could get a state press award for something like that, to say nothing of a Pulitzer. You could also, hike like that, get yourself a coronary. He rolled the cigar to the other corner of his mouth and took a hard look at Gus Thayer.

"You a native up here, Gus?"

"You bet."

"Know the place like the palm of your hand."

"Right."

"You're in shape, too."

"Not bad."

"The thing is, I might hold you up, city guy and all. So what do you say to this? You hike in by yourself, I'll hang out in town. Maybe grab a bite to eat while I wait. Maybe talk with the sheriff, see if I can squeeze out a few quotes. But you'll be doing the serious legwork. When you get back, we'll get together, share our dope. A collaboration thing."

There was a full blaze in Gus' eyes now. And something else—something, Phipps realized, Gus might have picked up from looking into *his* eyes. "We got a deal?"

"You bet."

"By the way," Phipps asked, "what's this lake called?"

"Lost Finger."

"And it's where?"

"Far end of the county going north."

"Okay. I got an idea now where you'll be. When you get back give me a ring, Wolverine Motel. Leave a message if I'm not there. We'll get together, share what we got."

"Sure thing," Gus said.

"We'll figure out where we go from there."

"You bet."

Like hell, Phipps thought.

A GREASY SPOON down the main drag from the newspaper office served breakfast all day, so Phipps edged into a wooden booth and had his second while he planned his next move, the one that had come to him in the midst of talking with Gus Thayer. Gus had turned out to be shrewd rather than wacky—shrewd enough, at least, to know you didn't tie yourself down with collaboration when you were on a story that could turn a career around.

Gus had played along, but Phipps wasn't fooled. Gus would check out the lake, all right, and if it proved to be what Phipps suggested, a base camp for a militia outfit, the information would go no further than his notes. The story Gus dreamed of would carry only a single by-line—which was only fair, Phipps acknowledged, since the story he had in mind would only carry one, too, when it appeared on the front page of the *Free Press*. No doubt Gus had realized as much, understood the sheen of deception in Phipps' eyes. But he hadn't understood everything.

Gus said it would take time to paddle down the river, hike overland to the lake. Phipps could be in and out well before that. By the time Gus called the Wolverine Motel, assuming he did, Phipps would be long gone, rolling back to Detroit, writing a story in his head as the miles slipped by. Phipps asked for a refill of coffee and relit the stub of his cigar. The Wolverine Motel, it seemed, was an aberration in Ossning. Everyone in the greasy spoon was puffing away like a furnace, the air gray with smoke, the ceiling tile yellow from nicotine. Phipps inhaled with pleasure. He leaned back in the booth, plenty of time at his disposal, feeling deeply content.

The tricks of the trade were coming back to him.

TWELVE

"IT'S THAT IMPORTANT?" Frank Connery asked.

Willard Stroud took a sip of coffee before he answered. "Put it this way: Deke doesn't meet me out there, talk to me straight, you don't keep the place open."

The voice on the other end of the line was smooth as oil, if oil could set like concrete. Frank Connery owned a string of seedy taverns and motels around the state and was used to dealing with sheriffs who had something in their craws. He knew when to bend, when to harden. "Why would that be, exactly?"

"Take your pick. Maybe Deke isn't checking IDs the way he should. Maybe minors are getting beered up. Maybe the state boys are planning a raid."

"I don't believe so."

"Believe it."

Frank Connery paused and Stroud thought he could hear classical music in the background. He had never met Frank, only talked by phone with him at his home, a place in Muskegon where Frank also maintained his office. At times Stroud imagined the home as ultra modern, all wood and glass and abrupt angles, and at other times it seemed a big country colonial set off by white horse-farm fencing. He could never get the house in sharp focus, no more than he could Frank Connery himself, a seemingly intelligent man who ran businesses that brought him one headache after another. And an income that would probably knock his socks off if Stroud actually got a look at the house.

"And you wish to speak with Deke about our liquor supplier?"

"The main thing."

"Perhaps I can satisfy you. We have our own distributor. If you wish, I'll—"

"That's not what I'm interested in," Stroud interrupted.

"Then I don't understand."

"You don't have to. Just tell Deke to be there, ten-thirty sharp."

"You could tell him yourself."

Stroud listened again to the music in the background, violins twanging softly while Frank Connery, as he imagined him, rubbed a perfectly shaved chin and labored to control the concrete in his oily voice.

"True," Stroud said. "But I've got an idea a call from you would improve Deke's memory."

"Perhaps."

Stroud smiled into the phone. "I'll put in a word. The state boys might hold off a while."

"That's all then?"

"Except one thing. This distributor you use—"

"The company," Frank Connery said before Stroud could continue, "is called Lakeland Distributing. A holding of mine, as a matter of fact."

"Thought it might be. And the company has customers other than the joints you own?"

"It does."

"I'm wondering," Stroud said, "who they might be up here."

"In Tamarack County? I believe the only significant accounts are the Keg O'Nails and the Borchard Hotel. I'd have to check the records for others, but they'd be on the order of the Elks, Moose, VFW, convenience stores."

"You've got competition, Frank?"

"In your county? It hardly pays for a large distributor to service a sparsely settled area."

"Smaller distributors then?"

"In a market economy competitors are always springing up."

"And you keep an eye on them?"

"Not personally. I have employees who do."

"Like Deke," Stroud said.

"Whom you will be seeing," Frank Connery replied, "at ten-thirty."

STROUD CHECKED his watch: ten after nine. Frank Connery gave the impression of being a morning worker, which maybe you could be if you owned taverns rather than worked in them. Roused out of the sack before nine, Deke Musso, the manager of the Keg O'Nails, wouldn't have remembered his name. Ten-thirty was still early by Deke's standards, but by then a call from the boss would have done wonders for clearing out the cobwebs. So would Stroud's presence at the bar rather than a deputy's. Deke would have two reasons for providing answers.

After Mercy Virdon called him that morning about the classified ads Ray Thorne had run in the *Call,* Stroud sent Zack Cox around to the newspaper office to examine the back files, making sure she had the story straight. According to Mercy, plenty of people in town knew about the ads—knew what they meant. Eventually, Stroud would have a talk with Gus Thayer, finding out if *he* knew what they meant. If Gus did, Stroud planned to raise holy hell. Even if Gus didn't, he would. A publisher had a responsibility for what he printed in his pages.

So did a sheriff for what went on in his county.

Mercy hadn't said as much, but she hadn't needed to. Stroud got the message. Ray Thorne had made a fool of him, running a bootlegging business right under his nose, running it in such public fashion that it was advertised in the local paper. People, the ones in town who knew about the business, had been laughing behind his back and he hadn't heard a sound. When he got to the bottom of it, finding out who Ray Thorne's customers had been, making a complete list, there would be hell to pay in the county for more than Gus Thayer.

In the meantime there was the matter of two murders to solve. "Consider this," Mercy had said. "The telephone number in the *Call* ads was the same one Allison Thorne gave the *Free Press*. Fitzgerald called Detroit, had a secretary check. That means Allison could have been involved in the bootlegging operation, handling calls that came in, making records. If I were you, I'd check her computer files in the mobile home."

"Anything else?" Stroud asked in a tight voice.

"That could explain everything," Mercy went on. "Once Allison teamed up with Ray, they expanded the operation. She was there to handle calls and make records while he made deliveries. That could have been their downfall, expanding. Maybe some bigger types didn't like it, didn't like the way Ray and Allison were cutting into business. So they did something about it."

Stroud said, "Any bigger types in mind?"

"I'm just saying that could be it. The big picture. I don't have the specifics."

"I don't suppose Fitzgerald does, either."

"Look," Mercy said. "We're not telling you how to do your job. It just seemed important to let you know about the phone number."

"All right," Stroud said. "I can take it from here." Then, swallowing first, he said, "Thanks."

Mercy didn't say that he owed her one. Her tone did. "You know me, Stroud. Always helpful."

When Zack Cox returned to the office he confirmed what Mercy had said. The classified ads were in the *Call,* under a heading of Firewood for Sale, with a phone number to call. And the ads had lately increased in number. Zack had spent only enough time to look back three months in the weekly, but the increase was evident. During the past month an ad had appeared every week. Stroud told him to keep the information under his hat for the time being. He didn't want it getting mixed up with the murder investigation. Then, on second thought, he told Zack to go back to the *Call* office and see if anyone there remembered who placed the ads, Ray Thorne or Allison.

"Guess what?" Zack said.

"What?"

"She did. Phoned 'em in. Paid on time, too."

"Nice of you to let me know."

"You think it's important?"

"It's evidence," Stroud said sourly. "That's what I think."

It was more evidence that Allison was involved in the bootlegging operation, though not, any more than the phone number given in the ads, that she knew exactly what was going on. She might have believed Ray *was* selling firewood. That seemed doubtful—how could she have answered phone calls believing that?—but it was a possibility, however remote. Stroud told Zack to go back to the mobile home on Lime Creek Road and run through Allison's computer files, looking for anything that appeared to be a record of liquor sales. Or, for that matter, firewood sales.

"Both?" Zack asked.

"Since you're there," Stroud answered.

ALONE IN THE OFFICE, time on his hands before he went out to the Keg O'Nails, Stroud thought about what he would say to Allison Thorne's parents. The Wardlows came from a small town north of Grand Rapids, Cedar Springs, but were living in retirement in Sun City, Arizona. The state police had located them down there and broken the news about their daughter. That evil task he had been spared. But the Wardlows were coming to Ossning to claim the body. He would have to look into their stricken faces, explain the circumstances of Allison's death.

Saying what, exactly?

That their daughter had hooked up with a no-account and was innocently dragged into his bootlegging business? Or had it been the other way around, Allison developing an on-going business, expanding it, improving the cash flow? Who, in fact, *had* been in charge, Allison or Ray? In the final analysis it didn't matter. Whatever had happened had gotten both of them killed. "You have my sympathy," he would say to the Wardlows, saying what he always said, knowing how little it was.

Stroud shook his head, trying to clear it, and called to Elsie to get the medical examiner on the phone.

"Where?" she called back.

He took a long drink of tepid coffee before he answered. "What would you think about starting with his office?"

"Okay," Elsie said.

It took three calls before Slocum Byrd was located having breakfast at the Six-Grain Bakery. When Stroud picked up the phone he could hear a din of voices in the background. "Damnit," he said, "call me from somewhere private."

"I'll stop by."

"Call, I said. I've got an appointment."

When Stroud picked up the phone again he listened to the background silence before he said, "Well?"

"We found a relative, second cousin, to give a positive identification. The body's Ray Thorne, all right."

Stroud drank more tepid coffee before he said, "What about the time of death?"

He could almost hear Slocum shrug over the telephone line. "Looks like they were both killed about the same time."

"About?"

"More or less."

"That's not good enough. I have to know the order of the killings. Who died first?"

"She did, I'm pretty certain. But it couldn't have been much before he did. I'll give you the details about the state of the bodies, if you like."

"Thanks anyway," Stroud said. "But it's important, Slocum. I have to know the time frame."

"Then she died a little before."

"You can't be more exact?"

There was a pause then before Slocum said, "You could bring somebody in, Willard."

Stroud released his breath in a muffled sigh. Slocum Byrd never had qualms about a forensic expert from the state police, even a medical examiner from another county, looking over his shoulder and giving a second opinion—a character trait, Stroud realized, that stemmed either from a lack of professional paranoia or Slocum's awareness of his level of professional competence. Whatever the explanation, Stroud liked the trait. Against his better judgment he said, "Not for now. Got anything else?"

"The shots, they never knew what hit 'em."

"A small mercy."

"There's another thing."

"Go on."

"The bullets you dug out at the mobile home and the cabin—I hear from Zack they're the same caliber."

"They are."

"But fired from different guns."

"Zack thinks so. But we're waiting on Lansing."

"It's strange."

"What is?"

"Two people killed at opposite ends of the county, killed about the same time and the same way, same caliber guns used, but not the same guns. We've never run into one like that before.''

"Thanks for reminding me,'' Stroud said before he hung up the phone.

BOTH BULLETS, one removed from the trunk of a pine after passing through a stud in the framing of the mobile home, the other from the log wall of the lake cabin, were .38 caliber Winchesters, 130 grade MC. Nothing special about that. Both the weapon and the ammunition were common enough around the county. Stroud had had a deputy drive the bullets down to the state police laboratory in Lansing for routine ballistic analysis—analysis that no longer seemed so routine. Since the bullets were the same, Stroud had assumed they were fired from the same weapon, but Zack didn't think so. He had examined the bullets with a magnifying glass and thought the firing markings didn't match.

Another deputy had checked the distance from Lime Creek Road to Lost Finger Lake, seeing how long it took to drive from one to the other, south to north across the county. It worked out to just under an hour if you circled around Ossning and drove a moderate speed. The times of death Slocum Byrd had given were rough, Ray Thorne dying slightly later than Allison, but if Slocum was right they gave a window of time for a lone killer to drive from one place to the other. But why had he changed guns? If he had.

Stroud cautioned himself to be patient, not to jump to conclusions. He wouldn't know about the guns until Lansing faxed a report. But he couldn't stop possible conclusions from running through his head.

He might not have a single killer on his hands but a pair, a pair who had calibrated their actions to kill at approximately the same moment. They might have intended the moment to be exactly the same but circumstances had intervened. He could imagine the circumstances—getting the victims to feel they had nothing to fear, waiting to get their backs turned, any number of things you couldn't time right down to the second. Or he might be faced with a lone killer who had shot Allison, then driven to Lost Finger Lake and shot Ray, using different guns to leave the impression there were two killers. Either way, a single killer or a pair, the murders were planned and deliberate—murders in the form of executions. More and more they looked like that: cool, calculated, professional executions.

On the way out of the office Stroud told Elsie to call him at once if a fax arrived from Lansing. He was anxious to get moving, quit trying to solve the case in his head, get on the trail of some hard evidence. *Any* evidence.

"Call you where?" Elsie asked.

"What would you think about trying my car phone?"

"Okay," Elsie said.

THIRTEEN

THE KEG O'NAILS was located in a hacked-out opening in the pine barrens on the highway to Traverse City, a log tavern and restaurant with a blinking orange neon sign anchored on the roof. Out behind, across a crushed-stone parking area and set tight against a wall of pines, was a motel, a dozen cabins that, if log walls could talk, would tell a dark history of Ossning, one Willard Stroud didn't care to ponder. Most of what was down and dirty in the town began in the tavern and ended up at the motel.

Periodically, he thought about closing down both places. It wouldn't be hard, though there would likely be an expensive wrangle with Frank Connery's legal eagles. But what he had told Frank on the phone wasn't entirely hot air. Serving alcohol to minors was only one of the violations he could pin on the tavern, and the county health officer could find a litany of reasons to pull the plug on the food operation. But as often as he thought about closing the place Stroud came back to the central reason he left it alone.

You couldn't eliminate what went on in the Keg O'Nails, human nature what it was. So, since it would anyway, you let it express itself—but at a place you knew about, that held no surprises, a place you could draw a circle around and contain. From the conferences and short courses he went to down in Lansing, Stroud had learned that every sheriff in the state thought more or less the same way. They talked about battle zones, red-light districts, DMZs. Though the terms didn't apply to a scruffy north woods establishment like the Keg O'Nails, that orange neon sign, blinking away in the pine barrens, drew the troublesome element in Tamarack County like a magnet. If Stroud didn't care for what went on there, he could take comfort in knowing where it went on at.

Ten-thirty sharp, he pushed open the entrance door of the Keg O'Nails and peered into an interior gloom laced with a permanent odor of beer, cigarettes, and stale cooking oil. Deke Musso was behind the bar, leaning over a cup of coffee, a column of steam washing over a long, sallow, night-worker's face. When he saw Stroud he wiped his eyes with a hand, slowly straightened behind the bar.

"Been a while," Stroud said. He stood across the bar from Deke, one foot resting on the rung of a bar stool. He wouldn't sit, and Deke wouldn't waste time offering him coffee. This was business, the shorter and sweeter the better.

"Way it should be," Deke said. Though he was heeding his boss' message, his eyes, blurred with lack of sleep, revealed an unhappy man. Stroud took a measure of pleasure in that.

"That's true. No problems, no morning chats. Way to keep it."

"So?"

"I've got a dead body on my hands, murdered, man by the name of Ray Thorne. You heard about that?" Stroud didn't wait for an answer. By now everyone in Ossning knew he had not one but two dead bodies on his hands. "He came in here a while ago, tried to sell you liquor. He was overheard."

"By who?"

Stroud smiled thinly. "What did you tell him?"

Deke sipped his coffee, wiped the moisture from his eyes. "To take a hike. We sell, we don't buy. He got prickly about it so I threw his ass out. All there was to it."

"Go slow," Stroud said. "What exactly was Ray Thorne's proposition?"

"Said he could supply what we wanted, as much as we wanted. It was bullshit but he kept going on. And he'd sell cheap. Whatever we were paying now, he'd sell for less."

"How much less?"

"We didn't get that far. Like I say, it was bullshit."

"You mean you never get offers like that, some independent out to undercut your distributor?"

Deke shook his head. "We get offers, but from new distributors trying to start off. We don't get offers from customers."

"So you knew Thorne?"

"He came in."

"But this was the first time he'd tried to sell liquor?"

"Yeah."

"That night, the night he tried to sell you, was a woman with him? Quite a bit younger than he was?"

Deke hesitated. "Mr. Connery said it was liquor you wanted to know about."

"Now I want to know about this. I'm not in a good mood, Deke. I don't have a lot of patience."

"There were broads around that night. But I don't remember one hanging with him."

"All right. You said Ray Thorne got prickly with you. What's that mean?"

"He wouldn't take no for an answer."

"And you didn't like that?"

"He was causing a disturbance. When he gave me some lip I hauled him to the door."

"He let you do that?"

Deke straightened behind the bar and rolled his shoulders inside a sweatshirt with a Detroit Red Wings logo on the front. "Wasn't much choice, was there?"

FROM HIS CAR in the parking area of the Keg O'Nails Stroud called his office and asked Elsie if Zack Cox had reported in yet. He had, and Stroud had to wait while Elsie hunted for the message she had written out on a slip of paper. The gist of it was that Zack had found a file on the hard drive of the computer in Allison Thorne's mobile home that could be what Stroud was looking for—a list of names, dates, and dollar amounts. Elsie added, "He said to tell you the file was named Firewood."

"Tell Zack to run a printout," Stroud said.

"He said he did."

"Good."

"But he said it can't be a record of firewood sales. Too much money's involved."

"One other thing," Stroud said. "Tell him to keep his mouth shut around town."

After he finished talking with Elsie, Stroud sat in the car, looking beyond the Keg O'Nails at the string of motel units set against the black wall of jack pines. The tawdry appearance of the place fit his mood. The one encouraging piece of information Deke Musso had given him, encouraging for Allison Thorne's reputation, was that a young woman hadn't accompanied Ray Thorne the night he tried to sell liquor at the Keg O'Nails. Now Zack Cox's report canceled out the feeling.

Allison was a town girl, so she might not have known much about the price of firewood—that much could be said in favor of her innocence. But it was a stretch. The evidence leaned strongly in the other direction—that she had known exactly what was going on, that she and Ray were partners in the bootlegging business. And the odds were that that was what got them killed. They expanded, crossed some barrier, found themselves on someone else's turf, ended up with bullets in the back of the head.

The turf was Frank Connery's. His company was the

main liquor supplier in the county, so it was his business Ray Thorne was cutting into. But would Frank Connery have taken such penny-ante competition seriously enough to eliminate it? It seemed another stretch.

Frank Connery wouldn't have done anything himself, leaving that home in Muskegon, leaving the classical music, coming up north, getting his hands dirty. That was what he had people like Deke Musso for—employees, Frank had said, who looked after his interests. So had Deke gone further than tossing Ray Thorne out of the Keg O'Nails?

Deke had seemed oblivious to the implications of what he had told Stroud—that he'd had an altercation with a man who was later found murdered. Maybe he thought the only implication was that Ray had a grudge against him, not the other way around. Or was Deke blowing smoke, saying he wanted nothing to do with Ray and his liquor proposition, covering his tracks—tracks that had taken him to Lime Creek Road and Lost Finger Lake?

But what if there were two killers, not one? That meant Deke had a partner, and Stroud had no clue who that might have been. He could have a deputy do some checking on Deke, see who his pals were around Ossning, see what he did with his spare time. And he could have the state police run a check, seeing if Deke had any criminal record. But—

Stroud gazed out again at the motel units beyond the Keg O'Nails, his eye moving methodically from one closed door to the next. Something told him Frank Connery and Deke Musso were the same—closed doors, dead ends.

FOURTEEN

"YOU'RE UP from Detroit," Max Ringwald asked Fitzgerald, "that what you're saying?"

"Not exactly. I'm living here for the time being. Place at Walther Bridge."

Mercy said, "You must have heard. He won a lottery and came here to fish and write a book."

Max ignored her. He kept studying Fitzgerald. "And you're with the paper?"

"He told you," Mercy said. "It's the *Free Press* and he's on leave of absence."

They were standing outside a screened porch that wrapped around the front and one side of the white clapboard house, having progressed that far from a separate building, a garage, where Max Ringwald had been standing when the Cherokee emerged from the jack pines into the former fishing club. Inside the garage, Mercy had noted, was a Volvo station wagon and a pair of pickup trucks. Before her now an emerald lawn stretched from the porch to the dark splendor of the river.

Seeing the lawn, calculating the fertilizer it took to maintain the look, she had bitten her tongue. With the Borchard's designation as a scenic river under the Wild and Scenic Rivers Act, riverbanks were supposed to be left in a mostly natural state, but a management plan worked out with local property owners allowed pre-existing development to remain. Mysterious Max hadn't been content with that. He had enlarged and improved the lawn of the old fishing club until it resembled a manicured golf green.

"And it's about the story the girl didn't get in?"

"Allison Thorne's story. You've heard what happened?" Fitzgerald added when Max didn't respond.

"I heard."

"I feel I owe it to her, a colleague, to see if I can do anything with the story. I realize it's not much."

"Hell it isn't," Max bristled. "The story's important."

"Not much insofar as her memory goes."

Max grimaced, dismissing the thought. He was a head shorter than Fitzgerald, a solid, well-conditioned, fireplug of a man, standing close and squinting upward through half-glasses hung on a braided cord around his neck. Looking at him, Mercy was inclined to say, *This is the north woods. You got some obsession with grass, live down in the 'burbs.* But that would likely stall completely a conversation that wasn't making much headway anyway. For Fitzgerald's sake she avoided looking at Max and his flawless lawn. Through a window off the porch she had noticed a woman sitting beneath a lamp inside the house, glasses on, reading.

"What I hoped," Fitzgerald said, "is we might go over the information you gave Allison. Unfortunately, I don't have her notes."

Max angled his head, skeptical. "She said she wrote the story up, sent it in, the paper said it stunk."

"My understanding is an editor wanted some additions. The paper's still interested. The story was scheduled for publication."

"Bull," Max sniffed.

"The paper gave Allison a go-ahead with the story. If there wasn't interest it would have been killed."

"Bull crap."

Fitzgerald smiled, more diplomatic than Mercy would have thought possible. For her part, she was ready to spin on her heels, leave Mysterious Max to his lawn and his grievances. The woman inside the house, she noticed, hadn't looked up at the visitors beyond the porch. Her eyes were cast down, fixed to her reading.

"Maybe we could sit for a moment," Fitzgerald suggested, "talk about the story."

"What's the point?"

"I'd like to know why you believe the paper wasn't interested."

"Yeah?" Then Max Ringwald tossed a hand in the air and said, "Come on if you want."

THE ROOM Max led them into looked as if it might have been the common room of the fishing club, a large open space with plank flooring, knotty-pine walls crammed with framed pictures, and at one end a stone-faced fireplace with a smoldering fire sending waves of heat into an already stuffy warmth. At the other end of the room the woman sat wedged in the corner of a sofa facing a large television set—a middle-aged woman with a bland, dough-colored face and, Mercy realized with a start, flaming red hair. The woman—presumably, Max's wife, Lucille—hadn't raised her eyes from the paperbound book.

Mercy shed her DNR jacket in the warmth and looked over the pictures on the walls: men in uniform, aerial views of what might be military bases, framed certificates. One wall, floor to ceiling, exhibited a collection of what she took to be antique military swords. In the room Max Ringwald had created a shrine to his career—one of them, anyway—which wasn't unusual for a retiree to do. Mercy had seen lots of walls in the north woods cluttered with recollections of the past, which in another way was odd because a retiree might be expected to put the past behind. She would. There wouldn't be any flotsam and jetsam of the DNR years on the walls during her sunset years.

But what stuck out about Max's shrine was where it was—in what appeared to be the main living area. No memorabilia remained of the fishing-club past, nor was there a hint about the room that a woman also lived in the house. Maybe the other rooms looked the same, the house an entire Max shrine. Mercy considered asking to use the bathroom, getting a peek along the way at Max and Lucille's bedroom. Swords there, too? She wouldn't be surprised.

They sat in deep chairs before the fireplace, Lucille behind them on the sofa at the far end of the room. Max didn't introduce her, didn't indicate he was aware of her presence. "Big city rags," he was lecturing Fitzgerald, "you're all the same. You've got a liberal bias. The story wasn't politically correct."

"Allison showed it to you?" Fitzgerald asked.

"She didn't need to. I gave her the information."

Fitzgerald scratched his head, giving an impression he was puzzled. He asked Max what was politically incorrect in a story about Borchard trout.

"*Keeping* 'em. That's the kicker. It's like asking for prayer in schools, like wanting to repeal affirmative action, like trying to keep smut off the boob tube. You'd think we were talking about going back to the Stone Age. Ordinary sense is what it was."

"Allison agreed?"

Max shrugged. "She didn't have to. She wanted a story, was all."

"About the Catch and Keep Alliance?"

Max nodded. Then he was glaring at Mercy. "She knows. Ask her."

Mercy smiled but didn't respond. From where she was sitting she could see a portion of the way down a long hallway off the living area. Regularly-spaced doors suggested they might open on bedrooms from the days of the fishing club. Why did the Ringwalds, apparently only the two of them, want to own such a big place? It was situated on a fine stretch of the river, but keeping it up would be an immense amount of work.

Mercy was pondering the question when she felt Lucille's eyes on her. She glanced in the direction of the sofa but immediately the woman looked away, back to her book. Her glasses, Mercy saw, had plastic rims in a shade of blue. Red hair, blue glasses, dough-colored skin—a color combination, okay for a flag, that only made a middle-aged woman look foolish.

"How do you respond," Fitzgerald asked, "to the argument in favor of catch and release fishing? There's strong support from the scientific community."

Again Max glared at Mercy, personalizing the scientific community at the same time he dismissed it. "Politics is what it is. The government puts fish in the river, using taxpayer money, then turns around, says taxpayers can't eat one now and then. We're saying we can. Simple as that."

"Trout in the Borchard are wild. The river isn't stocked."

Max rolled his eyes. "You learn that from the scientific community? You think the browns and rainbows dropped from heaven? There was nothing here originally but brook trout and grayling. Of course the river's stocked."

"Was," Mercy said, keeping her voice as flat as possible. "Stocking on the Borchard ended in the 'sixties."

"Shouldn't have. But that's another DNR blunder."

"By definition, a trout born in a stream is a wild trout."

"Your definition. We're talking about something else— getting rid of the blunder of catch and release. It's political, that's what I'm telling you. A question of taxpayer rights. We paid for the fish originally, we should be allowed to keep one when we want. Case closed."

Fitzgerald was quiet for a moment. Then he said, "What you're saying, the argument for keeping fish, it's part of a larger view."

"Of course it is."

"Did Allison's story take that into account?"

"She didn't show me the story. I told you before."

"But you talked with her about it—the larger view?"

"We talked about a lot of things."

Fitzgerald asked, "She came here? To your home?"

"A few times. I gave her our printed stuff."

"Could I see it—that material?"

"You're telling me you're going to read it?" Max turned to Mercy with a pained look. "She never bothered."

"On the contrary. I read every word. I just didn't agree."

"Bull." But Max rose from his chair, passed his wife without a sideways glance, turned down the hallway. When he came back he handed Fitzgerald a sheath of stapled paper.

"You produced the material for the group?" Fitzgerald asked.

"Not me."

Mercy said, "Sarah?"

"I don't fool with computers. Read it," Max said, "you want to know our philosophy."

That's one way of putting it, Mercy wanted to respond. *Utter nonsense* would be a better way. She was still trying to contain herself when Fitzgerald stood up, smiled down at Max. With relief she rose with him. As she did she took a last look at Lucille Ringwald, whose eyes, she realized, had been riveted on her. At once Lucille's gaze returned to her book, but Mercy had the distinct impression the woman wasn't actually reading, and hadn't been from the moment she and Fitzgerald entered the room.

"One other thing," Fitzgerald said. "If you were certain the *Free Press* wouldn't print the story, why bother meeting with Allison in the first place? It would have been a waste of time."

"It was."

"So?"

"Hope springs eternal."

"In the liberal media?"

"Like I said," Max said glumly, "it was a waste of time. The girl didn't get the story in the paper. Neither will you."

Fitzgerald smiled again, then pulled his wallet from his trousers and edged out a *Free Press* business card. He unclipped a ballpoint pen from his shirt pocket, wrote on the card the telephone number of the A-frame at Walther Bridge, handed Max the card. "In case you want to get in touch."

"Yeah?" Max said. "What for?"

"I'D SAY," Mercy said when they were back in Fitzgerald's Cherokee, driving out the long dirt lane from the fishing club, "that was full-stop pointless. Or did you pick up something I missed?"

"Let's go to High Pines, grab some coffee."

"You noticed that, too? Our genial host didn't offer anything. I consider it a triumph we got inside the house."

"With some coffee we can think."

"About what?"

When Fitzgerald didn't answer Mercy looked across the seat at him. He was gazing straight ahead, eyes narrowed. "I suppose," she said, and turned away, "there's always the weather."

At the convenience store they took their coffee containers to a lone picnic table set in a patch of limp, water-starved grass, the table's surface a scarred abstract of carved initials. A few yards away rose a wall of jack pine.

"Well?" Mercy said.

"Bad coffee."

"You expected Starbucks? I meant what we're thinking about."

Fitzgerald ran a hand through his hair and looked beyond

her, toward the wall of pine. "I'm trying to size up Max Ringwald."

"I wouldn't say that's difficult. Irritating through and through. They kill me, actually, types like Max. They spend most of their lives cashing government pay checks, then come up here and don't want any more government. Government was okay when *they* were government. Now they want to live in a state of nature or something."

"So maybe it's true."

"What?"

"What Allison said she was working on. That the Catch Keep Alliance has a connection with some militia group."

"They're *simpatico,* I suppose, in an ideological sense." Fitzgerald nodded but kept looking away from her. "I take it you disagree."

"Not exactly. It's just that Max Ringwald didn't seem like someone who'd have anything to do with a bunch of citizen soldiers, no matter how much he agreed with their views. They aren't his style."

"C'mon," Mercy said. "You think militia types are all unemployed loggers or wild-eyed survivalists? My guess is plenty of retired military brass are playing soldier in the woods, thinking they're the country's saving remnant. Plenty of shirt-and-tie types, too."

"Maybe."

"But you still disagree."

Fitzgerald shifted his eyes, looking at her now. "I'm trying to think of reasons to disagree. If a militia group is involved in the murders we're out of the game. We don't even know where to begin. The whole thing is beyond us—something for state or federal authorities."

"Oh, swell. The feds turn up here and half of Ossning will believe a United Nations takeover is next."

"What I mean is Allison's death has to be a local matter

if we're going to figure it out. If not, we might as well toss
in the towel now."

"It could be local and still beyond us."

"I know."

"So we forget the militia business," Mercy said.

"No," Fitzgerald said, "just hope to hell there's no connection."

ON THE DRIVE along the North Downriver Road to Walther
Bridge Mercy asked Fitzgerald for his impression of Lucille
Ringwald.

"I hardly noticed her."

"I think that's the point. You weren't supposed to."

"What?"

"Nothing. Just tell me what you did notice."

"She's on the odd side, I suppose."

"You call that odd?"

"The red hair, I meant. And she didn't say anything."

"And Max didn't introduce her or even look her way.
He acted like she wasn't there. She could have been a piece
of furniture."

"So what do you make of her?"

"That she's crazy, letting him get away with it. And for
what? To stay married to him? Unless I'm missing something, Max Ringwald's no bargain."

"That depends."

"Oh?"

"On what the options are."

"I suppose," Mercy admitted. "I'll tell you something
else. That woman may be beaten down but she heard everything we said. She was paying attention."

"And?"

"I don't know. It's just a hunch."

"About what?"

"That if we ever got her talking we'd learn a lot more than Max told us."

THEY PASSED THROUGH a stretch of pine barrens that had been burned over a half-dozen years before, the fire started from a trash burn by a homeowner during a period of severe August drought. Mercy had seen to it that he was brought up on charges, trying to set an example for other fool trash burners in the county. But there was nothing she could do about the devastation. The pine barrens had a raw beauty about them, but after a fire swept through there were blackened trunks, eroded soil, nothing to love. Pine seedlings and scrub oaks had emerged, yet the area still held its sa~ ravaged look.

Mercy sighed and said, "I didn't know you still carried around business cards."

"I nearly forgot I had them."

"They signify something? You may go back to work for the paper?"

"There's a lot of old junk in my wallet, that's all."

"Maybe."

Fitzgerald shifted in the seat, looking at her. "Something else on your mind?"

"You told me Max Ringwald had complained to the *Free Press* about Allison. You didn't bring that up."

Fitzgerald nodded. "I wanted to keep him talking. Max had his back up already."

"But he wanted a story in the paper about the Catch and Keep Alliance. He gave Allison information. Why would he turn around and complain? It doesn't make sense."

"It doesn't," Fitzgerald agreed. He kept looking at her. "That's not all, is it?"

"I keep thinking about Lucille," Mercy said. "There's something I can't get out of my mind."

"What?"

She shook her head and said, "Go back to Allison and the militia business. How'd she ever get the idea the Catch and Keep Alliance had any involvement in that direction? From Max's anti-government talk? You know, she just assumed it? Or did she get it from someone entirely different?"

"Ray?"

"A possibility. But he doesn't strike me as someone who'd get mixed up with a militia group. For one thing, he'd have to take orders. That doesn't fit with the Ray Thorne I've got in mind."

"There's another possibility—that she made the whole thing up."

"I know," Mercy said. "I've heard newspaper folks do that. But let's say she didn't."

"Okay."

"I've got another hunch. I don't suppose you ever heard of a character up here named Wesley Wallace Dawes?"

"No."

"Before your time. There's someone who'd remember."

FIFTEEN

THE MOMENT the Cherokee came through the pines to a low house of weathered logs set back from the river among scattered white birch, a tall, angular, gray-haired woman appeared from a rear door, watching them. She wore khaki trousers, a blue denim shirt, and around her neck was a knotted bandanna. When Mercy waved from an open window, the woman leaned forward, rigid, hawk-like, then seemed to relax. She waved back.

"She doesn't see all that well," Mercy said to Fitzgerald, "and she won't wear glasses, at least not in public. She's a little vain that way. But she knows everything that goes on around here. You'll see."

"I heard the sound," Sarah Nunemaker said when she came up to the Cherokee. "It gave me a start."

"Oh?" Mercy said.

"I wasn't expecting anyone." Sarah smiled in at them, brown eyes alive in a long, brown, sun-etched face. "When I saw it was you— How nice."

"Afraid we can't stay, Sarah."

"But you must. I'll put on coffee."

Mercy shook her head. "We were driving by and I wanted to show Fitzgerald the river from here. The way you and Cam left the bank wild. Could we take a look?" When Sarah peered in at Fitzgerald, Mercy said, "He's the one who won a lottery."

Sarah looked from Fitzgerald to Mercy. "The writer you're living with. How nice." Then she said, "You're certain you won't come in?"

"We'll take a rain check."

"I won't forget."

"Sarah doesn't forget anything," Mercy said to Fitzgerald. "Believe me."

From the log house Sarah led the way through high grass in the direction of the river. Except for a long, tunnel-like opening, the view was obscured by a dense growth of spruce and cedar.

"Sarah can glimpse a bit of the river from the house," Mercy said, "but that's all. You float by, you have to look quick to notice a place back in here."

"My husband insisted," Sarah said to Fitzgerald. "He wanted everything as natural as possible. Of course there aren't many cedars anymore, not with the deer, so he put in seedlings. He had to protect them with wire fencing, building the fences higher every year. It's fifteen years before they're any size at all."

"Sounds like he was a fine environmentalist," Fitzgerald said.

"Ahead of his time." Then Mercy was looking at Sarah, telling her, "We stopped at the Ringwalds' place before we came here. The way Cam treated the river bank as against Max's way—it's day and night. I wanted Fitzgerald to see. He's renting the A-frame—"

"—at Walther Bridge. Such a grand part of the river."

"It is," Mercy said, "and has to be kept that way. Your place is a model."

"That's kind."

"I mean it. You and Cam worked wonders here."

Sarah smiled, then drew Fitzgerald's attention to an area of tiny cedar seedlings encircled by chicken-wire fencing. "I do it still, foolish as it is at my age. I'll never see them halfway grown." She turned to Mercy. "The deer population is quite out of control."

Mercy shrugged. "You know the problem. People feed

them through the winter, there aren't any predators besides hunters. We need to bring back wolves."

"Cam used to shoot them for the bounty."

"Everybody did back then. That's when there were sheep ranches up here that had to be protected. Or so we thought. There's nothing now. There's no reason not to bring them back."

"I don't know, Mercy."

"Well, it's a whole other problem." Mercy turned to Fitzgerald and smiled. "Sarah and I can't get together on fish let alone wolves. She likes to grill a trout now and then."

"My husband did."

"Like I say, everybody did back then."

"I might be in Sarah's corner on that one," Fitzgerald said. "Doesn't seem unreasonable, grilling an occasional trout. I hear you have an organization around here working for that."

"Traitor," Mercy said.

"Would you be interested?" Sarah asked.

"Oh, no," Mercy said, "don't get started. We're here to look at the riverbank."

Sarah winked at Fitzgerald and said, "I'll see you're put on our mailing list. Everything you receive you must hide from Mercy."

Fitzgerald winked back. "It's a deal."

"All right," Mercy said, "no plotting."

THEY WERE BACK AT the Cherokee, standing outside it, when Mercy asked Sarah about the murdered young woman, Allison Thorne.

"She was right here, Mercy, visiting me. She was writing a story for her newspaper."

"About the Catch and Keep Alliance?"

"We had coffee. She was so intelligent."

"You must have been a help to her," Mercy said, "knowing so much about the area."

Sarah shook her head. "I'm afraid not."

"Oh?"

"She stopped coming."

"You told her all you knew?"

"She was a lovely young woman." Sarah looked down at her hands, the backs speckled with age spots, fingers knotted together. When her eyes lifted she said, "Did you know her husband, Mercy?"

"Only by reputation."

"He was killed in the same manner."

"So I understand."

"Don't you find that strange?"

"It is."

"So very strange," Sarah said.

"You cut that short," Fitzgerald said on the drive back to the A-frame. "I thought you were going to bring up the man you mentioned."

"Dawes," Mercy said. "And I changed my mind."

"So you brought up Allison instead."

"Started to. I changed my mind about that, too."

"Sarah might have said more."

"If I'd given her a chance, you mean." Mercy gazed out the window at the vista of pines, a checkerboard here of burnt-over patches within sections of healthy, mature growth. "Maybe she would have, but I doubt it. I realized it right away. Sarah's very polite, a real lady. But—"

"An attractive lady. I liked her."

"Attractive for her age."

"Any age. Cam was a lucky man."

Mercy waved a hand through the air. "C'mon, Fitzgerald. Keep tracking. Sarah's polite as can be. And she's lonely, living out there by herself. Still and all, she's guarded around me. Couldn't you tell?''

"No."

"Well, she was. I'm the DNR, and as far as the catch and keep people are concerned that means I wear the black hat.''

"You can be troublesome, that's so."

"I'm serious," Mercy said. "Sarah and I detour around certain subjects."

"You talked together like old friends."

"That's not the point. We go way back. But trust me, we'll learn more if someone else speaks with her about Allison.''

"Who?"

"You'll see."

SIXTEEN

PHIPPS PULLED his rental up beside the patrol car parked off the side of the road and rapidly rolled down the window. The officer rolled down his and looked back at him, eyes fogged with sleep. "Half-dozen miles down the road," Phipps said in a breathless voice. "Looks like a guy lost control on a curve, whacked a tree. Godawful mess."

The officer's eyes snapped to attention. "You stopped?"

"Long enough to see what happened. I was going for help when I spotted your car. You hurry, maybe you can save him."

The officer had put on his flat-brimmed hat and started the engine of the patrol car. "Follow me," he instructed Phipps.

"Sure thing."

The patrol car spun from the dirt siding, reached the asphalt, shot forward, vanished down the road. Phipps smiled into its wake. Then he turned his rental into the dirt two-track that had been blocked by the patrol car and moved along a narrow passage through a dark growth of pine. Why had he ever thought himself rusty? You never forgot how, like riding a bike. Away from a desk, out in the field again, he was as good a reporter as ever.

The road he was on had received some recent use. There were tire tracks in the dirt and weeds alongside were flattened. Nonetheless, he felt, leaving the asphalt road behind, as if he had dropped off the edge of the known world. At a gas station in Ossning, inspecting a map, Lost Finger Lake had been a pin-point of blue in an otherwise blank expanse. The map hadn't shown any road in.

He had gone what seemed a mile or so when the two-track dipped sharply from the pines and he was looking across a weedy meadow with a small lake in the center, blue water encircled with brown reeds. Off to the side was a string of tired-looking log cabins, one of them marked off with yellow plastic police tape fluttering in the breeze coming off the water. Gus Thayer had said the cabin was cordoned off, but the tape was a surprise. You saw it all over in Detroit but Phipps hadn't expected it here, a hidden-away place in the north woods.

But that the place *was* hidden was all to the good. It didn't take any imagination to see a guerrilla force training back in this wilderness, nobody the wiser. In his mind's eye Phipps saw the pictures a good photographer could take away, pictures that lent visual weight to an article blowing the whistle on the operation.

He followed the lumpy two-track down to the cabins and parked beside the one set off with yellow tape, the place where Allison's husband had been wiped out. Before getting out of the rental he pulled a pair of rubber knee boots over his tasseled loafers, the purchase made in Ossning at the Wal-Mart across from the Wolverine Motel. He placed his other purchase, a plastic flask he had filled in the motel room, in the inner pocket of his sport coat. He was prepared now, body and soul, for whatever lay ahead.

It was one thing to find the place looking like a training ground, another to turn up evidence militia had actually been here, doing whatever they did. But what kind of evidence? Spent shells, targets they had shot up, equipment left behind—he didn't know what he would find until he looked around. The murder site was the place to begin.

Did police really think yellow tape kept anybody out who wanted to get in? Phipps was wondering about that as he slipped under the tape and walked to the cabin's door. It was padlocked, a disappointment, but not unexpected. He

walked around to the side and peered through a window
into a sparsely furnished room—a room that seemed neat
as a pin, which wasn't the way you would expect a bunch
of backwoods warriors to leave it.

Disappointment deepening, he went to another window
that looked into a small room that had a pair of beds
pressed against one wall. Another wall was lined with
boxes, floor to ceiling, the window so streaked with dirt he
couldn't make out the lettering on the sides. He looked
around to see if the coast was clear, which he knew was
pointless considering he was as alone as anyone could be,
then began kicking through the weeds with his boots, hunting for a rock.

When he found one the right size he went to work. He
meant to chip a small opening at the edge of the window,
enough to see through, but ended up shattering half the
glass. Not that it mattered since the cabin was on its last
legs anyway. The opening afforded a good view of the
room. He read the lettering on three or four boxes before
the meaning finally registered. Christ almighty! The room
was stashed with booze.

But was it?

What he was looking at were boxes. There was no guarantee they were filled, or filled with booze. For all he knew
there was ammunition inside, enough for a decent-sized
war. Even if the boxes were full of booze it was a major
discovery, putting the militia in a whole new light—booze
hounds as well as backwoods warriors. In his mind's eye
Phipps saw a progression of photographs in the *Free Press:*
a wilderness with the lake in the center; a string of cabins
with one with yellow tape around it; an inside shot of the
room stacked with booze boxes; lastly a tight close-up of
the contents of one of the boxes, showing ammunition or
booze.

Or nothing.

A bitter possibility was that the boxes were empty, worth zero as evidence. He wasn't going to know unless he looked inside one, which meant getting inside the room, which in turn meant breaking the rest of the glass and crawling through the window. Phipps stepped back, estimated the width of the opening as against his own, decided he could make it, barely. He hefted the rock again and went to work.

When the glass was out, most of it resting in shards within the room, he braced his hands on either side of the opening and began to pull himself through. At once he jumped back, shot a hand to his mouth. A tiny triangle of glass had been missed, located—naturally—just at the spot where he had placed his hand. When he took his hand from his mouth, examining the wound through half-closed eyes, blood spurted from his palm.

IT TOOK A WHILE to get the blood stopped, a handkerchief wrapped around his hand. It took longer to ease the queasy feeling in his stomach, a sensation always brought on by the sight of blood, his especially. The wound, though, was minor. It wouldn't stop him. He thought of it as a minor casualty suffered in the course of reporting, a journalistic equivalent of a purple heart.

Phipps returned to the rental car and was sitting in the driver's seat, sipping whiskey from his flask while he prepared himself to venture again through the cabin window, when his eye caught movement at the edge of pines beyond the far end of the lake. It was an animal, he thought first—deer probably—about to emerge from the woods, drink at the lake. He felt a surprisingly keen interest. He was about to witness a picture-postcard moment in nature.

But deer had four legs and what he was looking at appeared to have two. Deer were brown and this was dark green. Phipps leaned close to the windshield, peering into the distance. And deer didn't carry guns.

So it wasn't a deer but a hunter, about to move from the woods toward the lake. Was some season underway? Ducks? Phipps still couldn't see the figure distinctly. He could only make out that he was wearing a dark-green coat, a cap of the same color, and had a gun cradled in the crook of one arm. But weren't hunters supposed to wear orange? Maybe that was when they were blasting away at deer. Maybe, duck hunting, they wore green.

Phipps cast an eye over the lake, checking to see if ducks were present. When he looked back the hunter had stopped moving. He was standing motionless at the edge of the pines, facing toward the cabin where the rental car was parked. Phipps had the impression he and the hunter were studying one another.

The hunter, it dawned on him, might have hunted here before, a regular at Lost Finger Lake. In which case he might know something about the use of the place for militia training. The hunter might, in other words, be a source— the only one, given the hidden-away nature of the place, it seemed likely he would find.

Phipps got out of the car and waved a hand vigorously in the air, then began moving off at a brisk pace in the direction of the hunter. For a moment the hunter remained motionless, looking back, then abruptly turned and retreated into the pines. "Hold on!" Phipps shouted into the distance.

If the hunter heard he paid no attention. He kept moving away, deeper into the pines. Phipps picked up his pace, half running now through high grass and thickets of low bushes, congratulating himself for having purchased the knee boots at Wal-Mart. In tasseled loafers he wouldn't stand a chance in terrain like this.

"Phipps here!" he called out. *"Detroit Free Press!"*

By the time he reached the end of the lake and was about to enter the wall of pines Phipps was certain he was gaining on the fleeing hunter. He was in better shape than he knew, or the hunter in worse. Surely the hunter could hear him now.

"I'll make it worth your while!" Checkbook journalism was a last resort in extreme cases, as when your one and only source was on the verge of vanishing. "That means I'll pay for your time!"

He stopped, breathing hard, waiting for the hunter to switch direction, emerge from the pines, agree to deal. But nothing happened. The wall of pine ahead was black and motionless in sunlight. What was going on? Was the hunter pissed off, Phipps having interrupted his hunting? If so, why wouldn't he have waited, angry, letting off steam? Phipps had planned to say he was sorry, but point out there weren't any ducks on the lake anyway. But the hunter had just taken off, ignoring even the offer of dough for a few minutes of his time.

The only explanation Phipps could come up with was that the hunter still hadn't heard. Maybe he was hard of hearing, only seeing a guy waving his arms and bearing down on him as a threat. Phipps resolved to try again. He would move faster, enter farther into the pines, allow the hunter one last chance.

"Phipps here!" he shouted from deep in his lungs. *"Detroit Free Press!"*

A FEW STEPS inside the woods he found himself stopped by a barbed-wire fence fastened to the trees. What was going on? You couldn't raise cattle or sheep in a wilderness like this, so why fence it off? He was pondering possible explanations when he saw a flash of green, though this deep in the woods, the whole world colored green, you could be fooled. But this green seemed darker—and it moved.

Which meant the hunter had gone over the fence, which also meant Phipps could.

He lifted a leg, felt the sting of a metal barb through his pants, lifted the leg higher. When he was over he worked his way through a tangle of deadfall and called out, "I've got identification, business cards, whatever you want! Just hold up a damn minute!"

There was another flash of green, just off to his side now, closer, and he turned to face it. He was catching up with the hunter. If the guy wasn't stone deaf he couldn't help but hear him now. Phipps was about to repeat what he had just said, barking it out, when the gun went off.

Everything came to him in a definite sequence: first the orange-red flash; then the big-bang explosion; finally the needles of pain coursing up and down his right leg, knee to ankle. He was on the ground in a bed of pine branches, exploring the pain with his hand, the wounded one still wrapped with a handkerchief, when it came to him what had happened. The maniac hunter had shot him!

Phipps was about to unleash a string of curses when second thoughts overtook him. Followed, the guy had shot him in the leg. Cursed at, he might blow his head off. Phipps tried to burrow deeper into the pine branches, gaining shelter, still feeling the pain in his leg. He was certain something was broken in there. He wouldn't be able to stand. He worked his good hand inside his rubber boot, edged the hand down to the cuff of his trousers, then up above his stocking until he felt skin—and the sticky wetness of blood.

There was no way he could manage to get the boot off, pull up his trouser leg, get the handkerchief off his hand and around the wound, stopping the flow of blood. He wasn't sure he wanted to even if he could—wanted to know for certain how bad off he was. What he needed to do was get out of the woods, find his rental, drive to Ossning, locate a hospital, get professional help, assuming the hick town had any—do all that and not get shot a second time by the maniac.

It amazed him how clearly he was thinking. His leg from the knee down blazed now with pain yet his mind was calm, orderly. Compensation had set in, he supposed, his head drawing the voltage that had once gone to his leg. He was considering that when his mind reminded him of a basic problem: He couldn't walk.

With his good hand he eased the plastic flask from his inside coat pocket, with his teeth unscrewed the top and let it drop, raised the flask and drained whiskey down his throat. He seemed to feel better at once. If he couldn't walk maybe he could crawl, pulling himself along with the parts of his body still in working order. It was worth a try.

Phipps closed his eyes and listened with all his might. He couldn't detect a sound. That might mean the maniac had kept retreating and was now out of firing range—or that he was hiding, stock still, waiting for another chance. Phipps weighed his options. He could stay where he was and hope somebody found him before he bled to death— or try to help himself and make for the lake, the cabins, his car.

He tilted the flask, draining the remainder of the whiskey. "Go for it!" he told himself then, and began moving.

He had pulled himself forward maybe twenty yards, in the woods still, when a fresh thought came to him. If he made it out, lived, he would have an even better tale to tell: *Free Press* reporter gunned down in pursuit of a militia exposé! A story like that, written in the first person, would be page one above the fold. Afterward, *20/20* or *60 Minutes* might come calling.

He inched forward, composing the story in his head, and as he did so everything fell into place. He had it wrong before, had been on a false track, entirely screwed up. Now he understood. Understood perfectly.

SEVENTEEN

MERCY GRINNED and explained to Fitzgerald, "Calvin's not good for much, but I knew he could handle this. Sarah's soft in the head when it comes to him."

"She's got good taste," Calvin said.

"Cam Nunemaker taught him about fishing with flies. That's when Calvin and Verlyn were kids, running wild, living in a tent on the South Branch, fishing with worms. Cam straightened them both out, but it was Calvin he really took under his wing."

"He had good taste, too."

"Eventually he gave Calvin a bamboo rod, a custom-made Nunemaker. That sealed things as far as Sarah was concerned. If her husband thought enough of Calvin to give him a rod, he must be God's gift to the world. Little did she know. Anyway, she still thinks Calvin uses the rod."

"Naw, you don't use something that good. I get it out, look at it now and then."

"I'd like to see it," Fitzgerald said.

"The point of all this," Mercy said, "is I knew Calvin was the one to talk with Sarah about Wesley Wallace Dawes."

They were sitting at the bar of the Borchard Hotel, where they had agreed to meet after Calvin returned from seeing Sarah Nunemaker. Mercy had laid out for him exactly what he should do. It was to appear to be a social call, Calvin realizing how long it had been since he had stopped to see her. Soon he would be off to New Zealand, where Sarah knew he spent half the year guiding, and he wanted to touch base with her before he left. Sarah would be delighted. She would make coffee and insist he have cake or pie.

"Coffee's bad for the ticker," Calvin had protested.

"Damnit," Mercy told him, "this is serious."

"I thought you said you had a hunch."

"A *serious* hunch."

Eventually he was to turn the conversation with Sarah to the murders, getting Sarah to recall her meeting, or meetings, with Allison Thorne. Then he should slip into the conversation Dawes' name, letting Sarah ramble on about him. Dawes was Mercy's hunch.

"Then what?" Calvin had wanted to know.

"See what develops. See if Sarah makes any connection between Dawes and Allison."

"Should she?"

"C'mon, Calvin," Mercy said. "Your job's to find out."

"SO WHO WAS DAWES?" Fitzgerald asked now.

Mercy waited until Sandy brought schooners of beer for her and Fitzgerald and a bottle of O'Doul's for Calvin. "A crazy who lived back in the woods out south in the county."

"Hold on," Calvin said. "He had his points."

"He was mad as a hatter. A survivalist type, wild hair, big mountain-man beard, living in a ramshackle cabin he built himself. Nobody paid any attention until he started turning out a newsletter, printed on some old hand press he'd bought and fixed up. He had a nearly rusted-out pickup and you'd see him chugging around the county stuffing the newsletter into mailboxes. Even if you didn't want it you wouldn't say anything to someone who looked as crazy as he did."

"I wanted it," Calvin said, "but Dawes couldn't get down to my place. Road was too bad. I had to read it at the bakery."

"He called it the *North Country Avenger*. You can imagine what it was like—an anarchist mishmash of antireligion, anti-government, anti-everything. The DNR came in for its share of abuse. But that's what the whole thing was, a steady stream of abuse. After a while the newsletter became a kind of odd-ball institution around here, showing up in your mailbox every other week, people halfway expecting it. That's when Cam Nunemaker got the brainstorm of running a small display ad in the thing. This was at the start of the rod business, before Cam began turning out catalogues, and Dawes' paper was the cheapest place to advertise. But there was more to it than that. There was a part of Cam that was as sensible as could be, another that was nearly as anti-everything as Dawes. That's where Calvin got a lot of his crackpot ideas, as a matter of fact, hanging around Cam as a kid."

"Hold on," Calvin said.

"Dawes and Cam got pretty chummy, and after a while Sarah got involved, turning out the *Avenger* when she got a computer, doing a better job than Dawes could on his old hand press. There was some talk that Dawes and Sarah got real chummy, though it was hard to believe since Sarah was a nice-looking woman, Cam was presentable, and Dawes was a wild boar. But Dawes wasn't married, so people talked. One day Dawes was shot dead by a deer hunter. That was the official verdict, a hunting accident, though the hunter was never located and people around town had their doubts. Dawes was cutting firewood when he took a slug in the chest."

"Doubts?" Fitzgerald asked.

"Dawes made enemies with the newsletter, needless to say. And there was Cam. Cam was a friend but he might have decided he'd seen enough of Dawes. Or maybe Sarah—maybe she'd seen enough. Anyway, Cam himself was dead a year or so later—fatal heart attack sitting in his workroom wrapping a new rod. Sarah was a widow.''

''All right,'' Fitzgerald said. ''But this was a while ago, right? Why bring up Dawes to Sarah now?''

''I told you. It's a hunch. Allison may have gotten her militia notions from Sarah. Sarah may have told her about Dawes.''

''He had something to do with the militia movement?''

Mercy shook her head. ''It was before anyone knew there was such a thing. But if Dawes were around now, still putting out that nutty newsletter, that's the first thing you'd think. You'd have him pegged for sure as a militia type. Allison would think that way.''

Fitzgerald asked, ''Did she?''

''Ask Calvin.''

''Really?'' Calvin said. ''I get to talk now?''

''Very funny,'' Mercy said. ''Just talk.''

''First I get Sarah to brew up some tea instead of coffee. Then I drink a gallon of it and have two hunks of German chocolate cake, arteries turning to lead, before we get around to what she knew about Allison. She said Allison sat right where we were, took notes, wrote down everything Sarah told her. So she started telling her about Cam and his rods, but Allison wasn't interested. She only wanted dope about the catch and keep outfit, so Sarah spun some tales about the old days when Cam would go out before dinner, wade the run in front of their place, bring in a couple twenty-inch rainbows for their meal. Sarah said that's all people wanted now, the right to do what Cam did. She didn't tell Allison you could fish for a week now on the mainstream and never pick up two big rainbows.

''Some time goes by and Allison comes back, wanting more dope for her story. Sarah's happy to see her but she's told her all she knows. Allison's got out pen and paper again, ready to take notes, but about what? Sarah can't think of a single thing. Then a lightbulb goes off. Allison had told her where she and Ray lived, the place near Cord-lee, and Sarah knows the location. That's near where old Dawes had his shack. So she starts in on Dawes and his newsletter, thinking this will interest Allison because Dawes had gone ballistic when catch and release came on the mainstream. He figured the next thing the government would say was you couldn't cut firewood, the billion jack pines an endangered species.

"So Sarah spins the story of Dawes, her point being that opposition to catch and release has a history on the river. It didn't hatch overnight with this new group. She even has some old *Avengers* around, kept them because of Cam's ads, and digs them out for Allison. Allison thinks she's struck gold. She writes down everything Sarah remembers about Dawes and wants to take the old copies with her, but Sarah says no, she doesn't want them out of the house. That was part of it—the other part was she wanted to keep Allison coming around. So Allison keeps showing up, reading the old copies and taking notes, and Sarah's happy. You hit her years, you don't have young women wanting to visit you.

"I let Sarah tell me all this, then I drop in the conversation the thing about the militia. She doesn't know what I'm talking about, so I say, 'Guys who put on camouflage and shoot up the woods.' She says, 'The national guard?' I explain some more but it's clear she doesn't get it. She's got the tube but maybe doesn't keep up. I can tell it's no use. Sarah told Allison about old Dawes and showed her old *Avengers* but never told her anything about the militia. So what I'm thinking now is how I make my exit.

"I change the subject, telling Sarah about the rod Cam gave me, how it's still the best there is. If we can get talking about Cam, I figure Sarah will forget we were talking about Allison and I can ease out. Big mistake. Sarah gets wound up again, about Cam now, and I'm stuck listening. I figure the next thing is more cake. But then she wants to show me what she'd have shown Allison if Allison was interested. We go through the house to the back room Cam used for wrapping and tying. It's the way Cam left it, all his equipment, gun collection, boots, tackle, the whole works. And Sarah's stash of Cam's rods—a dozen maybe. We take them out of the cases and I touch them all. Talk about striking gold—I'd never seen that many Cam Nunemaker rods together in one place. It was another half hour or so before I got out.

"Allison wanted to write about something, that was it— the rods. Forget catch and keep. Forget Dawes. Good story right there, right in front of her, and she blew it."

Fitzgerald said, "You think the rods are a good story. I'd think so. Mercy would. All serious fishermen on the Borchard would. But the *Free Press* wouldn't. Allison was savvy enough to know that."

"I always said the paper's a rag," Calvin said.

"Never mind," Mercy said. "My hunch was right. Sarah's old boyfriend, Dawes, is behind the militia connection."

"Hold on. Sarah and Dawes were never like that. And she never said anything about the militia. I told you, she didn't know what I was talking about."

"What Mercy means," Fitzgerald said, "is the story about Dawes, especially seeing copies of his newsletter, gave Allison the idea of a militia connection. She knew about the militia, if Sarah didn't. She'd have pictured Dawes as a militia type."

"One before his time," Mercy said.

"Hold on. That still doesn't tie in with the catch and keep outfit."

"True. The only connection was in Allison's head. So

that leaves us," Mercy went on, "with the possibility that Allison invented the whole thing. Made it up."

"I thought that's what you did," Calvin said, "writing for a rag."

Fitzgerald said, "It's why newspapers have editors. Allison might have come up with the idea that a militia group was involved with the Catch and Keep Alliance, but an editor would want to see the evidence. Dawes wasn't evidence. Both he and his newsletter were long gone."

"So Sarah might have given Allison the idea, but the idea was only a start."

"Exactly."

Calvin said, "I don't get it. I read stories all the time that don't have any evidence, just quotes, this guy and that guy."

"That's evidence—newspaper evidence. You hunt up somebody to say something you can put quote marks around, something that supports what you're trying to get across."

Mercy said, "So after she saw Sarah, Allison would have to dig up someone who'd support the militia idea."

"But she didn't. I read the story on her computer. There was no mention of the militia."

"What computer?" Calvin asked.

"I'll fill you in sometime," Fitzgerald said. "Let's stay on track. Either Allison didn't get anywhere with the militia connection—or she did: She *was* working on a new story, and the story was erased from the computer by her killer."

Mercy said, "A killer who also erased her notes. Remember Sarah told Calvin she took notes."

"I only checked her computer system. You would think she'd enter her hand-written notes in the computer so she'd have a backup record. That's the usual procedure. But I didn't find any notes in the computer and there weren't any notebooks on her work table."

"Okay," Mercy said, "let's summarize. We're guessing that Sarah Nunemaker put the idea of a militia connection in Allison Thorne's head. Then we're guessing that Allison tried to dig up evidence to support the idea. Either she didn't find any, or she did, but the evidence is missing. The only story that remains is the one the *Free Press* turned down. That about it?"

Calvin shrugged.

Fitzgerald raised his hands, palms up, in the air.

"In which case," Mercy sighed, "we better have another drink."

AFTER SANDY BROUGHT two schooners of beer and another bottle of O'Doul's she remained to talk, arms braced on the bar, her voice at the level of a conspirator's whisper.

"Stroud was in earlier. Guess what for?"

Calvin said, "Why he came to a bar? He wanted a drink."

"Ha, ha. He wanted to know about Ray Thorne, as a matter of fact. If he ever tried to sell me liquor. I told him I didn't drink hard stuff, not after what happened to my ex, Rollie Wink. But he said he didn't mean me personally, he meant the bar. Did Ray ever try to sell the bar liquor? I said we don't buy off who comes in, we buy from a distributor in Muskegon. Besides, Ray Thorne never came in. The hotel isn't his kind of place, thank goodness." Sandy paused, rolled her eyes. "Wasn't his kind of place."

"What's this all about?" Calvin asked.

"We'll tell you later," Fitzgerald said. He asked Sandy if Stroud wanted to know anything more.

"Just if I knew that Ray had peddled booze around the county. Boy, did I. I mean, I did after I learned that Rollie had been drinking his lunch every day out at Weyerhaeuser. Rollie bought the booze off Ray. Stroud tried to remember how long that was now, Rollie getting killed out there, and

I told him seven years. More like seventy, you want to
know how it feels. Anyway, he asked if I knew about the
ads Ray put in the *Call*, firewood ads, and I said sure. I
thought he was going to have a stroke, right in front of me.
Didn't I know it was illegal, selling booze that way, and I
said sure I knew, Ray was competition for the bar, but what
can you do about some people? 'Throw them in jail,'
Stroud said. So I said, 'You should have.'''

"I can imagine his muted response," Mercy said.

"Boy, let me tell you."

Calvin said, "Hold on. I didn't know Thorne peddled
booze."

Mercy said, "You don't read the *Call*, that's why."

"It's a rag."

"And you don't drink."

"That's so."

"So Ray never considered you a customer. Fact is, Calvin, you're out of the loop. *Every* loop."

"That reminds me," Sandy said. "It's why I got talking
about Stroud in the first place. He wants to see you."

"Who?" Fitzgerald asked.

"You. After he was in about Ray, a couple hours later,
he called. Said he was calling every place around town you
might be."

"He say why?"

Sandy shook her head. "He wasn't all that happy. You
could tell."

AFTER FITZGERALD LEFT the hotel for the city-county building Mercy told Calvin she had another job for him.

"I can't eat more cake."

"This doesn't involve Sarah. It's Max Ringwald."

"Never met him."

"You must have. He comes around Verlyn's fly shop.

You know the type—buys a few flies but actually wants to pick up fishing tips from the guides.''

"We never tell the truth.''

"He doesn't know that. Besides, the lies you tell are better than what fishermen like Max know themselves.''

"That's so.''

"He knows who you are. You call, tell him you're Calvin McCann, he'll be an eager puppy.''

"What do I say then?''

"You've heard about the Catch and Keep Alliance and want to know more. You're thinking of joining.''

"I don't join things.''

"He doesn't know that. All he'll know is that the Kabin Kamp's top guide is interested in his organization. He won't be able to contain himself. It would be a major coup, having you involved. Tell him you'll meet him somewhere, but it can't be the fly shop, not with Verlyn there. Tell Max you're in town.''

"I am.''

"So you'll meet him somewhere here. Set the time.''

"Then what?''

"You call me at the office, tell me the time, then show up and get him talking about the organization. Tell him you don't believe in catch and release.''

"I don't.''

"So there you go. Tell him every half-baked thing you think about it. Tell him anything. Just keep him there at least an hour.''

"So you can do what?''

"Play another hunch.''

EIGHTEEN

WILLARD STROUD SHUT his office door, came around the desk, lowered himself into his chair, took a long look at Fitzgerald. Then he drew a slip of paper from his drawer and passed it across the desk.

"Name you gave me before?"

Fitzgerald looked at the paper, nodded.

"Fellow in Detroit who asked you to check on Allison Thorne? One you were doing a favor for, you said?"

Again Fitzgerald nodded.

"Then how come I got him in the hospital with buckshot in his leg? Next room they're checking out Gus Thayer, seeing if his heart blew up. How come I've got that, too?"

"What?" Fitzgerald said.

Stroud kept looking at him, his gaze as fierce as he could make it. "That means you're surprised?"

"Of course I am."

"You told me you wouldn't write anything. That isn't how it looks. It looks like your fellow came up here and you two were getting together. Next thing I'd know there'd be a story in the paper."

"But we didn't get together. I didn't even know Phipps was in Ossning." Fitzgerald asked then, "He was shot?"

"Below the knee, one leg. He'll live."

"Where?"

"Where'd the shooting take place? That's what I thought you might tell me."

"How can I? I didn't know Phipps was here."

Stroud said, "Then I'll tell you. I've got deputies stationed at Lost Finger Lake keeping busybodies from taking the two-track in, gaping at the murder site. So my deputy is out there, sitting in his patrol car, when Gus Thayer comes up from the lake and says there's a fellow back in the woods, shot in the leg. So the deputy gets Gus in the car and they drive in the two-track and find the fellow, your fellow, where Gus left him when he went for help, in high grass at the far end of the lake. He's passed out and now Gus is having chest pains. So the deputy gets them both in the car and whips off to the hospital, calling me on the way. When I get there your fellow is still out and Gus is feeling worse, so there's nothing to do but get them both into the emergency room.

"But I learn from the deputy part of what happened. He recognizes your fellow as the one who pulled a stunt on him, drove up and told him there was an accident down the road. But there wasn't. When the deputy comes back he doesn't think to go into the lake, check the place out. Only when Gus comes up the two-track does he figure out what happened. Your fellow got him off chasing his tail, then drove down to the lake."

Fitzgerald said, "What for?"

"Bust a window."

"What?"

"The back window of the cabin where Ray Thorne was killed was busted out. The deputy noticed."

"What for?"

"I asked your fellow that when he came out of emergency."

"Let's start over," Fitzgerald said. "Phipps isn't my fellow. I don't have anything to do with him."

"Except you were doing him a favor."

"That was before. This doesn't have anything to do with that."

Stroud shrugged. "He told me he was getting background, looking over the place where Ray Thorne was

killed. He saw the cabin marked off with tape and tried to
look in the window. Breaking the window was an accident.
Then he saw someone down by the end of the lake—a
hunter, he figured—and tried to get his attention. When the
hunter moved off, Phipps followed him into the woods.
Next thing he knew he was shot.''

"By the hunter?''

"He thinks so.''

"But why was he trying to get the hunter's attention?
And background for what?''

"That's what I got you in here to tell me. Phipps won't
say any more. I threatened to charge him with something
but he wouldn't budge. Maybe I'll charge him anyway—
disturbing the scene of a homicide.''

"Is that a crime?''

"In Tamarack County.'' Then Stroud said, ''You're on
the up and up with me? You don't know anything about
this background Phipps was working on?''

Fitzgerald nodded.

"Then get over to the hospital and talk to the fool. Whatever he tells you, tell me. I want to know why he busted a
window out there and why he wanted to talk to the hunter.
He still won't budge, you make him understand he's looking at jail time, *Free Press* fellow or not.''

"You want my help, in other words.''

Stroud waited before he said, ''One way to put it. Another is you're proving you and Phipps weren't working
behind my back. You're proving you're on my side.''

Fitzgerald smiled. ''What else? You're the law.'' Then
he said, ''You haven't told me what Gus Thayer was doing
out there.''

"I haven't talked to him. He was all hooked up to mon-
itors. If he's out of the emergency room when you go over,
leave him to me. There's some other business I've got with
him—about some classifieds in the *Call*. Mercy tell you?''

"She mentioned something,'' Fitzgerald said.

PHIPPS WAS BEING kept overnight in the community hospital for observation, only a moderately irritating prospect now that the pain killers had set in and he was soaking in a warm bath of tranquility. The old man snoring in the next bed, gallbladder case, hardly edged into his attention. Still, Phipps was giving the hospital a single night only. First thing in the morning, doctor's okay or not, he would be back in his rental car, racing south, hunting up a real doctor in Detroit to check out his wounds. What did they know about modern medicine in the north woods?

"I changed my mind," he told Fitzgerald. "The story's all yours."

Fitzgerald had pulled a chair beside Phipps' bed, sitting close so they would have privacy. Not that it mattered. The gallbladder case was dead to the world. "About what? And what story?"

Phipps leaned toward the edge of the bed and summoned up a scowl. "The story right under your nose. *Allison's* story. I was going to write it myself, win a goddamn Pulitzer. That was before Gus found me, half dead."

"I understand you weren't hit that bad."

"The hick sheriff tell you that? I'd have bled to death if it weren't for Gus."

"Maybe we should back up," Fitzgerald said, "to why you came to Ossning in the first place. You didn't let me know."

"Remember telling me if I needed more dope on the story to send someone up?" Phipps sniffed. "I did. Me. And I found plenty," he added before Fitzgerald could reply.

"About what?"

"What else? What Allison was working on—the militia connection."

"Maybe you could explain."

"Look," Phipps said. "I came up here, I knew you were no use, I hunted up the local rag. Gus tells me about the husband getting shot out in the woods, a secret place."

"Not secret," Fitzgerald interrupted, "private."

"I'm saying nobody knows about the place, what goes on out there. So it could be a militia layout—compound of some sort. That's why the husband got killed. He was out there, doing some digging for Allison. So Gus and I decide to check out the place, see if our theory holds water. Gus says he can walk in, some back route he knows through the woods. He'll let me know what he finds. But I get to thinking that maybe I can get in the easy way, on the road, if I can outfox the cop out there. I give it a try and it works."

"A sheriff's deputy was out there to prevent gawkers from entering a crime scene."

Phipps rolled his eyes. "You better stay up here, the fish expert. You've lost it for the paper."

"Go on," Fitzgerald said.

"You'd gone out there, a reporter, you'd have seen it—cabin full of booze boxes. The place is marked off with police tape, so I know it's the place the husband got it. My guess is he'd found the booze and put two and two together. It's for the militia, out there boozing as well as banging away with guns. So he's in the cabin, looking it over, when they find him. After that it's lights out."

"You said booze *boxes*."

"The cabin's locked up but I can see them through a window. I've got to make sure there's real stuff in them, so I bust the window to crawl in. Then I have a little accident, cut my hand, and I'm stopping the blood when I see a guy at the end of the lake—guy in green with a gun, so I figure he's a hunter, and if he hunts around here he'd know if militia types used the place. So I head off to talk to him but he goes the other way, back into the woods. I holler that I'm with the *Free Press*, I want to have a talk, I'll even make it worth his while. I keep following, he keeps retreating, then I lose sight of him—and bang! I'm shot. I can't walk so I crawl, trying to get back to the car, drive in here to the hospital. I make it as far as the edge of the lake when I run out of steam. Later, in here, I learn Gus found me, got the cop up on the road to help. I was in a coma or something."

"You passed out from loss of blood."

"What I said. Gus hadn't found me, I was finished. You heard about Gus?"

"He was having chest pains."

"Worse. I got the story from a nurse. His arteries are junked up—they're doing a bypass. You believe that? Here in this hick hospital."

"I was here myself once. They have good people."

"For sawing your chest open? It was when I heard about Gus I decided to hand you the story. I'm checking out first thing in the morning."

Fitzgerald said, "I'm not sure what story you're talking about. You getting shot? Gus having a bypass?"

"Christ almighty!" Phipps snarled. "*Allison's* story. Now we've got evidence—the secret place in the woods, the booze boxes in the cabin. To top it off, the husband getting bumped off."

"Evidence of what?"

"Ha!" Phipps nearly shouted. He rolled closer to the edge of the bed, his face inches from Fitzgerald's, paused then, checking the rhythmic snoring from the other bed, before he said, "Out there, crawling on my belly through the woods, I suddenly got it straight. You know, an epiphany. I thought the guy I'd been chasing was a hunter. Like hell! The guy in green was a militia member in military duds, patroling the training compound. He must have had orders—media turn up, shoot on sight.''

"Wait," Fitzgerald said. "He didn't shoot on sight. You said you followed him into the woods."

"He didn't know who I was. Not at first. I was just somebody on his tail. He didn't blast away until I said I was with the paper."

"All right, but that still isn't evidence. You don't know he was a militia member."

"Guy all decked out in green, lugging a gun, patroling the edge of the training compound? That's evidence."

"It's inference, if that."

Phipps rolled back to the center of the bed. He was tired of talking, especially to Fitzgerald. There was no point to it. Fitzgerald didn't understand, didn't want to understand. It went to show you what happened when a newspaperman came into money. When he got back to civilization he would give Gus Thayer a call, assuming Gus lived through his surgery, and pass on to him the dope he had given Fitzgerald. Maybe Gus would pick up the story for the local rag. Whatever happened, Phipps himself was out of it. If he could forget the dull ache in his leg, starting to work its way now through the pain killers, the trip up to the woods hadn't been a total washout. He had discovered his reporting skills were still there, rusty but ready.

"I got to rest," he said to Fitzgerald. "Doctor's orders."

"Anything you want me to tell the sheriff?"

"Goodbye, is all."

"It may not be so easy. He's got his back up over you entering a crime scene. And the shooting—he's got to find out what happened."

"I told him."

"Find out who did it."

"Yeah?" Phipps said, letting his eyelids drift downward.

"If I were him I don't know I'd push that. The militia don't care any more for sheriffs than reporters."

"You only got hit in the leg," Fitzgerald reminded him.

"And half bled to death," Phipps said.

THE FIRST THING Fitzgerald did when he returned to Stroud's office was tell him about Gus Thayer's bypass.

"I heard. But not here. They're running him over to Traverse City. I can't talk to him for a couple days."

"Too bad."

"Not if you got something from your fellow."

"Phipps," Fitzgerald said. "And he didn't say much."

Stroud listened as Fitzgerald went over what Phipps had told him. It didn't amount to much beyond the fact the broken window in the cabin wasn't an accident, which Stroud had figured out himself. He assumed Phipps had spotted the liquor boxes and was climbing in for a closer look, or to help himself. A nurse at the hospital told him there was a flask in Phipps' clothes when he was brought in, empty. And it was no surprise that Phipps was looking around the murder scene with the intention of writing something for the Detroit paper. That was what he meant about getting background—background for a story. What else could he have meant?

"I'd told him on the phone I wasn't interested," Fitzgerald said, "so he came up himself. He hooked up with Gus and the two of them went out to the lake."

"My deputy said only one man was in the car out there."

"Because Gus took another way in."

"What other way?"

"Overland."

"From where?"

"All I know is that's how Gus happened to find Phipps. Gus didn't have a car himself, so he had to get your deputy for help."

"All right," Stroud said. "Phipps and Gus Thayer were in on this together. But why'd they want to look at that murder scene rather than the mobile home?"

"I don't know," Fitzgerald said, "other than Ray Thorne getting shot seems to rule him out as Allison's killer."

Stroud waited, studying Fitzgerald. "You been talking to Slocum Byrd? Or Elsie?"

"You hear things, is all."

"Then you might as well hear it from the horse's mouth. Slocum says Ray and Allison died about the same time but Ray a little after her. Lansing ran a ballistics check on the bullets used. They're the same caliber, thirty-eights, but fired from different guns. So the way it looks, I'm hunting for two killers working together or a single killer who shot Allison, then drove to Lost Finger Lake and shot Ray, doing it the same way, one bullet, back of the head, but using different guns. You understand what I'm saying? The killings weren't the kind we usually get, spur of the moment. They were planned, worked out."

Stroud paused, watching Fitzgerald's reaction, wondering again if trusting a reporter was a mistake. It probably was, generally speaking, but for some reason he trusted this one, and this one was already involved in the case. Fitzgerald had found Allison's body and Mercy, his live-in, had found the other one. Stroud patted his empty shirt pocket, thought for a moment about asking Elsie to bring in coffee, decided to put his cards on the table. Such as they were.

"I told you before—I never figured Ray killed her. The way it was done, it didn't have his signature. I figured Allison got mixed up in something Ray was doing, not that I knew what it was. Then we find the liquor supply out at Lost Finger and I learn Ray's been bootlegging around the county. But that's small potatoes—bottle here, bottle there. The supply at the lake suggests he'd expanded. You with me?"

Fitzgerald nodded.

"Now I'm going to tell you something that stays in this room. Agreed?"

"Yes."

"Absolutely?"

"Yes."

"I know Ray had expanded. He tried to sell booze at the Keg O'Nails and Deke Musso out there gave him the heave-ho. But we turned up on Allison's computer a file of customers who bought, and bought in bulk. Not huge amounts but beyond the small-time stuff. Who do you suppose is on the list? Your pal Verlyn Kelso.

"So I went out to the Kabin Kamp and had a talk with Verlyn. He was as big a pain in the ass as usual, so I had to tell him the state alcohol people would be up in a flash if he didn't cooperate. What I learned is that Ray Thorne showed up at the fly shop one day and offered to supply liquor for the lodge at a better price than Verlyn was paying. Thorne claimed he could handle any amount. Verlyn didn't believe him, but he decided to take a case to see. Right away Ray goes out to his van, hauls it in, tells Verlyn to give him a call when he needs more. Verlyn's impressed. He claims he had no idea it was against the law, buying like that. He's not that stupid, of course, but I let it go. It's something he's got hanging over his head, something to use when I want.

"But that's not what I'm getting at. The point is that Ray, expanding the bootlegging business, may have come to somebody else's attention—somebody bigger. Maybe Ray was given a warning: cease and desist. He didn't, so—"

Fitzgerald said, "But why kill Allison?"

"Because she was up to her neck in it. She handled the calls that came to the mobile home, kept the computer records. And remember me telling you how neat the mobile home was inside, how that didn't fit with Ray? The cabin was the same—neat as a pin inside. My guess is Allison was out there, picking up after Ray. I'll tell you something else. My guess is the expansion was Allison's idea. Only when she comes into the picture does Ray get big ideas.''

"So much for sweet Allison." Then Fitzgerald asked, "Mind if I have a look at the list?"

"You're not on it."

"I know that."

Stroud sighed and said, "No use drawing the line now. But keep it to yourself." He took the computer printout from a file folder and passed it across the desk. "So the way it looked to me," he said while Fitzgerald scanned the list, "is the killings were professional executions—one gunman or maybe two, experts, leaving no traces behind. Quick, neat, lethal."

"You said looked—past tense."

"Not because I've changed my mind. I've worked myself up against a blank wall, that's the rub. Professional killings mean types from outside the county, maybe outside the state. Tell you the truth, I don't know anything about professional killings. We've never had any up here. I've only heard about 'em. So it looks like I've got to ask for help."

"And you don't want to do that."

"Would you?"

"You know who handles liquor distribution in the county?" Fitzgerald asked.

"One company out of Muskegon takes care of the Keg O'Nails, the hotel, VFW, a few other places. I've talked to the boss. I don't think he's involved. He might have somebody pay a call on Ray Thorne, straighten him out, maybe even bang him around, but I can't believe he'd order killings. Too much to lose if they came out."

"But isn't that the point? Professional killings don't come out."

"So they tell me."

Stroud leaned back, patted his shirt pocket, looked up at the tiled ceiling. "I'll give it another day or so, see what develops. I've got two deputies at Lost Finger, checking out where Phipps said he was shot, seeing if they can turn up anything. If he was hit the way he says, by a hunter, I don't see any connection with the murders. Then I'm going to run up the white flag, call in help. After that I'm thinking about retiring."

"Seriously?"

"Might as well. Outside law, you bring it into Tamarack County, you couldn't get yourself elected dog catcher."

NINETEEN

"TELL ME AGAIN," Bonnie Pym said after Mercy picked her up in a DNR Suburban at Bonnie's home, a manufactured house on the fringe of Ossning that had been included among the spoils of a divorce settlement. A high-school girl had taken over for her at the Six-Grain Bakery, giving Bonnie the free time Mercy needed her for, but Bonnie insisted she couldn't leave directly from work. If she and Mercy were going calling, she wanted to do something with her hair and put on a new blouse. You never knew who you might bump into.

"I just want your opinion about someone," Mercy told her. "That's all there is to it."

"Someone I know?"

"Doubt it."

"And you can't tell me more?"

"That would ruin it. We're going to visit for a while, afterward tell me what you think."

"That's mysterious, Mercy."

"Not much. I just want a fresh opinion."

"And you really want mine?"

"Can't imagine a better one."

Bonnie was flattered, and it was nice to be off work during the day, driving out on North Downriver Road. A wall of pine blocked a view of the river, but knowing it was there was nice, too. The Borchard was the reason, the only one she could think of, why anyone lived in Ossning, an otherwise boring place. She didn't fish or canoe herself, but she liked watching people who did—and liked watching the river itself, seeing water that came from some swamp farther north on its way to Lake Huron. Watching the river, she would concentrate on a small section of water and try to imagine it making the long journey.

Feeling as she did about the Borchard, she ought to have a home with a view of it, if only a sliver. But a home on the river these days meant big bucks, so the only way to swing it would be with a guy. Off the top of her head Bonnie could think of only two who fit the bill, meaning unattached and with both feet still out of the grave. There was Calvin McCann, but Calvin's place on the South Branch was a log cabin that was too wild and remote for her taste. That left Fitzgerald, whose rental at Walther Bridge was a place any girl would die to live in. The problem was that a girl *was* presently living in it, the one sitting right next to her, who happened to be a friend.

Bonnie was pondering how good a friend she really was when Mercy slowed the Suburban and turned off in the direction of the river, following a dirt road through the pines. At the turnoff Bonnie caught sight of the name lettered on a black mailbox. "Ugh. Him?"

"You know Max Ringwald?"

"Know of. He comes in the bakery now and then. He's picky as all hell."

"About what?"

"Bread. He wants to know the kind of oil we use, I tell him the best there is, canola, he asks again the next time."

Mercy grinned and said, "Tell him you've switched to Pennzoil."

They parked near a big garage building and walked along a crushed-stone path to the house, heading to a side entrance. Toward the front of the house, beyond a screened porch, Bonnie caught sight of the river at the foot of a long green lawn. "Wow," she said, and reached out, holding Mercy back for a moment.

"I know," Mercy said, "it doesn't look real. As a matter of fact, it isn't—not with that damned lawn."

"Couldn't we go around the front way?"

"Too distracting. We have to concentrate, Bonnie."

On what? she was about to ask. But then she noticed that, ahead of Mercy, a woman was standing behind the screen door of the side entrance, watching them come toward her. Bonnie couldn't see her well through the screen, but well enough to notice the color of the woman's hair, a flaming red.

Beside her Mercy was smiling and waving at the woman.

"ACTUALLY," MERCY SAID after Lucille Ringwald explained that her husband was in town, "Bonnie and I came to see you."

"Me?"

"Bonnie works at the bakery in town. We went to school together, way back when. Would it be okay if we came in? When I was here before we didn't have a chance to visit."

Lucille examined them through the screen, turning a soft pale face from one to the other, cautious. Bonnie could see now that she was wearing moccasin slippers, faded jeans, and a shapeless sweatshirt—an entirely nondescript middle-aged woman except for the weird color of her hair.

The door was pushed outward and Lucille stepped back. "We'll only stay a few minutes," Mercy said as she and Bonnie moved into a spacious kitchen with a large oak table in the center. "Isn't this nice?" Mercy said, and Bonnie understood that Mercy wanted her to join in, filling the uncomfortable air with talk.

"Sure is," Bonnie said, though the room they were in seemed to resemble the kitchen of a restaurant rather than a home. All the appliances appeared oversized. An array of pots and pans dangled from a rod above a long, tiled counter.

"We remember when it was a fishing club, not that we were ever in it then." Mercy was looking about her, taking in the room. "But probably nothing's the same. You've done so much."

"It must have been fun," Bonnie said, "fixing it up. I've always wanted to take an old place, make it just the way you want." It wasn't true—she hated the mess of remodeling. But it seemed to be the thing to say.

"Could we sit for a moment?" Mercy asked.

Lucille hesitated, then nodded. When Mercy and Bonnie took chairs at the oak table she remained standing, looking down at them. "Please," Mercy said, "join us."

"Would you like something?"

"Oh, no. Don't go to any bother." Mercy waited then, smiling at Lucille, waiting until Lucille lowered herself into a chair. "The reason we're here—it's to see if you're all right. If there's anything we can do. It must have been a terrible shock."

Bonnie didn't know what Mercy was talking about, but she gazed at Lucille with somber eyes and nodded her agreement. "Your husband said Allison Thorne came here," Mercy went on. "You got to know her."

"Yes," Lucille murmured.

"That would have been pleasant for you, not having any close neighbors out here, women friends to get together with. There's Sarah Nunemaker, of course. You know Sarah through the Catch and Keep Alliance."

Lucille nodded.

"The isolation out here, that's the hard thing. Men like it well enough living on the river but it can be difficult for a woman. Bonnie wouldn't like it at all. She's a town person."

Bonnie supposed that was her key to say something, but it took her a moment to get her bearings. It was eerie, Mercy bringing up where she lived, since back in the car

she had been thinking about living on the river, how great
that would be. The appeal was the river itself, looking out
at moving water, but the isolation would be all right as long
as she had a dependable car to get back and forth to town.
Did Mercy really believe that where she lived now, on the
edge of town, she sat around with neighbor women in the
kitchen, talking? If Mercy stopped to consider the riffraff
neighbors on Bonnie's street the notion would never cross
her mind.

Bonnie blinked back her thoughts, fluttered her eye-
lashes, said to Lucille, "That's for sure. You work in a
bakery, there's people in and out all day, a real parade.
Never a dull moment."

"You must enjoy that."

"Well, I do." What she said had caught Lucille's attention. For the first time a spark of life flickered in the
woman's dull eyes. "What you hear is a lot of small talk,
mostly about the weather and sports and how the fishing
is, but the main thing is the people. You get to know them,
sort of develop relationships. When you see them at other
places in town they always remember you. You know what
I mean?"

"I think so."

"You ought to stop in next time you're in town, gab
with the regulars. I could introduce you around. You drive,
Lucille?"

"No."

"That's a real shame." Bonnie tried to catch the
woman's eyes, look into them, but Lucille had turned away
to Mercy.

"We didn't have an opportunity to know Allison per-
sonally," Mercy said, shifting the conversation back.
"We've heard she was a sweet young thing. Haven't we,
Bonnie?"

So that was what Mercy was talking about—the murdered girl, Allison Thorne. Lucille must have known her, the girl stopping at the Ringwalds' place on the river for some reason, and Mercy wanted to console her for the loss. But why hadn't she explained that in the car? Why be so mysterious? Again Bonnie blinked away the thought. For some reason Mercy wanted her to wing it, making up everything as she went along.

"Sweet as pie," Bonnie said. "She never came in the bakery herself but I heard people tell about her."

"She was too busy."

"Pardon?"

"With her work," Lucille said to Mercy, explaining to her. "She was a journalist in Grand Rapids before she married. She wanted to continue."

"That's what we've heard," Mercy said. "That's why she came to see you, wasn't it? About the Catch and Keep Alliance. She interviewed your husband."

"She was writing an article," Lucille said. "For a newspaper in Detroit."

"I imagine you sat right here, the three of you, while she took notes."

Lucille nodded.

"Did she always come for work? Were there ever social calls?"

Lucille didn't answer. Her eyes had dipped away from Mercy, cast down now at her hands clasped together on the table. For the first time Bonnie noticed the ring on Lucille's finger, a diamond caught in a beam of sunlight that nearly matched the size of her own, though with a setting that was badly out of fashion. It struck her as surprising that someone like Max Ringwald, fussing about bread, had anted up for a rock that costly. But someone should tell the poor woman to have the ring updated, just as someone should tell her to tone down the color of her hair. And ditch the blue-rimmed glasses. The color combination was bad—a bad miscalculation.

"Allison must have enjoyed coming to a nice place like this," Mercy went on, ignoring Lucille's silence. "Where she lived, down south in the county, it wasn't a good location. And so remote. She must have liked coming up to the river."

"Yes."

"She did?" Mercy picked right up on Lucille's response. "But of course your husband would have been here, so you talked business about the article Allison was writing. You wouldn't have gotten any time alone with her. Or were there times she came when your husband was gone?"

"Yes."

"Like now?"

"Yes."

"You must have been a comfort to one another. That's what makes it so dreadful, losing her the way you did."

Lucille's shoulders sagged, and Bonnie was tempted to reach out, place a comforting arm around her. She glanced at Mercy, hoping to get some signal, but Mercy was looking at Lucille without any expression on her face. Sometimes Mercy could be as hard as stone.

Bonnie reached out, but only as far as Lucille's hands, patting them. "It's all right, sugar. She's in a better place."

"Is there anything we can do?" Mercy asked.

Lucille shook her head.

"If there is," Mercy said, "you just pick up the phone and call. I'm at the DNR office and Bonnie's at the Six-Grain Bakery."

"That's right, sugar. You just call."

"Thank you so much," Lucille managed to say.

"WELL?" MERCY ASKED when they passed the Ringwalds' mailbox and she turned the Suburban onto the asphalt road.

"What?"

"What you felt about her."

"Sad lady," Bonnie said.

"Only that?"

"And she must work her behind off, kitchen that size."

"At least there weren't any swords."

"What?"

"Nothing. The kitchen's left over from the fishing club days."

"What's that about an article Allison was writing?" Bonnie asked.

"It was how she got involved with Lucille and Max, through the article. Something about the Catch and Keep Alliance."

"The cranks who want to keep fish?"

"She was writing it for the *Free Press*," Mercy said. "Max Ringwald was one of the people she interviewed. I came out here with Fitzgerald and we talked with Max, trying to get a handle on Allison's story. Fitzgerald was interested because of the *Free Press* connection. Lucille was there, in the house the whole while, listening, but she didn't say a word. Max didn't pay a drop of attention to her. Yet there was something—something in the air. I could feel it, or thought I could."

Bonnie said, "That Allison and Lucille had a thing going?"

Mercy turned in the seat, gave her a sharp look. "You felt it?"

"Sure."

"What sort of thing?"

Bonnie shrugged. "What you said before. They gave each other comfort."

"Because they were both lonely and isolated and living with husbands who were jerks?"

"Sure."

"And that's all?"

Bonnie looked back at Mercy and said, "What're you asking me, exactly?"

"What you felt back there. Your opinion of Lucille."

"I told you. She's a sad lady. She liked Allison and she lost her."

"C'mon, Bonnie. Liked her how?"

Bonnie kept looking across the seat. "Fancied her. That's what the hair job must have been about, trying to make herself look attractive to a younger woman. The color of the glasses, too. Allison would have picked up on it right away, how sad it was, a bad miscalculation, unless she was dead between the ears. You felt it yourself, the time you went there with Fitzgerald. There were vibes in the air."

Mercy nodded.

"You want to get down to it?"

"Yes."

"Maybe with Lucille it wasn't just Allison. More like a general thing. A little more opportunity, she might fancy you, too."

"But not you?"

"No offense, but she could tell. I don't incline in that direction."

"Good Lord," Mercy protested, "neither do I."

"All I know," Bonnie shrugged, "is she eyed you more than me."

TWENTY

TWO MESSAGES WERE on the telephone answering machine when Mercy returned to the DNR office after dropping off Bonnie Pym at the Six-Grain Bakery. "You owe me a buck for the coffee I bought him," Calvin McCann said on the first, "a grand for wasting my time. The old fart's blowing smoke about keeping fish." Mercy was going to phone him back, find out what he meant, when the second message played. "Call me," Willard Stroud snapped. "Now."

"It's me," she said when Stroud answered.

"About time. Don't you people ever work?"

"Something on your mind?"

"You know Max Ringwald? Has that fishing club on the mainstream."

"You know I do."

"You know anything about his property lines?"

"He thinks they're sacred, is all."

"The extent of them—where they go. I think he's bought up all the way to the outfit that owned the property at Lost Finger Lake."

"That we own now," Mercy said.

"That's why I called—to see what the DNR records show. Can you check with somebody?"

"I can, but why not ask the county recorder's office?"

"Irene Derba's out with flu. The other women over there can't locate their pencils."

"I'll call Ted Tinnery, see what he knows. But what's it all about?"

"Max Ringwald came in here, told me he was walking his property line, checking for trespassers, when he ran into a fellow who started chasing him and shouting. The fellow followed him into the woods and wouldn't stop, so Max lets loose a shotgun blast. He meant it as a warning. But he comes in and tells me he thinks he hit him.''

"And?"

"He did. I already had the fellow in the hospital—Fitzgerald's pal from Detroit. He went over and saw him.''

"Fitzgerald did?''

"You live together," Stroud said. "You ever talk?''

AFTER SHE PLACED a call to Ted Tinnery, Mercy tried the round of places Fitzgerald might be, home first of all, then the Six-Grain Bakery and the Borchard Hotel before she called Calvin McCann's cabin. Fitzgerald wasn't there but Calvin knew where she should try next.

"Verlyn's fly shop. I was leaving when he showed up.''

"What's he doing out there?''

"Talking to Verlyn.''

"I figured as much. About what?''

"I didn't hang around.''

"Forget it. Tell me what you meant on the answering machine about Max Ringwald blowing smoke.''

"Like I said. The old fart doesn't care about keeping fish.''

"But that's the whole point of the Catch and Keep Alliance. Max thinks it's his constitutional right.''

"I'm telling you," Calvin insisted. "He's not serious. I could give him a half-dozen better arguments.''

"All right. Maybe he's not serious about keeping fish, but he is about Big Brother telling him not to. He's serious about the principle of the thing. Lord, Calvin, I heard him say it.''

"Then you weren't listening good. He's got something else in his craw.''

"What?"

"No way," Calvin said. "I'm done jawing with him."

"LET'S MEET AT HOME," Fitzgerald said when she reached him at the fly shop.

"I'm stuck at the office a while. I'm waiting on a call to Ted Tinnery."

"I've got plenty to tell you."

Mercy said, "Not as much as I have."

It was full dark when she turned off the North Downriver Road and drove the narrow lane through the pines to the A-frame. Fitzgerald had the lights on, the house glowing like a tall-masted ship floating in black night. For a few moments she stayed in the Suburban, taking in the house, thinking of Fitzgerald in there, waiting for her. She could smell wood smoke from the fire he had started and he would have poured a whiskey for himself and one for her. They would kiss and Mercy would get out of her work clothes and with their drinks they would settle into deep chairs before the fire and the only question to settle was which one would start talking first.

One part of her couldn't wait to get inside, to see Fitzgerald, begin the long, comfortable evening, but another part hesitated. Was it because everything was so comfortable? In her eagerness was she overlooking something—about Fitzgerald, about her own feelings? Was this the man she truly wanted to spend the rest of her days with, this man who was only testing out a new life on the river, fishing through the seasons and writing a book and living off a winning lottery ticket? She needed time to think, think hard—and resolved she would the moment she returned to Michigan State and the bland dormitory room with metal furnishings and outside the window a sugar maple beginning to turn.

Fitzgerald was standing in the doorway, looking out,

waiting for her, drinks in hand. "Anything wrong?" he asked.

"Not a thing." She gave him a brush on the cheek as she moved past and through the kitchen and down the hallway to the bedroom. When she came back, changed into jeans, a flannel shirt, and fur-lined slippers, Fitzgerald had her drink waiting beside a chair pulled up by the fire.

"We've become predictable," she said. "You know that?"

"Drink, fire, both?"

"Everything."

"We could sip cocoa, freeze out on the deck."

"Very funny. Tell me your news first."

"You said you had the best scoop."

"Damnit, Fitzgerald, tell me. Stroud said Phipps came up here and got himself shot out at Lost Finger Lake. What was he up to?"

"He'd linked up with Gus Thayer. They'd gotten it into their heads a militia group was training out there. They went to look, Phipps driving in and Gus going overland on some route he said he knew. Phipps noticed someone down near the end of the lake who looked like a hunter, tried to catch up and question him, got buckshot in the leg for his trouble. Gus found him, which may have saved Phipps' life. They're both in the hospital. Gus had chest pains from the exertion and they took him to Traverse City for a bypass. Phipps says he's heading back to Detroit first thing in the morning."

Mercy said, "That all you know?"

"About Gus and Phipps."

"Then I'll give you some of my scoop. It wasn't a stray hunter who shot Phipps. It was Max Ringwald."

Fitzgerald stared at her.

"Max admitted it. He waltzed into Stroud's office and told him he was checking his property line when some trespasser started chasing him and hollering. Max let off a warning shot and kept going, then he must have gotten worried. He came in and told Stroud he might have hit the person. Stroud already knew about Phipps being in the hospital. He called me to see if Max's property extended all the way to the lake property. That's why I was waiting to hear from Ted.''

"And?"

"Max owns up to the tree line at the far end of the lake. He's got fencing inside the boundary. There's something else,'' Mercy added. "All that, Mysterious Max shooting Phipps, was yesterday. Today he spent time in town with Calvin, haranguing him about the Catch and Keep Alliance.''

"Why?"

"Tell you later. Now it's your turn.''

Fitzgerald went into the kitchen to freshen their drinks. When he came back he dropped into the chair before the fire but said nothing.

"Well?"

"Maybe we ought to slow down. Maybe we're jumping to a conclusion.''

"C'mon, Fitzgerald. Tell me.''

Fitzgerald sipped his drink and said, "Stroud turned up a file on Allison's computer—a list of people Ray Thorne was presumably selling liquor to. All very neat—names, dates, amounts. It looks like Allison was keeping records for Ray, which proves she knew what was going on. Verlyn's name was on the list. Apparently he bought some liquor from Ray for the lodge.''

"Lord, Verlyn's dumb.''

"And Max Ringwald's name.''

"You're kidding.''

"Stroud let me see the list. He's getting desperate about

the murders. There was Max's name and the amount, six cases of Jack Daniel's.''

"Good Lord."

"Stroud's got the idea the killings were retaliation for Ray treading on some other liquor distributor's turf, ordered killings carried out by one or two professional gunmen. He didn't turn up Allison's story on the Alliance—at least he hasn't yet. So he doesn't know Max figures in the story."

"And you didn't tell Stroud he does."

"The story's there—on her computer. He can find it himself."

"But he knows about Max shooting Phipps."

"That doesn't connect with the murders—not yet it doesn't. Stroud thinks Max was just guarding his property from a trespasser."

Mercy said, "Okay. Go back to Ray Thorne. How did Max get mixed up with him?"

"Maybe Max just knew about the ads in the *Call,* like everyone else in town except you, me, and Stroud. Or maybe he heard about Ray from Verlyn. You said he buys flies from Verlyn. But it doesn't matter. The fact is he knew Ray, did business with him. And he knew Allison, met with her about the story. Max Ringwald is the only one we know like that."

"What are you saying, exactly?"

"I think you know."

"Tell me anyway."

"Max could be our killer, for some reason we can't figure out."

Mercy said, "You're right. We've got to slow down. We're going to finish this drink, have supper, brew coffee, come back in here. Don't say another word 'til then."

BUT SIPPING COFFEE from mugs, the fire the only source of light in the room, they found themselves back at the same point—and the same name: Max Ringwald. Fitzgerald got up, added a fresh log to the fire, stood looking into the flames before he returned to the chair beside Mercy.

"Well?" Mercy broke the silence.

"Maybe we ought to go over everything again. See where it's leading."

"We know where. The question is why."

Fitzgerald nodded into the flickering light.

Mercy said, "There's something I skipped over before—why Max and Calvin were together in town. It was my idea—a way to get Max out of his house for a while. I told Calvin to tell Max he was interested in the Catch and Keep Alliance. I got Bonnie and we went out to visit Lucille Ringwald together. I wanted to talk to her."

"Why bring Bonnie?"

"You probably won't understand."

"Try me."

"When we were out there before, you and me, I had a feeling about Lucille."

"That we could learn more from her than from Max."

Mercy shook her head. "Another feeling. She pretended to be reading, but she wasn't. I could feel her looking at me."

"So?"

"Just listen. This isn't easy to say. There was something in the look—vibes, Bonnie called them. The reason I took her out there was to see if she felt them. You can't beat Bonnie when it comes to sex. She's got radar."

"Sex?"

"Damnit, Fitzgerald, just listen. We talked with Lucille for a while, sitting in her kitchen, talking about Allison, how Lucille felt about her. Bonnie picked up the vibes. Lucille had a thing about Allison—a physical thing. I don't mean it was reciprocated or that anything happened. It probably didn't. But Lucille had feelings that way. Bonnie could tell.''

Fitzgerald said, ''We're talking about the same woman—older, red hair?''

''Of course the same woman. Bonnie thinks the hair was an attempt to make herself attractive to Allison. And age has nothing to do with it. Lucille's a lonely woman, living out on the river with no one around except Mysterious Max. Allison came into her life—and she had this feeling for her.''

''Sexual feeling.''

''Yes.''

''But how do you—you and Bonnie—know? Allison's dead. The vibes are still in the air?''

''In a way.'' Mercy sighed, gazed into the fire, turned back to Fitzgerald. ''I'm saying this just once. When you and I went out there I felt something in the air, something directed at me. I wanted Bonnie to confirm it. She did. Lucille fancies me—Bonnie's way of putting it—in the same way she did Allison. I don't expect you to understand. Just believe it—as a possibility. It has nothing to do with how I feel or anything I did or said. It's Lucille. Probably that's the way it was with Allison. It's just something in Lucille, something always there or maybe the result of living with Max. I don't know and don't want to know. It's simply the way it is with some women. All right?''

Mercy kept looking at him, making sure there wasn't a hint of a grin on Fitzgerald's face. He only nodded. ''Just one question. Lucille didn't give off these vibes toward Bonnie. Just you?''

''It might have happened with any woman who came into her life after Allison.''

''But not with Bonnie?''

''No.''

Fitzgerald said, ''I'll tell you what. I'm going to go into

the kitchen and get the whiskey and bring it in here and splash some in this coffee.''

"You're shocked, huh?"

"I wouldn't put it that way."

"Then you see what it means?"

"I think so. But let's fortify the coffee first."

BEFORE, THERE WAS one name: Max Ringwald. Now they had another: Lucille. And a whole other possible explanation. "Any time you're ready," Mercy said when they finished the coffee.

"What you and Bonnie did—it may be the big break."

"Tell me how."

Fitzgerald said, "Everything points toward Max. The question is why. You said that before—and now we've got a second answer. The first is he killed Allison because she'd dug up a link between the Catch and Keep Alliance and a militia group. He didn't want that disclosed, so he silenced her."

"Maybe that's why he's so obsessed with his property lines—for that matter, why he wants to own such a big place. The old fishing club had room for lots of people. He could have something going on in there, something Phipps stumbled into. And got shot."

Fitzgerald nodded. "We know Max is willing to pull a trigger. But there's a large difference. In the case of Phipps he came to Stroud and admitted it."

"What choice was there? The shooting happened on his property. Stroud was bound to find that out and have a talk with him. Calling it an accident, admitting he did it, was smart. Shooting Allison and Ray was entirely different. He *killed* them."

Again Fitzgerald nodded. "Let's keep going with that, Max as the killer. What you turned up is another explanation—Allison's involvement with his wife. Max killed her to end it. But how'd he know about the involvement?''

Mercy shrugged. ''There's lots of ways. Maybe he and Lucille had a quarrel and she blurted it out. It doesn't matter how he learned. It's a male motive for murder. A damned good one.''

''So is disclosing a militia connection. But we're forgetting something. If Max killed Allison, why kill Ray? He was better off leaving Ray alone. Everyone's first thought was that Ray was the killer.''

''I know.'' Mercy got up, jabbed at the fire with a poker, turned to face Fitzgerald. ''But we've got to keep thinking Max did it. If Allison knew about Ray's bootlegging, maybe he knew about the story she was writing. And the business with Lucille. So there was no point in Max silencing Allison if he didn't silence Ray, too. Otherwise Ray could have blackmailed him or something. Maybe that's it.''

''Maybe.''

''You've got a better explanation?''

''No.''

''What then?''

Fitzgerald lifted his hands, then dropped them back in his lap. ''We're sitting here deciding on the killer and his motives. Let's say we're right. So what? It's all theoretical. Even if we dumped it all in his lap Stroud couldn't do a thing. There's no proof.''

''I know. The one certain thing, Phipps getting shot, Max admitted.'' Mercy looked at Fitzgerald again, examining him now, shifting to the side so the light from the fire was on his face. ''Oh, no. I can tell what you're thinking.''

''It's probably the only way.''

''Then we give up right now. You're not going to get Max to shoot someone else.''

''Give me a better idea.''

Mercy said, ''Let's sleep on it. In the morning I will.''

TWENTY-ONE

BUT SHE DIDN'T. As they sat over breakfast at the trestle table in the kitchen, hazy morning light flooding the room, all Mercy could think to try was one thing for her. And another for Fitzgerald.

"Talk to Calvin," she suggested. "He said something odd about Max—about his catch and keep talk. You know Calvin, hearing what he wants to hear. But he's got it in his head that Max isn't really serious."

"What good will it do?"

"Talking to him? It's just something to look into. If Max isn't serious, why'd he get involved with the Catch and Keep Alliance in the first place? Why make a big public stir? That's what brought Allison into the picture."

"All right," Fitzgerald said. "How about you?"

"I'm meeting Ted Tinnery at the office."

"What about?"

Mercy was vague. "District matters. Give me a call after you see Calvin. We'll get together at the hotel."

"All right."

"And nothing else. No dumb schemes. Promise?"

"Sure."

WHY HAD HE said that?

After Mercy left for Ossning, Fitzgerald cleaned up the breakfast dishes, then took a mug of coffee into the living room and stood at the glass front of the A-frame, looking down through the cedars at the river, still night-dark before the sun touched it. He would talk with Calvin, assuming he could find him. Otherwise he would go on his own. Was it a dumb scheme? Maybe—but, lying half-awake through the night, it was the best he could come up with.

Beside him the leather armchair and end table were still drawn up by the glass, the place where he was working, laptop on his lap, when Phipps phoned. That morning he was eager to switch off the machine, switch on to hunting for Allison Thorne—eager for an excuse to quit work on the novel, quit thinking about it, letting it take shape somewhere back in his head while he got off his rear and began moving. Phipps' call had been a relief.

Was it still?

He could make a good case that he was using the call, it and all that had unfolded since, to avoid returning to work. The same went for his high-minded talk about Allison as someone he felt connected to, responsible for, a colleague. He could make a case that that was merely rationalization.

So why was he planning to get in even deeper?

He tried to summon up what had happened after Phipps' call, remembering driving down to Lime Creek Road, locating the mobile home, going in the open door, finding slumped before the computer the young woman with red-brown hair that was actually matted blood and gore, losing control then and vomiting from the half-finished wood deck. It wasn't entirely rationalization. He owed it to Allison Thorne, simply one human being to another, to learn what happened to her.

The world wouldn't be a better place with his novel. Rid of her killer, it might be.

WHY HADN'T SHE told him?

She hadn't told Bonnie Pym, either. She wasn't certain it was true, or that it meant anything if it was, so she had to find out for herself. She didn't want to cloud the situation more than it already was.

But why, deep down, hadn't she told Fitzgerald?

Mercy was on the North Downriver Road, heading into Ossning, the radio turned to morning news from the public station in Interlochen, steam lifting from a travel mug of fresh coffee in the dashboard holder. She had picked up Fitzgerald's tastes—NPR, Irish music, Woody Allen films, whiskey and water without ice, big log fires at night, reading before the warmth and sipping whiskey and listening to CDs and going to bed late and then, first thing in the morning, grinding good coffee beans to fill the kitchen with the best aroma in the world.

Was she complaining?

She had moved in with Fitzgerald of her own free will. Though they hadn't actually said as much, it was understood they were conducting a trial run to see how it would go—for the long haul. He kept asking her to marry him and sometimes she said she would, but neither of them was serious. They both knew it. They knew they were waiting, enjoying the moment but watchful, keeping something of themselves separate.

So was she complaining?

No, but there were moments—last night had been one, sitting in the Suburban outside the lighted house that seemed floating in darkness—when she felt the need to stop and think what was happening to a woman named Mercy Virdon who was a DNR district field officer with a career and a life and a history that belonged to her alone. When was the last time she listened to Patsy Cline or watched Clint Eastwood? Was she in danger of losing everything, swallowed up in Fitzgerald's tastes, his life, his history? She made that mistake once before, with Verlyn, and, damn it all, wasn't making it again.

She told Fitzgerald about her hunch, about the kind of woman Lucille was, and he claimed to understand. But he couldn't, not fully. There was more to it, more that she didn't understand herself but would. She would get to the bottom of it—the bottom of her hunch. It was what she could do and Fitzgerald couldn't.

Lucille had told Bonnie she didn't drive. But Mercy had seen her in Ossning, putting groceries from Glen's supermarket into a Volvo. She couldn't swear Max hadn't driven her to town, but each time she had seen Max tooling around Ossning he was alone in a pickup. So if Lucille did drive, why had she lied to Bonnie?

Mercy had spent the night keeping the question from Fitzgerald—and the possible answer: Lucille Ringwald was covering up the fact that she did more than shop at Glen's. She paid visits, including visits to the south edge of the county.

There was one way, Mercy realized, she could find out for certain.

FITZGERALD DROVE INTO Ossning before heading out on the highway to Traverse City, the route to Calvin's cabin. He passed the Six-Grain Bakery and the Borchard Hotel and at the end of the main drag pulled into the parking area of the city-county building, idling the Cherokee.

The wise thing would be to go in, have a talk with Willard Stroud, have Stroud accompany him. But that would mean telling Stroud about Max Ringwald's name in the story on Allison's computer. It would mean telling him about noticing Max's name on Ray Thorne's whiskey list. The biggest thing, it would mean telling Stroud why Phipps was out at Lost Finger Lake when he was shot by Max, the whole business about a possible militia connection with the Catch and Keep Alliance. If he laid out all that—all that, up to then, he had held back—could he expect Stroud to go along with his plan?

Could he expect it in any case? Would Stroud run the risk? He already had two people shot dead and one

wounded. He would insist on another approach, and at the
moment Fitzgerald couldn't think of one that had a chance
of succeeding.

Did this one?

He put the Cherokee in gear and wheeled from the parking area, letting the question hang in the air.

TED TINNERY WAS IN the office—that much of what Mercy
had told Fitzgerald was true—but the work he was doing
that morning didn't involve her. After they exchanged
greetings Ted asked if the information he had given her
about property lines at Lost Finger Lake had been of use
to the sheriff.

Mercy shrugged. "Stroud and I only talk when we have
to."

"There's something else. I kept checking after you
called. The man in question—"

"Max Ringwald."

"He made an offer to buy the Panatics property. They'd
already decided to give it to the state."

"How'd he know it was available?"

"I don't know that he did. He found out they were the
owners and made the offer. When they told him the land
was going to the state he got huffy—the usual complaint
about government removing property from the tax rolls. It's
prime land for our purposes, but I can't see why an indi-
vidual would want it."

"Except that it joined property he already owned."

"To do what with it?"

"Catch and keep bluegills." When Ted looked blank
Mercy said, "Just kidding. Actually, I haven't the faintest
idea."

In her office she closed the door and made the first call.
There were pleasantries to get out of the way about the

continuing good fall weather before Mercy could ask Sarah
Nunemaker about Lucille Ringwald.

CALVIN'S PICKUP was there, parked in front of the garage
building where he kept canoes and fishing gear, Calvin
peering out at him from a window of the cabin. Fitzgerald
waved, then went around to the front of the cabin and in-
spected the river through the scrub vegetation.

Upstream the view was long and unobstructed, downstream the river braided around an island where, Calvin had
told him, beavers had taken down a stand of mature aspen
the previous winter. Around the far side of the island the
river bent sharply, the water deepened and wading was
treacherous, but big browns held against a thick tangle of
woody debris. It was Calvin's kind of fishing, requiring
long casts to present tiny flies that drifted tight along the
edge of the cover.

The whole stretch of the river up and down from the
cabin was, in fact, Calvin's personal fishing ground. He was
acquainted with every inch of cover and current, probably
every trout that lived therein. It was a mastery of the river
Fitzgerald envied, and knew he would never attain. It required more single-minded concentration than he was capable of—required living here, alone in a cabin in as much
wilderness isolation as northern Michigan provided, giving
the river full attention. Calvin was capable of that and he
wasn't. He wanted more—like understanding Thoreau and
finishing a novel and Mercy Virdon and—

Fitzgerald cut off the train of thought and turned up a
path to the cabin. Calvin was waiting on the porch, mug of
tea in hand. "Thanks anyway," Fitzgerald told him.

"Your life," Calvin said. He led Fitzgerald inside the
cabin where half-filled boxes were strewn about. "Trying
to remember what I need to send."

"To New Zealand?"

"Only place I go."

Fitzgerald said, "I've got another. Quick trip. At least I hope it is." He sat in one of the wooden rockers in front of the fireplace and waited for Calvin to join him. "First I need some information. Mercy told me about your meeting with Max Ringwald. She said you thought he wasn't serious about the Catch and Keep Alliance."

Calvin nodded. "It's hot air. You can tell."

"How?"

"I didn't argue. Mercy said not to. But I'm on the old fart's side and I could still shoot him to pieces. He hasn't done his homework. Mercy talks about studies, but you can find studies that refute her studies. Everybody thinks catch and release is a quick fix for streams in trouble, but the reality—it's up in the air. Some studies show catch and release even has a negative effect, increasing fishing pressure because people think it means more available fish. So what you end up with, in the long run, is more fishermen and fewer fish."

"And Max hasn't looked into the literature?"

"He's just yakking, trying to get attention."

"Or divert it." When Calvin looked at him Fitzgerald said, "He's got a big thing about privacy—buying up adjoining property, fencing it off with barbed wire, putting up no-trespassing signs. Mercy said people in town got a little testy. So the Catch and Keep Alliance might have been meant to get them thinking about him in a different light. It fits with his views about government—less is better."

"One thing he's got right," Calvin said.

"So it's plausible. But suppose the real reason he got involved was to keep attention off something he was doing on his property, something he wanted to keep secret. Buying the former fishing club, buying more land—he had something going on. Something he didn't want known."

"The militia business?"

"That's what I want to find out. I need your help."

"Hold on," Calvin said. "I thought you were nosing around about the killings."

"I am."

"And you think Ringwald's involved?"

"He may be the killer."

Calvin got up from the rocker. He went into the kitchen, poured more tea from a glazed pot, looked back at Fitzgerald through a curl of rising steam. "Friend of mine in New Zealand, a potter, turned this out." Calvin dipped his head toward the teapot. "Nice work—but I don't get how he makes a living. On the other hand, he doesn't get how I make a living showing high-rollers how to fish."

"Interesting."

"So what do I have to do?"

Fitzgerald smiled at him. "First I've got to tell you what happened when Gus Thayer and a newspaperman named Phipps went out to Max's property. Then dig out your case of topographical maps."

"DOES LUCILLE ever stop by," Mercy asked, "pay a visit? You're the Ringwalds closest neighbor."

Sarah hesitated. "Not recently."

"Not after Allison's death, you mean? You'd think she would. Both of you knew Allison."

"No, Mercy. She hasn't come by."

"When you were organizing the Catch and Keep Alliance," Mercy pressed on, "weren't there meetings at your house? Lucille and Max must have come."

"There were several people interested."

Mercy leaned back in her desk chair. Sarah was behaving oddly. Ordinarily eager to talk, she seemed reluctant to say anything about Lucille Ringwald. Mercy wanted to learn if Lucille had lied to Bonnie about driving, and it seemed likely that Sarah would know. But maybe it didn't matter. *A little more opportunity,* Bonnie had said, *she might fancy you, too.* Mercy clung to the feeling that Lucille was the key, but maybe the only way to find out for certain was to meet with her alone. And if Bonnie was right? She would cross that bridge when she came to it.

As soon as she was off the phone with Sarah, she would make another call, arranging a time to visit with Lucille. Then a better way occurred to her. She would show up at the Ringwalds' place unannounced, playing it by ear. She wanted Lucille alone but couldn't risk another ploy to get Max out of the house. She could hang up if Max answered the phone, but that alone might arouse his suspicions.

If Max was at home when she arrived she would say she was on DNR business—about the signs he kept posting on the river. She wanted an end to the cat-and-mouse game of Max putting them up, the DNR taking them down. Couldn't they reach some compromise? Of course Max wouldn't agree to any such thing, so she would keep coming out, unannounced, badgering him about the matter. She was bound, one time, to find Lucille alone.

"Listen, Sarah," she began.

"Why are you asking about Lucille?"

Mercy paused. Sarah didn't sound like herself at all. "No particular reason. I was just wondering about her, alone out there. She might need help."

"You saw her. You and Bonnie Pym."

Again Mercy paused. She had told Fitzgerald that Sarah knew everything that went on in and around Ossning, and here was more evidence. Sarah must have a network of phone correspondents. "We did—a sympathy call. I was thinking another might be in order."

"I wouldn't."

Sarah could be decisive when she wished, but the abruptness of the remark was startling. Mercy drew forward over her desk, frowned into the phone. "I'm not sure I understand. Lucille might still be disturbed because of Allison's death. Max is with her, but you know how men are. Sensitivity isn't a strong suit."

"I wouldn't trouble her, Mercy."

"Just calling on her, that would?"

"She isn't a strong woman."

"All the more reason to see her."

"No."

"But why?"

"She isn't the way we are, Mercy."

Mercy pressed the phone into her chin, waiting. She didn't want to misunderstand. Did Sarah mean that Lucille wasn't as strong, as resilient, as able to cope in an emotional sense with something like murder? Or did she mean something else entirely—something akin, that is, to what Bonnie had said of Lucille? Was she concerned that Lucille, alone with Mercy, would reveal the interest—*physical* interest—that had previously been directed toward Allison? Was she concerned, that happening, how Mercy might react?

Mercy was still thinking of a response when Sarah said, "I don't care to speak more over the telephone."

"Sure," Mercy said quickly. "I understand." Sarah was of a generation in which certain things were spoken of only in private, and the telephone wasn't private enough. "Listen, how would it be if I drove down your way? I could do that before I call on Lucille."

"I wish you would."

"Right now?"

"Yes," Sarah said.

TWENTY-TWO

THE AREA LOOKED the way Mercy and Phipps described it: a string of deserted cabins, the finger of lake fringed with reeds, in the far distance a dark wall of jack pines. Passing around the side of the lake, moving through high brown grass, Fitzgerald pondered the bluegill population. When all this was over he might come out, cast poppers along the reeds, see what happened. But that was jumping ahead. He was still at the beginning of the scheme, one that would have gone easier with Willard Stroud's help.

Before leaving Calvin's cabin he had phoned Max Ringwald, identifying himself as the newspaperman who had stopped at the former fishing club with Mercy Virdon. "I left my *Free Press* card."

"So?" Max said warily.

"The reporter shot on your property—"

"The trespasser?"

"—was a colleague. So was Allison Thorne."

"So what?"

"It seems odd—one of our people killed, another wounded. The paper's assigned me to look into it."

"You're on leave of absence, Mercy said."

"That was before the attacks on our people." Fitzgerald leaned into Calvin's phone, adding more edge to his voice. "I've talked with the sheriff. I know what happened on your property."

"What I told him. Trespasser got a warning."

"The reporter didn't know he was trespassing. He went into Lost Finger Lake from the highway, hunting for something out there. I think he found it. That's why he was shot."

"Bull."

"I'm going out myself, follow his route, see if I can locate what he found. That's why I'm calling—so you'll know. I'll be out there between one o'clock and two. I don't want any trouble. If there's nothing to hide, there's no reason for trouble."

"Get it through your head," Max snapped. "We're talking about private property."

"It can't remain private if there's evidence of unlawful activity taking place."

"*Unlawful?*"

"I haven't told the sheriff any of this. And I haven't said anything to the paper. There's no reason to unless I find some evidence. For now it's just between you and me. If I find something, on the other hand, it goes right to the sheriff's office. Afterward you'll read about yourself in the *Free Press*."

"Wait!" Max roared into the phone. "That a threat?"

Fitzgerald said, "The paper rejected Allison's story. It won't mine."

THE NEXT THING had been to work out from Calvin's maps an alternate route into the lake. With Stroud's help he could have driven in on the two-track off the highway, the deputy out there waving him through with the sheriff's blessing. Phipps' ploy, or a variation on it, was a possibility, but it was unlikely a deputy would fall for something like that twice. So Calvin had picked out an overland route that would be tough going through up-and-down terrain and downed timber but was actually a shortcut into the lake compared to the two-track entrance. Calvin could drop him off at the spot, a half-mile or so from where the deputy was stationed, on his own drive to the river.

"You up to it?" Calvin wondered.

"I'll find out."

"Keep dead northeast. I'll lend you a compass."

Fitzgerald nodded. "Now show me your route."

Calvin smoothed out another map. "It's probably the same way Gus took. I'll put in at the second TU access, float down to just above the old fishing club, get out and stash the canoe, circle overland. I'll reach the place from the opposite direction you're coming." Calvin paused. "Wherever the place is."

"I know. We have to play it loose." Fitzgerald drew a line on the map with his finger. "Just keep moving from the vicinity of the fishing club in the direction of Lost Finger Lake. Stick to that line. We'll meet up somewhere along it."

"That's a lot of territory."

"And we've got to keep track of the time. Max Ringwald thinks I'll be out there between one and two, so if he's going to act that's the time frame. That's when you've got to be in the area."

"An area we don't know exactly, at a time we don't know exactly."

"True."

"And the old fart's not supposed to see me, but I'm supposed to see him."

"All true."

"I'd say we've got a lot of variables here."

"That's what might make it work."

"How do you figure?"

"I don't," Fitzgerald told him. "I'm hoping."

After that he made a hurried drive from Calvin's cabin to the A-frame and put on a pair of walking boots and a canvas jacket and wolfed down a sandwich. Back at the cabin he helped Calvin load a canoe, an Old Town solo, into the back of his pickup. They watched a clock in Calvin's kitchen then until the hands drew near eleven, calculating that gave them enough time to drive through Ossning and out north to Lost Finger Lake, then begin Fitzgerald's walk and Calvin's float.

"There's one thing," Calvin said on the way. "Let's say you get lost and I'm at the place alone. What then?"

"See if there's any sign of militia activity."

"Running into Ringwald, I was thinking of."

"Don't. Remember what happened to Phipps."

Calvin nodded. "I don't spot you by two o'clock, I'm out of there. Right?"

"You wouldn't mind," Fitzgerald said, "give it a few minutes' leeway."

HE CHECKED HIS WATCH: coming up on twelve-twenty. The deadfall in the woods made for slow going, but the walk into the lake hadn't been bad. He took some spills and was breathing hard by the time he reached the open meadow and the string of dilapidated cabins, but the important thing was he found the place—and the timing had worked out. He could enter the woods at the far end of the lake, enter Max Ringwald's property, begin looking around before Max showed up.

If he did.

No dumb schemes, Fitzgerald had promised Mercy. But this one wasn't dumb. If Max had something to hide, he would appear. If not, he wouldn't—and one of the motives for Max as the killer of Allison and Ray Thorne, to hide militia involvement with the Catch and Keep Alliance, would be closed off. It would prove as well that Phipps had been shot solely for the reason Max claimed: He was trespassing on private property. The scheme, in other words, was foolproof.

Fitzgerald paused at the end of the lake, studying the wall of pine ahead. Phipps had spotted Max among these trees, given chase, called out he was with the *Free Press*. Looking at them now, it was hard to imagine any human presence intruding on the silence and isolation. The day was warmed by a milky sun, windless, hawks circling high in the dry air. Fitzgerald glanced over his shoulder at the lake, serene in the soft light, then lifted his eyes across the water to the distant cabins, black against the brown meadow. Yellow police tape singled out one—the place where Phipps broke a window, where Ray Thorne died.

He turned back to the line of trees, began moving ahead, eyes narrowed, tense now. Within this silence and isolation a man had been wounded, another murdered.

CALVIN COULDN'T REMEMBER when he last floated the mainstream. He guided now only on the South Branch of the Borchard, the mainstream clogged during the peak summer months with canoeists coming down from the liveries in Ossning. The South Branch was still okay, the river still flowing through long wilderness tracts, the only canoeists mostly fishermen.

But this fall day he had the stretch of mainstream below the TU access to himself. It was like seeing again an old friend, noting what had changed, what was the same. The big change was the absence of woody debris lining the banks, the livery operators keeping it thinned out, the river an open canoe run. The loss of good trout cover was one of the things that screwed up fishing on the mainstream.

If Calvin had a place here he would build up the banks with fallen timber, leaving just enough room for a single canoe to ease through. He would wage guerilla war with the canoe liveries, industrious as a beaver. He was relishing the thought—and thinking, too, he wouldn't mind having a rod with him, sinking a streamer up close to the banks where woody debris should be—when he realized he was coming up on Sarah Nunemaker's place.

He recognized the big cedars along the bank, a couple of them angled out over the river, sweepers low to the water, and through them a hint of white birches close by the log house. A narrow opening in the cedars gave him a quick view of the place as he rode by on the current. He leaned his paddle across the gunwales of the canoe, looking.

He couldn't see much, or see it long, but parked beside Sarah's house he glimpsed a brown Suburban.

FITZGERALD CROSSED the barbed-wire fence, moved deeper into the pines. Walking was easy, no undergrowth or deadfall to speak of here, the ground mounded with pine needles. He checked the compass, then his watch. He was on line and making good time. He was still ahead of Max—if Max showed.

Fifty yards or so into the pines he came into a clearing of rotting tree stumps. The devastation seemed natural, a result of one of the innumerable pine diseases. A resident now of the north woods, this was something he ought to look into—after he mastered Thoreau and novel writing and fishing the Borchard through all the seasons. The wiser thing was to ask Mercy what she knew; she probably knew a lot. It was her job to know, she'd tell him.

He moved on, through the clearing and back into dense pine, aware that his tension had lessened, that he was actually enjoying the walk. He could imagine Max taking the same route, not to defend his property lines but for the sheer pleasure of it. He shook his head, trying to regain his attention. A good scheme required good execution. He was getting somewhere, proving something—one way or another. He came into another clearing, smaller, a creek trickling through it, one of the feeders that came from the springs filtering into the Borchard. He walked along it through the opening, sensing he was nearing the mainstream. Before the pines closed in again he knelt on the cushion of needles, reached out, felt the vivid cold of the earth-stained water.

He stayed there, kneeling, letting water drain through his fingers. He hadn't, he realized, seen a single sign of human activity on Max Ringwald's property.

WHY WAS Mercy at Sarah's?

Though he caught only a quick look through the cedars, Calvin was certain he had seen her vehicle parked beside the house. Fairly certain. There were other brown Suburbans around Ossning, but the DNR's were a distinctive shade.

So if she was there, why? Mercy had him talk to Sarah about Allison Thorne because she hadn't wanted to do it herself. So was this a social call?

But Mercy wasn't the sort to pay social calls, at least not during hours when she was supposed to be working. So was it about the catch and keep outfit, Sarah killing trout and Mercy reading her the riot act? But that didn't figure. Mercy could be a hard case but she wouldn't bother with Sarah. Sarah probably couldn't find a trout worth killing on the mainstream anyway.

Calvin turned his attention back to the river. He checked his watch. Plenty of time. He would read the water the rest of the way, figuring out where a trout might hold in a stretch of water stripped of woody debris.

WHAT WAS HE searching for, exactly?

Some indication that militia activity had taken place on Max Ringwald's property.

What would that be, exactly?

Tents—or an open area, the grass flattened, where tents had been. Fire pits. Latrines. Maybe an exercise course. Maybe a firing range. Maybe—

He couldn't figure it all out in advance. He would know the indications, recognize them, when he saw them. They had to be obvious. You couldn't hide a militia training area.

Fitzgerald pushed on, searching.

WHEN CALVIN SAW the spot, the bank low and grassy, pines starting just a few yards back, he nosed the canoe in. This was state land, adjoining the old fishing club. He would circle through the woods and be inside Max Ringwald's property in minutes.

He hauled the canoe up the bank and through the grass, took his time getting it hidden inside the pines. He walked back to the river and took a look from there. Nothing of the green sides of the canoe showed. He was satisfied. Lending Fitzgerald a helping hand was one thing, losing an Old Town solo was another.

Not that anyone was lurking around, thinking to swipe it. From the TU access down he had the river to himself. He glanced around, marking the spot in his mind, then set off into the woods.

He had taken only a few steps when he noticed a patch of red showing in the green of the pines. When he looked, parting low branches, he was face to face with another canoe, fire-engine red, an Oscoda, paddle inside. He stood there, looking down, trying to figure. The canoe was meant to be hidden, like his. So he wasn't alone on the river, after all. On the other hand, the canoe might have been left a while back, left and forgotten. Was that possible with a good Oscoda?

Calvin looked back to the Old Town, marking the distance and angle in his mind. When he came back he would check to see if the other canoe was still here. If it was, he would keep an eye on it, off and on, until he left for New Zealand. He wasn't partial to red as a color on the river, but if it was still there—

He turned away, moved into the woods. He had to get his head back on straight, remember what he was doing. He settled into a steady pace, looking hard to both sides, hunting for Fitzgerald. And the other things.

TWENTY-THREE

MERCY DECLINED chocolate cake but coffee was already made. They took their cups to a breakfast alcove off the kitchen with a view from narrow windows of the lane through the pines to the log house, the comfortable cocoon in the woods Cam and Sarah Nunemaker had created for themselves.

Of all the river places she knew, Mercy had thought before, this was the finest. The A-frame at Walther Bridge was more dramatically situated above the river and more thoroughly modern, but nothing about it compared with the way Cam and Sarah's place fit seamlessly into its setting. The log house appeared as much a part of the north woods as the white birch surrounding it, the cedars and flashing river beyond.

One couldn't say that, it occurred to her now, about the fishing club Max and Lucille Ringwald had fixed up so carefully. Appealing as it was, a house of white clapboard and black shutters was an addition to the land, distinct from it, a statement finally of opposition. No matter how much the members of the fishing club might have valued the river, or how much the Ringwalds did, the house stood for town life, not the life of the woods.

Gazing out the windows to the pines, Mercy considered that she might, if the sordid business of murder was ever finished, tell Sarah about her feelings for the log house. Sarah had no children to leave it to, and as far as Mercy knew no kin in the area with a hope of inheriting. Sarah was quite alone. Whatever her resistance over the years to the DNR, she might wish to see the place in the hands of someone who cared for it, who would leave it just as it was. It was a delicate business, though, letting someone know you had an eye on their property after they passed on. It could easily be taken the wrong way.

"Mercy?"

Sarah was peering at her across the table, head thrust forward above a bulky cardigan over a denim shirt and a blue bandanna at her throat. When she met Mercy at the door, the cardigan, reaching halfway to the knees of her khaki trousers, had seemed odd given the pleasant weather. Now Mercy shook her head and smiled. "Sorry, Sarah. Your place is so lovely I nearly forgot why I came."

"About Lucille."

Mercy slid her cup in a slow, methodical circle on the scrubbed wood of the table. Sarah had been decisive on the phone, but in person there was an unmistakable look of caution in her eyes. Mercy decided to tread lightly. "When I called—what I really wanted was to ask a question. I was wondering if you'd ever seen Lucille driving a car. You might have, out on Downriver Road. Or in town."

"Why would that be important?"

"I'm not sure it is. But I think I've seen Lucille in a Volvo at Glen's. Max drives a pickup in town. It's just strange," Mercy added when Sarah didn't reply. "The time we went to see her, Bonnie tried to interest Lucille in coming to town, stopping at the bakery, getting acquainted that way. Lucille was down in the dumps about Allison's death and Bonnie thought it would help. But Lucille said she didn't drive."

"And you knew she did?"

"Not exactly. It's only what I told you. I thought I'd seen her in the Volvo."

Sarah stood up, went to the counter, refilled their cups with coffee. Mercy sighed at the prospect of more liquid.

Before she left for the Ringwalds she would have to use Sarah's bathroom.

Sarah remained standing when she returned to the table, looking down at Mercy with a pained expression. "I can't understand why you and Bonnie went to her home."

Mercy cocked her head. Was Sarah losing her memory? It was short-term memory, wasn't it, that went first? "Like I said on the phone, Sarah, it was a sympathy call. We thought Lucille might be upset over Allison's death. And she was."

"But who told you to?"

"To visit her? Remember the day Fitzgerald and I stopped here, looking at how you and Cam kept the river bank wild? We'd just come from the Ringwalds' place. Lucille hadn't said a word to us while we were there. It was spooky, actually. Max acted like she wasn't even there. Later, thinking about it, I suppose I felt sorry for her, alone out there, stuck with Max. Nobody told us to go. It was my idea to bring Bonnie along."

"I wouldn't have suggested you go." Slowly Sarah lowered herself into the chair. Her eyes fell away from Mercy's and fastened on her hands clasped together on the table. "I wouldn't have made the same mistake."

"Mistake?"

"The young woman—" Sarah stopped, began again. "I should have kept her here, Mercy. I should have tried harder. I shouldn't have let her go."

"To see Lucille?"

"It was a dreadful mistake."

"Why, Sarah?"

"It ruined everything."

Mercy edged her chair closer, placed a hand on Sarah's wrist—hard and sinewy under her touch, the wrist of a woman who had spent a lifetime casting fly lines in long, gorgeous loops, an outdoor woman, firm and vigorous despite her age. Now was the time. Sarah might come from another generation but she knew what was what. There was no reason to keep beating around the bush with her. Mercy lifted her hand and said, "On the phone you said Lucille isn't the way we are. Tell me what you meant."

"You know."

"I'm not sure I do."

"You and Bonnie went there. You must know. She isn't strong."

"You said that. Because she's dependent on Max, you mean? She hasn't had to live by herself, take care of herself?" Mercy tried a thin smile. "She doesn't have our tough old hide?"

Sarah looked up but didn't return the smile. "She couldn't protect herself."

"From Max?"

"She wanted to. She tried so hard."

"Sarah, wait a minute."

"I should have done more to keep her away."

"Allison, you mean?"

"Yes."

"Something happened between Lucille and Allison?"

Sarah turned away, dropped her gaze. "The worst thing."

"RIGHT THERE! Hold it!"

Fitzgerald froze. He recognized the voice but could see nothing. He was in a small clearing of limp grass, a tangle of deadfall just ahead, the pines thickening beyond into a dark wall. The voice had come from the deadfall but he could determine nothing more.

"Max?" he called back.

"Hold it right there!"

Fitzgerald hunched his shoulders, squinting ahead. "Why should I?"

He saw the burst of orange fire in the deadfall before he heard the explosion, felt waves of searing heat pass above. He dropped to his knees, braced his hands against the ground. He wasn't hit. He knew that much. Max hadn't tried to kill him. But the shotgun blast hadn't missed by much.

"That's why!" Max shouted.

Fitzgerald pulled himself to his feet. He realized he was trembling. But there was no point staying on the ground, crouched in the grass. Max, an open view from the deadfall, could hit him as well that way. He could hit him easily if he wanted to. "What's going on?" he managed to call out.

"I got your attention? You understand what I'm saying?"

He was certain now where Max was, prone behind the deadfall. He couldn't make out the barrel of the shotgun but it was there, poking out through the tangle of timber and brush, aimed at him. "You've got trouble on your hands. That's what I understand."

"*Me?*" Max called back. "You got your wires crossed."

"You shot Phipps. Now you shot me."

"You aren't hit." There was movement behind the deadfall, a patch of dark green showing for an instant, then disappearing, Max edging into a different position. Fitzgerald peered ahead, tried to fix the position. It seemed important to do so even though he could think of no reason why. "Not yet, you aren't."

"All right," Fitzgerald said. He gulped, trying to squeeze up saliva, his mouth bone-dry. "I'm not going anywhere. You've got me covered. Why?"

"You people won't leave us alone."

"People?"

"I told the girl. Then I put some buckshot in the other one. Now you. You won't stop coming."

Fitzgerald tried to think. But how could he think when

he was being covered by a shotgun in the hands of a man he couldn't see? "I told you I was coming out here. You knew. There was no secret about it. But okay, I'm willing to sit down and talk."

"Willing?" Max shouted. "I'll tell you who's willing. I'm willing to blow your head off."

"Okay," Fitzgerald called back. "I'm not moving. You can see. I'm not armed and I'm not moving."

"Damned right you're not."

The tone of Max's voice had dropped a decibel—an encouraging sign, Fitzgerald decided, the second one after the realization that Max could have killed him but hadn't. He only wanted him scared. He'd succeeded. But scared was on a different scale than dead. The thing to do was to stand stock still, play for time. He had that on his side. He better have.

"SARAH," MERCY ASKED, "go back. Tell me what you mean about Allison, about keeping her here. She was writing a newspaper story and came to see you about the Catch and Keep Alliance. I know that much. She wanted information. Do you mean you wish you'd given her more?"

"I wanted to help," Sarah said dreamily.

"Of course you did."

"She'd made a bad union. That's a terrible thing."

"Allison said that? About Ray Thorne?"

Slowly Sarah shook her head. "I knew what he did— his business of illegal liquor. Everyone knew. Allison had only a life of misfortune ahead of her. She needed to find a way of her own."

"Through the story, you mean?"

"After the newspaper refused it she visited me again. I helped her every way I could."

"By giving her all the information you had."

Sarah studied her hands, the palms flat now on the

scrubbed table, age spots on the backs distinct in the light from the windows. "The newspaper wanted a different story. She came back but I'd told her all I could."

"Of course you had."

"I told her to visit you, Mercy. You would know more. She said that wasn't the story the newspaper wanted. There was nothing I could do."

"That would hold her here?"

"Yes," Sarah murmured.

"So she went for information to other people? To Max and Lucille Ringwald?"

"Yes," Sarah repeated.

FITZGERALD SAID, "Why do you say we won't leave you alone? You wanted a story about the Catch and Keep Alliance. You cooperated with Allison."

"It wasn't my idea," Max barked back from the deadfall. "I shouldn't have."

"Whose idea was it, then?"

"When I saw it was a mistake I tried to shut it off. But the girl kept coming around. I'd go out, when I'd come back she was there. I couldn't get rid of her. She kept digging. I called your goddamn paper, told them to get her off my back. It only made it worse."

"Digging for what?"

There was sudden, spasmodic movement in the deadfall. Fitzgerald could see it then, the shotgun barrel protruding through the tangle of branches, a sheen of black against patterns of brown. For what good it did him, there was no question now where Max was located. "Don't get excited," Fitzgerald called out. "I'm just asking. What was Allison looking for?"

"You know damn well. What the other one was. What you are. You think I'm up to my ears with a bunch of play soldiers. It's bull."

Fitzgerald waited. He had to keep Max talking. He had to buy time. He wanted to lift his wrist, glance at his watch, but couldn't risk making the movement.

"You see anything out here? I didn't let the other one get all the way in but I let you. There's nothing to see, you still aren't satisfied. You want to keep looking. Next thing you'll be in my house. Like she was."

"I'm looking for a militia connection," Fitzgerald ventured. "I admit that. So was Allison—a connection with the Catch and Keep Alliance. So was the reporter you shot. If there's nothing to hide, why worry?"

Again the black barrel shifted abruptly in the deadfall. "You're on my property is why. You got no business here. I let it go too long. This is where it ends."

"Wait!" Fitzgerald called. "I'm not moving. You can see I'm just asking. The idea of a militia connection—it didn't come out of the blue. Allison was following a lead she'd gotten somewhere."

"The old lady," Max growled back. "That's where."

MERCY SAID, "I've got to admit something. I know Calvin was here, seeing you. He said you told Allison about Dawes, showed her old copies of the *Avenger*. I understand why: You wanted Allison to know about the resistance to catch and release, back when it first came in. The history of it. She could work that into her story."

"Yes," Sarah said.

"That may have given Allison the idea your group was connected to something bigger—some radical movement, resistance to the government, that sort of thing."

"Yes."

Mercy looked at her. Sarah's eyes remained fixed on her hands. "You know?"

"The militia, Calvin said."

Mercy cocked her head and said, "Calvin had the impression you didn't know."

Slowly Sarah lifted her eyes. "I knew he would speak to you. You and Calvin—"

"A long time ago, Sarah."

"He was questioning me for you and your friend."

"Fitzgerald."

"I've known Calvin since he was a boy. Cam said if Calvin ever told a falsehood it would be revealed on his face."

"Having him talk to you was my idea," Mercy said. "I had the hunch Allison might have gotten the idea about the militia from hearing about Dawes—that you'd mentioned him. I guessed she might have jumped from that to the idea that a militia group had some involvement with the Catch and Keep Alliance."

"She did."

"You knew?"

"I wanted her to."

Mercy stared.

"I wanted to help her. Don't you understand?"

BEYOND MAX, far to the right, Fitzgerald caught sight of movement. Another flash, green against green. He had bought enough time but had to keep filling the air with talk, covering the sound. A hidden twig could snap while Calvin advanced through the blanket of pine needles.

"Sarah Nunemaker?" Fitzgerald called out. If Max heard noise behind him, turned to it, the shotgun leveled in the other direction, he would have to move fast to reach the deadfall. Fitzgerald rolled slightly forward on the balls of his feet. "She told Allison your group was involved with the militia?"

"Didn't *tell* her. How could she? It wasn't true. She let her *believe* it, filling her head with rubbish about the past.

It didn't make sense but the girl sucked it up. She was ready to believe anything. She thought I was training a paramilitary force out here. Once we got catch and release off the river we'd take over the county."

"And you're saying that isn't so?"

Again the black barrel shifted in the deadfall. "Goddamnit all to hell," Max shouted, "you're just like her. You see any evidence? I'm here, you're here. You see anybody else?"

"Okay," Fitzgerald said. "Take it easy. If Allison had it wrong about the militia why didn't you just tell her so?"

"She didn't want to hear. None of you do."

Despite himself Fitzgerald paused, silence hanging in the air. Allison wanted her story in print, wanted it badly, but she couldn't have pushed ahead with it in the face of Max Ringwald's denial. Without something else—some evidence of militia activity, another source contradicting Max, something—she would have abandoned the story. She was experienced enough to recognize a dead end when she came to one. There had to be more than Max was admitting. Fitzgerald let his eyes search the distance beyond the deadfall. He hadn't seen more movement. But it didn't matter what *he* saw. What mattered was what Max heard.

"No," Fitzgerald called out.

"No what?"

"I don't believe it. Allison kept on with the story. She must have found something."

"*Found?* What she found was in her head. Everything fit together, in her head. That's the way it is with you people. You never saw a fact you couldn't ignore."

"No," Fitzgerald repeated. "It doesn't work that way."

"I'm telling you it goddamn well did."

"Allison had experience on a good paper before she came up here. She'd know she needed more than suppositions to hang a story on. She needed hard evidence. She'd know that." Fitzgerald steadied himself on the balls of his feet, concentrating his attention on the gun barrel poking through the deadfall. Could he hold Max off much longer? If the barrel shifted again he could dive to the ground, crawl through the grass on his belly. Stretched flat he wouldn't be out of Max's firing angle but he would be a tougher target. He scanned the distance beyond Max, saw no movement. Had he, really, ever?

"You're not telling the whole story. Allison found something. She wouldn't have stayed with the story otherwise. You're holding back."

"I'm lying, you're saying?"

Fitzgerald sucked in his breath. "I'm saying it."

An instant before orange fire colored the air the barrel of the shotgun jerked violently in the deadfall. It was enough. Fitzgerald dropped flat to the ground, felt the furnace blast sear the air above, rolled to his right, kept rolling, kept trying to reach cover, knowing he would never make it. Max might have to stand behind the deadfall to get the right angle for another shot. There might be that much delay. But, upright, Max would have an open view. Cover was too far away. He would never make it before Max fired again.

What Fitzgerald heard then wasn't what he expected. Not a shotgun blast but a high-pitched whine—a shrill cry of released air. He held tight to the ground, not daring to look up.

Then heard a long, anguished moan of defeat.

TWENTY-FOUR

SUDDENLY THE SUN slipped behind a bank of clouds, gray light descending on the woods beyond the windows of the breakfast alcove. An ominous sign, it seemed. Mercy felt tension grip her body. She was approaching something, some clarity of vision, just as the light of the world fell about her. "It was wrong," Sarah was saying to her. "I knew it was."

"Because there wasn't any militia connection?"

"I was grasping at straws. She wished so badly to finish her story. There was nothing else I could think of, nothing that would help."

"Sure, help Allison with her story."

Sarah shook her head. "Her entire life, Mercy. She had to escape from that man. When I told her about Wesley Dawes she was thrilled. She saw a way ahead. She would write a fresh story, one that would have the attention of the newspaper. She would gain her freedom. We sat right here, talking together. What I told her wasn't all true—I realized that. Dawes had no interest in joining with others. He wasn't like that. He only wished to be heard. But Allison wanted to believe otherwise and I did nothing to stop her. I brought out his newsletters and she read them so avidly, sitting at this table. She wanted to take them away, to duplicate passages, but I told her the newsletters had belonged to Cam and I feared something might happen to them. I wanted her to read them here, to stay with me. She made notes. She said she would enter them later into her computer."

When Sarah stopped, one hand slowly caressing the other, Mercy prompted her, "And then?"

"She left me. I'd exhausted everything I could think of to keep her here. There was nothing more."

"Allison left you," Mercy asked gently, "to go to Lucille Ringwald's?"

"I couldn't bear it. I wished her free of that man. I thought I'd helped. I'd succeeded only in sending her off to poor Lucille."

"But why did she go there—to Lucille?"

Sarah looked up, her seamed face creased into a painful frown. "Don't you see? I'd put it into her mind that our little group was linked with something larger. But for her story she needed documentation. I could only tell her of the past; she needed to learn about the present. I should have foreseen she'd go to the Ringwalds."

"Because Max had been in the military. Sure, it was natural she'd turn to him. She'd guess he'd be the present connection."

"Yes."

"And seeing Max meant she'd also see Lucille. Did something happen then," Mercy asked after a moment's hesitation, "between Allison and Lucille? Can you tell me about it?"

Again Sarah shook her head.

"Nothing happened?"

"I told you." Sarah looked away, her gaze receding into sadness. "It was the worst thing."

"YOU'RE *CRUSHING* ME, you bastard!" Max gasped when his voice returned.

"That's the idea," Calvin said.

"Hold him still," Fitzgerald said. He pulled the shotgun free of the deadfall and held the barrel angled down at Max's head. The gun was excessive given that Calvin was sitting on Max's back, both his arms pinned tight to the ground, his face forced into the cushion of pine needles. But Fitzgerald wasn't taking chances. Excess seemed reasonable after escaping two blasts from the shotgun. The second one hadn't been a warning.

"I can't breathe!" Max managed to say.

"That's the other idea."

Fitzgerald said to Calvin, "I caught a glimpse of you back in the pines, then I couldn't see you again. I didn't know if you'd get here in time."

"He fired the first one," Calvin said, "I had his location fixed. You had him talking so I came on slow. I figured you wanted to hear."

"Not that much."

"When he let off the second I figured he was done talking. I came up quick. He was pumping another shell in the gun when I took off. Mess of downed limbs where he was so I took a flying leap over the top. Flattened him like a pancake."

Fitzgerald inched the barrel of the gun closer to Max's head. "Here's the deal. Calvin gets off your back, you turn over, slow, then you sit up. Keep your rear on the ground. Any quick move and Calvin flattens you again. Clear?"

"Jesus, yes!"

"Two shots—you could have killed me. Calvin's a witness. We can go to Willard Stroud and swear out a complaint. That clear, too?"

"Yeah, yeah, yeah," Max moaned.

Sitting up, back pushed against the deadfall, Max glared at Calvin, then shook his head, let his chin sink to his chest. Glasses hung forlornly on the thong about his neck, both lenses smashed. Fitzgerald suppressed a momentary feeling of sympathy, kept the barrel of the gun directed downward. Calvin stood on the other side of Max, hands braced on his hips.

"We could go to Stroud right now," Fitzgerald said, "or you can tell us the truth about Allison. You do, maybe we won't go. There's no guarantee, but maybe we won't. I'd say it's your only option."

"You want me to flatten him again?" Calvin said when Max didn't respond.

"I thought you were on my side," Max said bitterly.

"Depends on the subject," Calvin said.

"We're talking about Allison," Fitzgerald said. "She found something or she wouldn't have kept on with her story. What? Tell us or tell Stroud."

"Nothing."

"I don't believe you."

Max met Fitzgerald's eye for an instant, then let his chin drop back to his chest. "You find anything out here? Nothing to find, that's why. Same with her. She poked around, came up empty. Everything she had I gave her."

"You?"

"She wanted garbage about some militia nuts and the Catch and Keep Alliance. Your paper wouldn't print the story otherwise. So I gave her garbage. It looked like we were a citizens' group fighting river regulations. In fact, we were tied into a network that meant to subvert authority in the north woods, then the state, finally the country. What she was seeing up here, it was the start of another American revolution. You get it now? That's what she found. Pure, total garbage."

Fitzgerald said, "Wait a minute. *You* told her this?"

"Sarah Nunemaker filled her head about an old coot up here who railed against the government."

"Dawes," Calvin said. "He had a name."

"That got the girl going on the militia. If you lived in the woods and were against the government you must be involved with some paramilitary group—that's how she thought. All she knew she'd seen on TV. So I told her, right, we're involved, but it wasn't with your usual militia nuts. Militia wasn't even the right word. The movement we were part of was serious. We were serious people with serious plans. She'd see. So would the country."

"And Allison believed you?"

Max looked up, glared at Fitzgerald. "Don't you get it yet? She wanted to. She was writing a story for a newspaper."

"But she needed evidence. It couldn't be just talk."

"You want to call it evidence. All the rooms in my place—I told her it was to bring in people, serious people, conduct planning sessions. It was why I'd bought the old club in the first place. She knew I had connections—military connections, and connections down at Dow. I showed her my gun collection. She knew I was buying more property, fencing it off, trying to keep the locals out. It all fit together in her mind. Then I added the clincher. I bought a half-dozen cases of booze off the low-life she said was her husband. I couldn't drink that much, so the booze had to be for big shots coming to the house."

Max stopped, looked from Fitzgerald to Calvin. "The girl knew all about getting around the law. The husband was the local bootlegger."

"We know," Fitzgerald said.

Max said, "So you got it now? She took down everything I said."

"And none of it was true?"

"What's true got to do with it? I told you—it was a newspaper story she wanted. I gave her one."

"All right. Let's say that. But why would you? You wouldn't want a story like that in print."

"I knew it wouldn't get in print."

"But you couldn't be certain. It was a risk. Why would you take it?"

"Why not?"

Calvin said, "You want me to flatten him?"

"Maybe you should," Fitzgerald said, "before we go to Stroud."

"It's personal," Max said thinly.

"I don't think that would make any difference to Stroud. Not with Allison and Ray Thorne dead, not after you wounded Phipps, took two shots at me. On the other hand, maybe it would to us."

Max looked beyond Fitzgerald and Calvin, took in the jack-pine woods. Then his eyes emptied out, his chin sank. "You wouldn't understand."

"Would Stroud?"

"I wanted to keep the girl around, that's why. I was stringing out the time, hoping it would run its course. It had before. Then something happened I hadn't figured on. How could I, something like that. Everything went straight to hell. Okay? That satisfy you?"

"You were interested in Allison—that's why you wanted her around? Interested personally? That what you're saying?"

"Jesus," Max managed to say, "I said you wouldn't understand. *I* wasn't. What do you take me for? *She* was."

"She?"

"Lucille," Max murmured.

"YOU HAVE TO tell me," Mercy said. "I can't understand if you don't. What happened between Allison and Lucille?"

Sarah shook her head.

"Then there's no other choice. I'll have to ask Lucille."

"No," Sarah said firmly. "You mustn't trouble her. It mustn't begin again. I won't allow it."

Mercy felt her back stiffen. She looked hard at Sarah, then took a deep breath and said, "Let's quit dancing around. What are we talking about—some affair between

Allison and Lucille? Something between two women, something physical? Sex? Is that what happened?"

Slowly, sadly, Sarah shook her head.

Mercy stared at her.

"I don't know what happened. Allison left me and went to poor Lucille. She went there over and over again. She wouldn't stop. I don't know what happened, Mercy. I can only imagine."

"Please, go on."

"I telephoned her. I went there—where she lived with that man. I asked her to stop seeing Lucille."

"Allison, you mean? You went to her mobile home?"

"She promised me, Mercy. She said she would. She needed to finish her story, then she would never see Lucille again."

"But she didn't—didn't stop seeing her?"

"It was only the story, you see. That was what she wanted. It wasn't Lucille. It never was."

"But Lucille didn't understand that?"

"She isn't strong, Mercy. Even if Allison kept her promise—it was too late. I knew it was."

Mercy waited, looking at Sarah, waiting for her to lift her eyes into the darkening light of the world. "Too late for what?" she asked.

Sarah shook her head. Then she raised her eyes, looked with level gaze at Mercy. "You said you were going to see her. I won't allow it to begin again."

"What, Sarah?"

"Don't you remember? I told you before. Everything is ruined."

"SHE WANTED HER AROUND," Max said, his voice a low monotone, "young girl like that. So I fed her the garbage, piecing it out, keeping her around. For Lucille."

Fitzgerald kept the barrel of the gun lowered. "And you

hoped your wife and Allison—it would fade away. You had reason to think that.''

Max nodded, a faint downward dip of his head.

"Because it had happened in the past, happened with others? But this time it didn't? Your wife wouldn't give Allison up? She didn't lose interest?''

"It wasn't that way.''

"What way was it?''

When Max didn't respond Calvin said, "Now?''

"I don't think you need to," Fitzgerald told him. "If we talk to Stroud, you know what'll happen. Stroud will want to see Max's wife. He'll bring her into town, question her about the relationship with Allison. He'll want to know everything that happened. Out here, just us, maybe it won't go any further. That's a possibility.''

"No," Max said.

"You don't want her involved?''

A bitter moan again arose from Max's chest.

"Go on," Fitzgerald said.

"Ah, Jesus. You won't understand.''

"Go on.''

Max made an effort to lift his head, failed. His eyes seemed fixed on the broken lens of the glasses dangling from his neck. "The girl wouldn't let it go. She kept coming to our place, every time you turned around. But that wasn't enough. She had Lucille going out to her dump, seeing her there when the crud of a husband was gone.''

"To Allison's mobile home, you mean?''

"It wasn't what Lucille thought. The girl didn't give a damn about her. She was pumping her for information for the story, is all. That's the only thing she cared about—the story. Lucille didn't understand. She never did. She *can't* understand. The girl's holding on to her for only one reason and Lucille can't see it. Everybody in the world can see it and Lucille can't. An old woman and a young girl like that—it was pathetic.''

"So what did you do?"

"What do you think?" Max said. His voice rose, a harsh whisper, then fell back. "What I had to."

Fitzgerald waited.

A last rush of air seemed to escape his chest. "I ended it," Max said, a spent balloon.

MERCY SAID, "All this coffee. Afraid I need to use your bathroom.''

Sarah looked at her but didn't seem to be seeing. Her eyes were abstracted, vacant. Or were they? Was Sarah, looking back, also seeing with perfect clarity, knowing exactly what must come next? Had she, in fact, known since the moment Mercy phoned her from the DNR office, known since Mercy arrived at the log house, known since they sat together at the table in the breakfast alcove?

"I can find the way. Just be a minute."

Mercy stood up, backed slowly from the alcove, watching Sarah. Her gaze didn't shift as Mercy turned into the hallway, leaving her alone at the table.

TWENTY-FIVE

BONNIE PYM could hardly believe it. You tell someone you just met, sure thing, ring me up whenever you want, but you never expect it. It was what you said to be considerate. But here she was, talking with Lucille Ringwald on the phone, getting the feeling the woman wasn't calling to pass the time of day. Something was on her mind. Something serious.

"Is this a bad moment?" Lucille's voice was so faint Bonnie had to put a finger in her other ear to hear.

"Now? We get some real down periods during the day. This is one. Good timing, Lucille."

"I'm glad."

"So how's it going out there?" Bonnie didn't mean to sound so casual, but in the bakery, some regulars hanging out at the tables, joking with her, it was the way you talked. She tried for a different tone. "You feeling any better, sugar?"

When Lucille didn't respond right away Bonnie thought she still didn't have the tone right. She was trying to come up with another when Lucille said, "You said to call if there was anything you could do."

"Sure thing," Bonnie said hurriedly.

"Could you come out here? Would it be possible?"

"To your house?" Bonnie was going to suggest that Lucille come to town if she wanted to talk in person, settle down at one of the bakery tables, when she remembered Lucille didn't drive. That took care of that. There was something else, too. If you said you were available to help, and someone—big surprise—took you up on it, you had to follow through. You couldn't say how you would help, or where. You had to just pick up and do it.

"Give me a half hour or so. There's a high-school girl here who can take over."

"My husband isn't home."

Bonnie didn't know if Lucille meant that was good or bad, or why she even mentioned it. Bonnie was thinking how to respond when Lucille said, "Please come quickly."

"Hey," Bonnie asked, "you all right?"

"I don't know."

The moment she put down the phone Bonnie wished she had asked if Lucille had called Mercy first, which she probably had, given the nature of her feelings for Mercy. But that was okay, calling Mercy first. You couldn't tell someone you were ready and willing to help, then get your nose out of joint when you found you were second on their list.

Given the urgency in Lucille's voice, there wasn't time to stop at home for a fresh blouse, so in the ladies' room Bonnie did the best she could, fluffing her hair and applying fresh lipstick of plum brandy, her current shade. She turned her head from side to side, inspecting her earrings, silver embedded with Petoskey stone. "What I call a weighty pair," Willard Stroud had said earlier in the morning, eyeing her in his office when Bonnie brought a box of sweet rolls to the city-county building. She had let him have a lingering sideways look. He deserved it, married to a prune like Elsie. "Best in town, sugar," she said, and gave him her usual wink.

She was still thinking about Stroud when she left the Six-Grain Bakery and drove down the main drag, on her way to Lucille Ringwald's place on the river. She wondered what it would be like, married to someone like that, a sheriff. Probably like being married to a minister, having to watch your every step, never able to let your hair down, at least not in public. Married to a sheriff, she would never again set foot in a dump like the Keg O'Nails. So what would she do when she needed a night out? Bonnie shook her head at the answer. There wouldn't be any nights out, which meant that the nights in would have to be plenty good. Being married to Stroud, something told her, would only be okay.

When she reached the Borchard Hotel, Bonnie turned off the main drag and drove to the DNR field office. It wasn't that she needed to know if Lucille had phoned Mercy first, but she couldn't get the possibility out of her mind. If Lucille had, why hadn't Mercy gone out to see her? Mercy was supposed to be attending some course at Michigan State, so, temporarily back in Ossning, it seemed unlikely she was tied down with office work. Was it possible that Mercy was avoiding Lucille—avoiding her now that Bonnie had told her what Lucille was? But that didn't sound like Mercy. Mercy wasn't the sort to back away, no matter what. Lucille Ringwald was just the way some women were. Mercy knew that as well as Bonnie did. No big deal.

Mercy's office was empty but a man was working at a desk in the next office, a man Bonnie didn't recognize. She cleared her throat to draw his attention. "Mercy not around?"

After he looked her over, taking his sweet time about it, the man stood up behind the desk. "Afraid she's gone out."

Bonnie gave him a smile, not her best but enough to fasten his attention. "She happen to say where? I'm a friend."

"She mentioned something on the way out—Sarah's, I think it was. A place on the river. She was going to stop there first."

"Business?"

The man shrugged. "I'm Ted Tinnery, by the way." He held out his hand.

"You're not from here."

"Traverse City office. But I'll be working over here more."

"Bonnie Pym," she said, and took his hand. She held it just a fraction longer than necessary. "You didn't catch where Mercy was going after Sarah's?"

Ted Tinnery shook his head.

"Or whether she might have had a phone call?"

"Afraid not."

"No problem." Before she left the office Bonnie smiled again, nearly her best but with some reserve, not overdoing it on a first meeting. "See ya."

On the drive along North Downriver Road she gave passing thought to what it would be like married to a DNR officer. Better, anyway, than to a sheriff. Mercy was a DNR officer, the head of the whole district, yet she hung out at the bar of the Borchard Hotel and dropped in at the Keg O'Nails, or did before she moved in with Fitzgerald. But that wasn't what Bonnie wanted to think about. It was Sarah Nunemaker—why Mercy was paying her a call. There wasn't anyone else named Sarah living out on the river, so it had to be Sarah Nunemaker.

Mercy might have some printing work for Sarah, though the DNR probably had its own equipment for that. And it might have something to do with fishing regulations. Sarah was one of the property owners on the mainstream who wanted to reverse the catch and release regulation. Bonnie had read about their group in the *Call*. Still and all, it struck her as an odd coincidence, Mercy calling on Sarah when, just a short distance downstream, she would be visiting with Lucille.

But lots of things were odd. Getting a phone call at the bakery from Lucille Ringwald was odd. Meeting a new man in Mercy's office was odd. Bonnie smiled and looked out the car window at the passing vista of jack pines, the odd landscape of her life.

GUS THAYER didn't look bad, considering he was just out of intensive care. Willard Stroud had expected a ghost, weak and white, but Gus, propped up with starched hospital pillows, had some color in his cheeks and a half-grin on his face. The fogged look in his eyes Stroud put down to the effect of drugs. On the other hand, it might always be there. He had never seen Gus before without his black-rimmed glasses.

"So you're feeling okay, considering?"

"A little tight," Gus said, and moved a finger in the direction of his chest, loosely covered with a rumpled hospital gown, "in here. Mostly I'm thirsty. I keep sipping water, I'm still thirsty."

"They let you up to pee?"

"You wouldn't believe it. I'm still hooked up, trailing tubes, they have me walking the hall."

Stroud nodded. "How they do it these days."

"Right."

Gus knew what was coming next, the pleasantries out of the way. Stroud could see it in his eyes, despite the fogged look. Gus knew this wasn't a social call. Stroud had phoned the Traverse City hospital first, getting the chief nurse in the cardiac wing, making sure Gus was able to hold a conversation. "Not too long," the nurse had cautioned him. "It's all I need," Stroud had told her.

He settled into the single chair in Gus' room and folded his arms across his chest. "I'll tell you what I know happened. You and Phipps, the *Free Press* fellow, met up at Lost Finger Lake. Phipps came in from the road, you off the river. You came through Max Ringwald's property. When you met up, Phipps had already been shot—by Ringwald. He was trespassing was the reason."

"Wait," Gus said. "How do you know Ringwald plugged him?"

"Because I do. Phipps was trespassing on his property and so were you. Ringwald didn't see you or you would have gotten shot, too. After you found Phipps you got hold of the deputy on the road and he hauled the pair of you to the community hospital. Sound right?" Stroud added after a pause.

Gus nodded.

Stroud pushed forward, his face just off the edge of Gus' bed. "What I don't know is what the goddamn hell you two thought you were doing. That's a murder scene. That's why there's a deputy stationed out there. He would have shot you if Ringwald hadn't." Stroud stopped, corrected himself. "Hadn't shot Phipps."

"You sure Ringwald did it?"

"I'm telling you he did. He was walking his property line, keeping an eye out. When he ran into Phipps he tried to back off but Phipps came after him. Ringwald didn't know what was going on. That's why he dropped Phipps."

"He knew, all right."

"What?"

"Ringwald was walking his property for a reason," Gus said, his voice strong. "The reason Phipps and I figured out. He had something to hide out there."

Stroud stared at him. "What are you talking about? You and Phipps went out to Lost Finger to work up a story. You were looking for background on Ray Thorne's murder. You—"

"Nope." Gus suddenly looked smug. Even his eyes seemed to clear. "Ray Thorne wasn't the story. We were hunting for the militia."

"*What?*"

"Michigan militia—some part of it, cell or something, brigade. Whatever they call it. We were just beginning to work on the story, the two of us, following what Allison Thorne had dug up, building the evidence. Looks like we found it.''

"Gus," Stroud asked, "you sure you're okay?''

On the pillow Gus shifted his head, bringing it closer to Stroud's. The smug look deepened. "You don't know, do you?''

"Know what?''

"Allison Thorne found out a militia outfit was behind the Catch and Keep Alliance, tied into it some way. She was working on the story when she was plugged. You think that was a coincidence? Phipps and I pick up the story, work on it, Phipps gets plugged. Another coincidence?'' Gus rolled his head back on the pillow, satisfied. "No way, Willard.''

THE OTHER TIME, with Mercy, Lucille Ringwald had offered to make something, coffee or tea or whatever. This time she said nothing. As soon as Bonnie was inside the door Lucille slumped into a chair at the big oak table in the kitchen and folded her hands in front of her. Bonnie didn't mind about the coffee or tea. During the day at the Six-Grain Bakery she drank enough to float a ship. But a mug of something, sipping it, was a way of easing into a conversation you were totally in the dark about.

Go with the flow, Bonnie told herself. She smiled and said, "This is real nice, Lucille.''

Lucille smiled in return but the look didn't hold. Her face faded back into the appearance Bonnie had found at the door, sad, colorless, middle-aged. The contrast with her hair—gaudy as before, though with a strip of steel gray emerging at the part—simply called more attention to her age. The same was true of the blue-rimmed glasses. Someone should tell her. Mercy maybe. Lucille might not be offended, given the eye she had for Mercy.

"But you wanted to talk about something," Bonnie said. "You mentioned on the phone."

"Yes," Lucille said, her first word.

"And this was a good time, your husband away and all."

"Yes."

"Maybe there was something I could do, you said."

"I don't know."

Bonnie glanced at her watch, hoping Lucille might notice. She was glad to help with whatever it was, but she didn't have all day. The high-school girl at the bakery was on a tight schedule. "Let's find out. Try me."

Lucille looked back at her, sad eyes in a sad face, as if she was trying to make up her mind. But what was there to decide? She was the one who had phoned.

"Please," Lucille said suddenly. "Excuse me."

Bonnie watched as she left the kitchen, disappeared back into the house. She was wearing the same outfit as before, moccasin slippers, washed-out jeans, baggy sweatshirt. The woman was no clothes horse, but who was out on the river? Bonnie wondered about that. If she had a river place would she let herself go, too? She didn't think so, but how could you tell? Someday she would reach Lucille's age, an unimaginable time when all you could change was the color of your hair. Maybe then—

It was a relief when Lucille emerged from wherever she had been, carrying a small cloth bag. She stood in the kitchen doorway and beckoned with her head.

Bonnie supposed that meant Lucille wanted her to follow. Maybe she had done some picking up before taking Bonnie into the rest of the house, which was understandable. Together they moved through a dining room with a long dark table in the center of it, a room that didn't look like it was used, and into a big living area with plank flooring, stone fireplace at one end, framed pictures on the walls, except for one wall hung with swords—curved, straight,

long, short, all old looking, probably valuable. Bonnie was
looking them over when Lucille led the way from the living
area and along a hallway with a number of doors off it.

Lucille paused before one, the door closed. "I had to get
the key. He keeps it locked."

"Your husband's key?"

"I had a duplicate made in town."

Bonnie cocked her head. "You went in yourself? I
thought you didn't drive."

Lucille looked away, a shy half-smile on her face. "I
shouldn't have said that."

She opened the bag she carried, took out a key, opened
the door. They stepped into a room, all fresh knotty-pine
walls, that looked like it was meant to be a den. A wood
desk strewn with books and papers occupied the center of
the room, facing another stone fireplace. More framed photographs lined the walls. In one corner was a glass-fronted
cabinet of expensive-looking wood, shotguns and rifles
lined inside. Beside it was a gray metal case, waist high,
with several wide drawers. Lucille bent down, opened one.
A display of handguns lay on soft cloth, the guns carefully
spaced and looking freshly oiled.

"Wow," Bonnie said. "I can see why he keeps the door
locked. Your husband's a collector, huh?"

Lucille didn't answer. She opened another drawer, then
another, five in all. In each, handguns were laid out on
cloth, barrels pointing the same direction. What Bonnie
knew about handguns was limited to the loaded Smith &
Wesson she kept in a bedside drawer, just to be on the safe
side. But she could tell the guns in Max Ringwald's metal
case were different types and different vintages. Some were
big cowboy revolvers, some military looking, some like the
stubby gangster guns you saw in movies. "Wow," she said
again, "that's something."

Lucille closed the bottom drawer of the case and re-opened the top. "Please, count them."

Bonnie looked at her. "Why?"

"Please."

The drawer had four rows, three guns in each—except for one row. A gun was missing. Lucille closed the drawer and reopened the bottom. Bonnie bent down to see. "Eleven again."

"Yes."

"It matters?"

"The other drawers have twelve."

Lucille shut the drawer and moved to the door. Bonnie had the impression she wanted to be out of the room, the door locked, back in the kitchen as soon as possible, which was understandable. She didn't want her husband to find out she had a key to his den. Was *den* even the right word, given all the fire power in there? *Arsenal,* maybe.

STROUD CONSIDERED going out in the hall, finding the chief nurse, seeing what kind of drugs had been pumped into Gus Thayer. Could they make him hallucinate? He leaned back in the chair beside the hospital bed, putting as much distance between himself and Gus as possible. "You want to tell me that one more time?" he said. When Gus did, enjoying himself in the retelling, Stroud said, "I thought that's what you said."

"What Phipps and I figured," Gus went on, "is Allison was right on the edge of cracking the story. It would have blown the lid off, made every paper in the state. So, to keep her quiet, she had to be plugged."

Stroud winced. Gus sounded like a cop on a television show.

"They thought they had it all figured. Then Phipps shows and we team up, on the trail of the story—bigger story now, a reporter dead. If we can crack it, it'll reach beyond the state, make every paper in the country. They've got themselves another problem, so they operate the same way. They plug Phipps. I'd come along, same time, they'd have plugged me, too." Gus paused. "One thing you got right."

Too bad you didn't come along, Stroud wanted to say. Instead he said, "Except Phipps wasn't killed. He got a load of buckshot in one leg."

Gus wasn't impressed by the difference. "Bad luck. Or maybe they didn't mean to plug him for good, knowing the stink it would raise, another reporter shot dead. They'd try scaring him off first. That didn't work they'd plug him."

"For good."

"Right."

"And *they*—you mean some militia outfit?"

"Right."

"And you're saying Max Ringwald's tied in with them? That he's running some kind of militia operation on his property?"

"That's why Phipps and I were out there, hunting for the evidence."

"But you didn't find any."

"We didn't have time."

Despite himself, Stroud lurched forward, scraping his chair against the tiled floor, narrowing the gap with Gus. His face burned. "Crap—pure unadulterated crap. There's no militia nonsense in Tamarack County. Never has been, never will be. Max Ringwald shot Phipps accidently. He thought Phipps was after him, he got panicky, let off a shot. That's all there was to it. It's got nothing to do with any militia. I'm telling you: there's nothing like that in the county. It's complete crap. I'd know otherwise."

Gus looked back at him, unimpressed, smug.

"Goddamnit, Gus. I'm telling you."

"Like you knew about Ray Thorne?"

Stroud stared at him.

"Like you knew what he had going at Lost Finger Lake?"

"THAT'S THE PROBLEM, huh?" Bonnie said. They were sitting at the oak table in the kitchen again, facing one another again. "Two guns gone from your husband's collection?"

"Yes."

"It couldn't have just happened?"

"No."

"How do you know for sure?"

Lucille said, "I had to tell someone. I thought you might—"

"Sure," Bonnie said. "Why I'm here."

"—tell me what to do."

Bonnie didn't respond. If she stopped talking maybe Lucille would begin. Really begin. Bonnie smiled at her across the table, looking into the sad eyes behind the blue-rimmed glasses. She kept smiling until Lucille met her gaze. "Go on," Bonnie urged.

"One of them's missing because I took it."

"After you made the key?"

Lucille nodded.

"You understand about guns? You wanted to shoot targets or something?"

"My husband was in the military. I learned—long ago. All wives learned. We were often alone."

"Sure," Bonnie said. "For protection." But that didn't explain why, now, Lucille had to sneak into her husband's collection to get a gun. If she thought she needed protection living out on the river, why didn't she tell him she wanted one? Most people living in the north woods, male and female, were armed to the teeth. Or had Lucille asked him and he refused? Was that it?

Bonnie was wondering how to put the question, tactfully, when Lucille said, "We were young then."

"Sure you were." Now, middle-aged, her husband no longer trusted her with guns—was that what Lucille meant? Bonnie bit her tongue, forcing herself to wait. Across from her Lucille twisted the ring on her finger, the big diamond with the out-of-fashion setting.

"Go on," Bonnie couldn't stop herself from saying.

"I didn't use it."

"The gun you took?"

"I couldn't."

Bonnie looked at her, waiting, but Lucille was intent on her ring, twisting it back and forth. "Hey, Lucille," Bonnie sighed, "we're not getting anywhere. You want me to help, you've got to tell me what we're talking about, straight out. Okay? Don't worry if it's hush-hush stuff. I can keep a secret. It's just woman to woman here."

Lucille looked up, the shy half-smile on her face again. "I'd hoped so."

"Well, you were right."

Lucille said, "I thought I wanted the gun. It wasn't for protection. I was angry—and so hurt. I had to do something. I wanted to—"

"Get even?" Bonnie prompted her when Lucille broke off the thought.

"I couldn't. I wasn't capable. The loss was so hurtful yet I couldn't. I just couldn't."

"But you kept the gun?"

Lucille opened the cloth bag she had placed on the table, withdrew a small, shiny revolver, settled it carefully in front of her.

"Wow. You had that in there, too?" Then Bonnie said, "You're sure there's supposed to be twelve guns in every one of those drawers?"

"Yes."

"So, figuring this, one's still missing."

"That's what I told you. My husband must have taken it. No one else could." Lucille was looking at her now, eye to eye, woman to woman.

"Go on," Bonnie urged.

"It's so hard to say."

"You want to get if off your chest," Bonnie said, "you got to."

"Yes."

"So?"

"I believe he took the gun," Lucille said after a moment's hesitation, "to kill Allison."

TWENTY-SIX

FITZGERALD LEANED the shotgun against the tangle of deadfall, then he and Calvin pulled Max to his feet, one on either side, got him in a sitting position on a downed limb. He was dead weight. Fitzgerald bent over, picked up Max's cap, handed it to him. It rested on his lap, beneath the shattered glasses.

"We can't let it stop here," Fitzgerald told him. "Not now."

Max didn't move, didn't look at either one of them.

"We have to go to Stroud. You understand that? If you can't walk, Calvin can go for help."

"I can walk," Max said without conviction.

"We'll go to your place, call Stroud from there, have him send a patrol car for us. Whenever you're ready," Fitzgerald added.

Max's eyes flickered. He looked up, his mouth a brief stubborn line before light faded from his eyes. "The day you showed up at the house I was ready."

"You don't have to say anything more."

Max shrugged. "What's the point? You showed up, asking about her, I knew it was over. You people wouldn't let go. Then the other one, sneaking around my property."

"Phipps."

"What I deserved, getting mixed up with a paper."

"Why did you? Allison was writing a story. You knew she was." Fitzgerald stopped, looking at Max, giving him time. "You should talk to Stroud. We'll go in."

"What's the point?" Max raised a hand, touched the bill of his cap, let the hand drop back. "I thought I could hold it together. The girl was trying to get on with the paper, she wasn't a regular. And the story didn't amount to anything. I figured the paper wouldn't want it. The girl—she'd go off to something else, everything would work out, we'd be back to normal. I was done running."

"Because of your wife?"

"I retired early. Promotion wasn't in the cards, not living on military bases, everybody looking over your shoulder, knowing everything. Down in Lansing was better, living in a regular neighborhood, away from snoops. Then it started up again, same thing, people smirking behind your back. In Midland—nothing different. It was the end of the line. We came up here, got the old club on the river, added property. I wasn't moving another inch." Max stirred on the downed tree, looked sourly at Fitzgerald. "You get it? Custer's last stand."

"Then why join the Catch and Keep Alliance?"

Slowly Max nodded, nodding to himself.

"If you wouldn't have—"

"Don't tell me. Sarah Nunemaker—it was her brainstorm. She pushed it. I believed in it, the principle. But the main thing was Lucille got a kick out of the meetings, people around, getting together. I couldn't see the harm, bunch of old-timers on the river, some older than we were. Like Sarah. So I went along, got mixed up with the group. Second biggest mistake of my life."

"Because of Allison?"

"She came into it, writing the story. I didn't take her seriously, wife of the bootlegger, showing up at the meetings, coming to the house, a notebook always out like she was some regular reporter. By the time I got wind of what was happening it was too late. Lucille—" Max shut his eyes, swung his head from side to side. "The girl wasn't even a looker."

"Your wife—" Fitzgerald stopped, began again. "You

thought the relationship would run its course, but it didn't. So you felt you had to end it. Was that it?'' Fitzgerald waited, giving Max time, letting him decide. ''You should talk to—''

''And tell him the same thing? What's the point? I killed the girl. That's what I'm saying.''

CALVIN CAUGHT Fitzgerald's attention, drew him off to the side. They kept an eye on Max even though he wasn't going anywhere.

''His wife had a fling with Allison?'' Calvin asked. ''That's the deal?''

''He thinks so,'' Fitzgerald said.

''I never heard that up here.''

''You have now.''

Calvin nodded. He considered himself enlightened on such matters. It was the way the world turned, even in the north woods. ''Surprised?'' he asked Fitzgerald.

''Mercy had a feeling when she met Lucille.''

Calvin nodded again. It was the sort of thing women probably picked up right away. ''Want me to go for Stroud? You hold the fort here, I'll paddle up to Sarah's, use her phone.''

''Not yet.''

Calvin looked back at Max, slumped on the downed limb. ''He's out of gas. No way he can walk out. We can get a deputy out here, rig up something, cart him in.''

''No.''

''He killed her,'' Calvin said. ''You heard him. What're we waiting for?''

''There were two, remember?''

For a moment Calvin didn't know what Fitzgerald was talking about. Then he did—the other murder, Ray Thorne. If Max Ringwald killed Allison because of what was going on with his wife, who killed Ray? And why? That was what

Fitzgerald must be wondering. "I get it," Calvin said, and led the way back to Max. "You want the deputy, let me know."

"I HAD TO MAKE SURE the crud of a husband wasn't around," Max explained when Fitzgerald asked how he had gone about killing Allison Thorne. "So I called her up, said I was coming to her place, I was going to give her more material on the militia, the big piece she needed to finish her story. She was hot to come to our place, but I told her no, Lucille wouldn't want her there, not now. She said okay. I got there, her place, she's got coffee made, friendly, big smile, because I'm giving her what she wants. When she sat at the computer, putting in what I said, I shot her. That's it."

"Shot her where?"

"Back of the head."

"And the gun?"

"One of mine—thirty-eight."

"You said Allison had coffee made. You drank some?"

"Yeah."

"Did Allison?"

"What's the point? I said I shot her."

"Then what?"

"I left."

"Did you close the door of the mobile home?"

"What?"

"Did you close the door or leave it open?"

"I don't remember."

"That's all you did—you shot Allison and immediately left?"

"What do you think? I was going to stay around?"

"And the gun?"

"What about it?"

"What did you do with the gun?"

"Kept it."

"Why?"

"I had a reason."

"To kill Ray Thorne?"

"WE DON'T NEED a deputy," Calvin said after he beckoned Fitzgerald to the side. "Let's drag him in. The old fart killed them both."

"He's lying."

Calvin stared back.

"I think he's lying."

"Hold on. You don't lie about killing two people."

"Unless you have a good reason."

"What?"

"Protecting someone who's important to you."

"Like his wife?"

"Let's find out."

"I WENT TO WHERE he stashed his stuff at the lake," Max said when Fitzgerald asked how he had gone about killing Ray Thorne. "I knew about the place—tried to buy the property once. I'd walked in from my place, looked it over. I found the cabin with the booze."

"The day you killed him," Fitzgerald asked, "that day you drove from the mobile home directly to Lost Finger Lake. Is that right?"

Max nodded.

"How did you know Ray Thorne would be there?"

"He had a phone in his van. He was at the lake, unloading cases. I called, said I'd be right out."

"You knew the number to call?"

"I told you. I bought from him one time. The way it worked, you called the girl first, gave her the order. She gave you the van number to set up delivery."

''So you called from the mobile home, using the number Allison had given you before. Then what?''

''He said he didn't do business at the lake. He'd deliver after he heard from Allison. I told him I couldn't reach her on the phone, it was a rush buy, big one, so I was calling him direct. I wanted to look over his stock, take delivery right now. Maybe he knew the garbage about the militia, knew from the girl, so he figured I had people staying at my place. He said okay, we'd do business out there this once.''

''Then?''

Max didn't answer.

''Then you shot him?''

Max dipped his head, a faint nod.

''How?''

''Same way.''

''How, exactly?''

''He was sitting at a table in the cabin, making a note in a little book. I'd told him I changed my mind, wouldn't take delivery until the next day. He could bring the booze around in the van and I'd pay him then. I wanted him sitting, back to me, writing the order down—that was the idea. Afterward I got two cups out of a cupboard, like with the girl, except there was nothing to make coffee. The place was bare. I wiped away prints and got out.''

''What happened to Ray's book with your order?''

''I got rid of it. What do you think?''

''The gun you used—it was the same one?''

Again Max dipped his head.

''I don't understand,'' Fitzgerald said. ''You killed Allison Thorne because of your wife. You wanted to end the relationship between them. There wasn't any need to kill Ray Thorne.''

Max's lips tightened. ''A loss to humanity?''

''You don't have to say anything.''

"What's the point? I had to think quick at the girl's place. I thought of robbery, ransacking the place, taking the computer, making it look like a robbery. But that would leave the husband on the loose. I didn't know what he knew—knew about what was going on. He might put things together, come looking. I didn't want the worry. I was done worrying."

"Your last stand. But why shoot Ray Thorne the same way as Allison?"

"I told you. I had to think quick. A crud like that, bootlegger, he'd have enemies. People he'd screwed, who didn't want to pay up, all sorts of creeps. But they'd kill him, not the girl."

"So who would kill her, too?" Fitzgerald prompted when Max stopped. "That's what you had to work out."

Max's shoulders drooped. A raspy sigh lifted from his chest.

"Someone who knew she was part of the business," Fitzgerald went on. "So the killer wiped the slate clean, got rid of them both. And killed the same way, wanting the liquor business to appear as the reason. That's the way you figured it."

"I had to think quick out there," Max said.

"YOU CAN SEE IT," Calvin said when he and Fitzgerald moved off from Max. "The way he figured, it makes sense. You shoot them both, same way, Stroud gets the idea it didn't just happen. He learns Ray and Allison were peddling booze, he's got the reason. Another bootlegger wanted to take over."

"Or get even."

Calvin looked at Fitzgerald. "Somebody Ray cut out? Revenge? That's possible. Stroud could think that way."

"He did. From the start he thought the killings were professional executions."

Calvin nodded in Max's direction. "What he wanted. Back of the head—sure, some hit man up from Detroit, contract killer. You read about that."

"Except Allison and Ray were killed with different guns. Stroud told me."

"Maybe that's the way it's done."

"Maybe. But it has nothing to do with this." Fitzgerald turned back to Max. "Didn't you hear him? He said he used the same gun."

"He forgot."

Fitzgerald said, "Not about killing, you don't."

"AFTER YOU KILLED Ray Thorne," Fitzgerald asked, "did you remove anything from the cabin other than the book he wrote in?"

"What?"

"From the mobile home, after you killed Allison?"

Max lifted his head, peered at Fitzgerald. "What is this? I told you what happened."

"You were going to give Allison a big piece of information about the militia and the Catch and Keep Alliance. That's what you told her. That's why she sat at the computer. She was putting in the information. Is that what happened?"

"Yeah."

"How much did she put in before you shot her?"

"Jesus," Max said, "I'm supposed to remember?"

"And what you told her, you were making it up?"

"Pure garbage."

"Then why wasn't any of it found?"

"What?"

"I checked myself. Allison had opened a word-processing program but there was nothing there. And nothing on her hard drive or disks. The only thing I found was the original story, the one the *Free Press* rejected. There was no mention of a militia connection—and no new story, no notes for a new story, nothing. You understand? Nothing.''

''What's the point? I told you I killed her.''

Fitzgerald shook his head. ''Whoever killed Allison erased the militia material, all the false information you'd given her, everything she'd entered in the computer. They shot her, leaned over her body, erased everything on the open file, went into the hard drive and erased more, went through her disks and got rid of any backups she'd made of the material. It wasn't you. That day at your house, with Mercy Virdon, you told me you don't fool with computers.''

Max roused himself, began a reply, slumped into silence.

''You said you killed Ray and Allison with the same gun. But different guns were used. Stroud had the state police analyze the bullets.'' Fitzgerald paused, shifted position, tried to get an angle to see into Max's eyes. ''You didn't kill either of them.''

Slowly Max raised his head, raked Fitzgerald's face, then Calvin's. A faint sheen had appeared in his eyes.

''You didn't kill Ray or Allison,'' Fitzgerald repeated.

''Goddamn newspaper people,'' Max hissed, ''you can't get anything right.''

Fitzgerald waited.

''Him,'' Max said. ''Him I did.''

TWENTY-SEVEN

THE BATHROOM WAS at the end of the hallway, door open, marbled green tile showing. Along the hallway two other doors stood open, a bedroom, bird's-eye maple furnishings inside, and a room arranged as an office, with a computer on a large desk and beside it what appeared to be a laser printer. It was a third door, closed, that drew Mercy's attention.

The windows of the room would be at the front of the house, facing the river. Someone working in the room could glimpse a narrow strip of moving water through the gap in the wall of spruce along the riverbank. It had to be the right room.

In the bathroom Mercy flushed the toilet, then opened both faucets, hoping the sound of the water pump would rumble through old piping, that Sarah would hear. From the bathroom she quickly crossed the hallway to the door of the closed room, eased the door open. When she saw what was inside she said a fervent prayer of thanks to Calvin.

One wall of the room was taken up with a long fly-tying table, an antique vise occupying the center beneath the swinging arm of a high-intensity lamp. Above the table an array of shelves were stacked with containers of tying materials. The table was probably just the way Cam had left it—except for an absence of litter, the detritus of feathers, thread, flecks of dubbing and tinsel. Swept clean, the desk was a shrine to a fly-tier long gone.

Mercy took in the rest of the room—gun cabinets, boxes of waders and wading boots, fishing vests hanging from wall pegs, a collection of wood-handled landing nets. What she was looking for was on an inside wall, a neatly stacked row of old-fashioned metal rod tubes, a dozen or more. Rapidly she took a tube from the end of the row, unscrewed the cap, removed the rod encased in silken material of deep maroon. When she slid the material down the rod emerged, a gleaming three-piece split-bamboo Cameron Nunemaker original. Despite her hurry she slid a finger from the cork grip along the richly lacquered surface until she touched the wrapping of the first guide. Idiotically, she had an impulse to switch on the desk lamp, inspect closely what she held in her hands, a work of art.

The rod with her, she left the workroom, moved swiftly to the bathroom, turned off the faucets. In the cabinet mirror she caught a glimpse of herself, hair a familiar chaos but a strange look in her eyes. Fear? She grimaced at herself, trying to change the look. She might be misreading the whole situation, have it entirely wrong. The rod was simply a precaution in the event she was right. Wrong, she would explain that she had taken it to admire, just for a moment. Sarah would understand.

Calm determination, Mercy told herself, *that's the look I need.*

BONNIE STARED AT Lucille across the oak table, dumpy, middle-aged Lucille who had just said she believed her husband killed Allison Thorne. It was like getting whacked in the forehead with a board, except Lucille had delivered the blow in a toneless voice, her eyes wide and innocent, the shy half-smile back on her face. But was it, exactly, shy? When Bonnie leaned forward, examining closely, she felt herself whacked a second time. How could she have gotten it so completely wrong?

Shy wasn't the word at all. *Coy* was closer. Lucille was flirting with her!

She wanted to phone Mercy, confess the foul-up that time, telling Mercy about vibes in the air, Lucille fancying Mercy if she had the opportunity, Bonnie acting like some sex expert you saw on television, when all the time the vibes were aimed the other direction. Toward her! *I don't incline in that direction,* she had told Mercy, which was God's own swear-on-the-Bible truth. But Lucille didn't know it was, or didn't care. She hadn't called Bonnie only after failing to reach Mercy on the phone. Bonnie had been at the head of her list all along.

When she finally did talk to Mercy, everything over, she would have to eat crow. In the meantime, there was Lucille, sitting across the table, flirting, saying her husband had killed Allison. "Wait a damn second," Bonnie blurted out. "*Killed* her?"

"Yes."

It seemed stupid, the stupidest thing in the world, but she asked anyway. "Why?"

"So I wouldn't."

"You said that," Bonnie said, "before. So you wouldn't what?"

Lucille didn't hesitate. "Do it myself."

"Kill her?" Bonnie felt herself ready to rise off the chair, explode into orbit. She released a stream of air through her nose, holding herself in place, before she said, "Why'd you want to?"

"Because."

"Aw, c'mon, Lucille, don't jerk me around. This is serious." Bonnie stopped herself. That was stupid to say, too. Of course it was serious. If what Lucille was saying was true, here she was, Bonnie Pym, sitting in Max Ringwald's own house—a house from which he was gone, but Lucille hadn't said where or for how long. If he barged in, found the two of them talking, what then? "Just tell me, okay? Because why?"

"I was so hurt."

"I know. You said that."

"I needed to lash out. I felt so betrayed."

"By Allison, you mean?"

"Yes."

"She said something to you? Something mean?"

"Yes."

"Real mean?"

"I wanted to kill her for it."

Bonnie edged back again from the oak table. She hadn't gotten anything right about dumpy Lucille. "But you think your husband did instead?"

Lucille's lips turned up into a fleeting smile. Absently she caressed the red hair, fluttered her eyes behind the blue-rimmed glasses. "For me," she said.

FITZGERALD STOOD on one side of him, Calvin on the other, looking down, Max speaking steadily now. "Where I keep guns—Lucille got my key to the room, made a duplicate in town. I knew about it. I should have changed the lock, shifted the guns, done something. But she was in bad shape, torn up inside, way I'd seen it before, way she'd get when she was dumped, riled up, near out of her mind. I cut her some slack before, let it peter out, so I figured it would again. She'd get over it. What choice was there? What I didn't figure—it was her last stand, too.

"I kept checking the guns. A Rossi thirty-eight turns up missing, gun she knew about, learned on once, but she might only be fingering it, working out what she was feeling. I wasn't sure. That day I came back from town and she's gone, the car gone, middle of the day. I didn't like the look. So I decided to drive to the girl's place, give her a warning, tell her Lucille has a gun, maybe it's nothing, but she should know, not take any chances. I took another gun with me, a thirty-eight, easy to handle, thinking to give it to the girl, maybe enough to scare off Lucille. I knew the route. I'd tailed Lucille to the girl's place before, not letting her see, keeping an eye on her. I got there—the girl's at the computer, fallen over, back of her head half gone.

"I had to think quick. I called up the husband, got hold of him in the van at the lake place, made a deal to meet out there. All I could think was to make it look like two killings, done the same, same caliber gun, bootlegging the reason. I told you."

When Max stopped, Fitzgerald looked at Calvin, who was looking at him. Then Fitzgerald said, "You're certain Allison was dead when you got to the mobile home?"

"She was dead."

"You felt for a pulse?"

Max's eyes flickered upward, fell back on his folded hands. "All right," Fitzgerald said, "but you should have called for an ambulance. You should have notified Stroud."

Max said, "Don't you get it? The girl was dead. I was trying to cover for Lucille. Why the hell would I get mixed up with the sheriff?"

"Because Allison had been murdered."

"By my *wife*."

"All right," Fitzgerald said, "go back. Something had happened, happened before the killing, between your wife and Allison. You said you phoned Allison, told her your wife wouldn't want her coming to your house, not now, so you'd bring information to her place."

"That was bull," Max said. "I never called the girl."

"But why wouldn't Lucille want Allison coming to the house? Allison wouldn't have been the one to break off the relationship, not if she was still trying to get information about the militia. So it had to be your wife. But she must not have been satisfied with that, just breaking off with Allison. What had Allison done?"

"Plenty."

"Enough to make your wife angry enough to kill her?"

"Yeah."

Fitzgerald waited.

"What's the point?" Max said at last. "The girl got herself knocked up."

"BUT YOU HAVEN'T TOLD anybody, huh," Bonnie asked, "until now?"

"No," Lucille said.

"You consider maybe telling the sheriff?"

"What would he do?"

"Bring your husband to town, question him. Maybe it didn't happen the way you think."

"It must have."

Bonnie said, "I don't know, Lucille. You didn't use the gun you took, maybe he didn't use the other one. He just took it, like you."

"He must have used it."

"But how do you know?"

"Because Allison's dead."

"There's another thing," Bonnie said. "Ray Thorne. You think your husband killed him, too?"

"I don't know."

Bonnie looked across the table—looked at the dough-faced woman with red hair fluttering her eyes behind blue-rimmed glasses. She had been in a lot of weird situations in her life but none matched this. She felt like someone about to play the final cards in a rotten hand. "Maybe we should call Fitzgerald," she said. "Remember, the one came here with Mercy? Newspaper guy. He'd know."

"I'd rather not."

"Mercy then?"

Lucille shook her head.

"You wanted me to tell you what to do," Bonnie said,

exasperated, her cards gone. "I can't think of anything else."

"That's all right."

"What?"

"Couldn't we just sit here? Wouldn't that be pleasant?"

Bonnie stared across the table. Then, suddenly, she smiled and said, "It would, sure enough. But your husband coming back and all—" She felt like someone who had been slipped another card, one from the bottom of the deck. "I've got a better idea." She reached out across the table, slowly slid the shiny revolver away from Lucille, toward her. "You'll like where we're going."

MAX SAID, "She let Lucille know. Maybe it was starting to show and Lucille figured it out herself. Maybe the girl, sick of Lucille, told her outright. How do I know? Lucille hit the skids—mad, bitter, weepy, depressed, all the misery we'd been through before but worse this time. She went on about the girl—didn't care for her, betrayed her, never cared for her, running at the mouth about it. Don't ask me—I never understood. Never wanted to. But I could tell it was worse. I had experience. When I found the gun missing—"

"Your wife didn't kill Allison," Fitzgerald said. Beside him he felt Calvin turn, felt his eyes, but he kept looking steadily at Max. "Maybe, Allison pregnant, she wanted to. But she didn't."

"She had the goddamn gun."

"It doesn't matter. You killed Ray Thorne for nothing."

Max stared back, mouth open. "Allison and her killer had coffee," Fitzgerald said. "They wouldn't have, not if the killer was furious with her, not if Allison knew that. Then Allison switched on the computer, planning to write something. The killer moved behind her, close to her, almost looking over Allison's shoulder. There's no reason to think Allison felt any alarm. After the shooting the killer got rid of Allison's notebooks and worked the computer, erasing everything she'd written about militia involvement with the Catch and Keep Alliance.''

Max said, "But I never gave her any information that day. What I told you, it was all bull. She was dead when I got to her place."

"Allison already had information—the false information you'd given her before. And that day someone was giving her fresh information—what she was entering in the computer, or was about to enter, when she was shot. The killer erased whatever was there."

"Jesus," Max groaned.

"Would your wife have known how to do that?"

"Jesus."

"Would she?"

"She can't work a typewriter."

"Sarah," Calvin said. Fitzgerald turned, feeling Max's eyes swivel at the same instant. "She'd know."

"Ah, Jesus."

"Grab the shotgun." Calvin was moving away already, heading into the jack pines. "Mercy's there," he shouted back. "I spotted her vehicle when I canoed down."

MERCY HELD THE ROD before her as she came down the hallway, entered the kitchen again, bearing it like a gift. When she realized Sarah wasn't there, the breakfast alcove empty, she stopped in mid-stride, turning, looking. Sarah was standing at the back door, blocking it, looking back at her, one hand deep in a pocket of the bulky cardigan.

Of course. She watched Sarah's hand rise, fingers gripping a dark revolver, feeling only foolish. *Of course that was why Sarah was wearing a sweater on a warm day.* Then a thought, equally foolish, sped through her mind: *I*

*won't be singing the praises of Cam's rod. There's no need
to pretend that's why I have it.*

As calmly as she could, Mercy crossed the kitchen to the
alcove, pulled a chair from the table so she would be facing
Sarah. Mercy sat down, crossed her legs, held the rod with
her hands at the ends of the sections, poised the sections
over her knee. Then she looked across the room at Sarah,
squinting back at her, Sarah unsure if she was seeing what
she thought she was—crime, sacrilege, the planned destruc-
tion of a work of art.

"Now bend down," Mercy instructed her, "put the gun
on the floor, slide it this way with your foot, real slow."
When Sarah didn't move, locked in place, Mercy said,
"Trust me. You don't, the rod ends up as kindling."

She held her breath then, waiting.

TWENTY-EIGHT

WILLARD STROUD could never decide about Traverse City. There were attractions, namely the location on Grand Traverse Bay with a long spine of the peninsula between the two arms of the bay and Lake Michigan out beyond, but the town was too crowded, choked with traffic in summer and fall, tourists crawling about. He liked to visit now and then, but living there was hard to imagine. He didn't think he would be comfortable in any of the lakeshore towns—Ludington, Manistee, Charlevoix, Petoskey. He should have known them when they were raw lumber ports. Now they were all the same, playgrounds for the leisure class.

He belonged in a small place stuck in the pines. Ossning was about right, but wouldn't be any longer, not after he retired, an ex-sheriff home all the time with Elsie. People would remember why he retired, unable to make an inch of headway with two murders, finally calling in state authorities with the lame excuse that the killer (or killers—he didn't even know that) was an outsider, maybe a professional gunman. People would recognize his retirement for what it was, forced, an admission of failure.

Probably he ought to move to the Upper Peninsula, way up near the edge of Lake Superior, find a good log house deep in the woods, hunker down through the winter, then fish every day from spring through fall. Elsie wouldn't like it. She would miss the chatter that went on in the city-county building. Would he? He thought briefly about Bonnie Pym, stopping in the office every morning with a box of sweet rolls, showing him her earrings. Showing more than that. One thing he damned well wouldn't miss was dealing with nitwits like Gus Thayer.

After leaving the hospital Stroud had driven into town, parked on tree-lined Front Street, walked up and down, looking in shop windows, trying to let off steam. He would deal with Gus later, getting even somehow or other. In the meantime he was stuck with the fact that Gus was right about one matter: he hadn't known a thing about Ray Thorne's bootlegging business. It had gone on under his nose, most of Ossning knowing while the person paid to know, the Tamarack County sheriff, knew nothing. His stomach tightened, a bitter knot, when he thought about that—that and Ray having the gall to advertise the business in the town paper. If he was adding up reasons to resign, here was another.

When Stroud came to what he remembered as a Big Boy restaurant he discovered it had been turned into something called the Mackinaw Brewing Company. He went inside, sat at the marble-topped counter, looked over the beer menu. Was Beadle's Best Bitter really a beer? After he retired he would come back, sample everything on the menu. For now, still on the job, it would have to be coffee.

"Coffee?" the young woman behind the bar repeated.

"You have it?"

"Oh, sure."

"Hot," Stroud said. "And black."

He left before he finished half the mug, found his car, drove to a parking area beside the power plant on the waterfront of the West Arm, a better place to walk. In town, walking Front Street, he had the impression the flow of people could read the sorry state of his thoughts by looking at his face. Out here, circling along the landscaped edge of the bay with an occasional jogger, they were his alone.

I'm putting off going home, he realized. *I don't want to face the music.*

He looked out at the bay, sailboats on it, power cruisers, a few fishing boats, the blue surface rippling in a soft breeze. Way out, choppy, blue-green, the big lake began. He was positive about one thing, at least: Gus Thayer was dead wrong about the militia operation in the county. Waco, Ruby Ridge, the massacre in Oklahoma City with its Michigan connection—he and every other sheriff in the state had been on alert ever since. There were briefings from the state police, even the FBI. He and his deputies had scoured the county, making sure nothing was going on.

Maybe that was why he missed Ray Thorne's bootlegging, concentrating on possible militia groups, giving them too much attention. He felt a stirring of justification, immediately cut it off. *I'm not letting myself off the hook. If I'd scoured everything in the county I'd have found the cabin at Lost Finger Lake, the one stacked with liquor. I'd have learned about Ray Thorne's business, maybe learned that Allison Thorne was working with him, keeping records on her computer. Maybe if I'd unraveled the bootlegging business, Allison would be in jail rather than dead and I wouldn't be walking up and down, looking at water, two unsolved murders on my hands.*

He walked until his legs were tired and he needed to sit down. He was back to his car, about to unlock the door, when he heard the phone ringing inside.

"I've been calling," Zack Cox said when Stroud answered.

"I was seeing Gus Thayer."

"A nurse at the hospital said you took off."

"Why'd you want me?"

"Wait a minute." He heard muffled sounds, as if Zack was shifting the position of the phone. There was still background noise on the line, people talking. Then Zack said, "Guess what?"

Stroud sighed. "What?"

"We solved the murders," Zack began.

WHEN STROUD ARRIVED at the city-county building Calvin, Mercy, and Fitzgerald were in the interview room, sipping coffee from Styrofoam cups with Zack Cox. When Zack saw Stroud in the doorway he got up. Together they went into a hallway.

"I put Max Ringwald in a cell. Sarah Nunemaker's in your office, talking with Elsie. Like you said."

"Bonnie Pym?"

"She's still got Ringwald's wife at the bakery, holding onto her gun. They're drinking coffee together, happy as two clams."

Stroud told Zack to relieve Elsie but not talk with Sarah in a formal capacity. He would have Sarah make a statement later. Max Ringwald and his wife, too. Then he poured a cup of coffee, entered the interview room, took a chair at the table. "Who wants to start?"

"About what?" Mercy said and grinned at him.

Stroud gave her a stern look. "I'm not in the mood."

"Odd," Mercy said, "since you're going to get written up in the *Call*. Local lawman cracks case."

He turned from her to Fitzgerald. "Ringwald thought his wife killed Allison, so he killed Ray Thorne to cover up. That's his story?"

"It worked. He had us thinking Allison was killed because of the liquor business."

"Had me thinking it," Stroud admitted. "But you believe him about wanting to protect his wife?"

"He's been doing it a long time."

"But not killing anyone before."

"He'd never believed his wife had. It hadn't gone that far before."

Stroud thought for a moment before he said, "He'll make a statement?"

"He talked to Calvin and me. But he didn't know about Sarah then. You'll have to see."

Stroud turned back to Mercy. "Tell me what she said."

"Why she killed Allison? Same reason as Max. Sarah was protecting Lucille."

"Ringwald's wife?"

"Actually, Sarah was protecting everyone. She wanted to have Lucille as a friend, another lonely woman out there on the river. Then Allison turns up and Sarah likes her, too. She wants to help her get away from Ray, so she works with her on the story Allison's writing. But the story brought Allison and Lucille together. Sarah must have known from the start, the moment she met her, the kind of woman Lucille was—and what might happen when she was alone with Allison. She tried to keep Allison away but she couldn't."

"So that's why Sarah killed her?"

"Sarah went out to Allison's mobile home, had coffee with her, they talked together. Sarah wanted a pledge or something that Allison would break off with Lucille. Allison said she wanted to finish the story, that was all, but Sarah knew the story was hopeless. She'd already told Allison all she could think of about a militia connection. She didn't think there was anything more. The affair would go on and on."

"So that's why she ended it?"

"Sarah felt she was responsible since she'd caused Allison to go to the Ringwalds. She found herself in a bind. She wanted to protect them both, Allison from Ray, Lucille from Allison, but it wasn't possible to do both. She felt she had to choose."

"And she chose to protect Lucille Ringwald?"

"When it came right down to it, that's who she felt the

most sympathy for—poor Lucille. She knew she couldn't change Lucille—change the way she was. All she could do was try to get Allison to end the relationship. When she realized Allison wouldn't, well—she chose Lucille. Still and all, maybe she thought she was protecting Allison. Maybe she thought she was protecting her both from a future with Ray and a story, so Sarah believed, that would only disappoint her in the end."

"Protecting her by killing her?"

"Strange as it seems." Mercy stopped, looked quickly at Fitzgerald, straightened in her chair before she turned back to Stroud. "Afterward she went into Allison's computer and removed all traces of the militia story. Now she was protecting Wesley Wallace Dawes. She'd told Allison about him, helping with her story, making up some of it. She didn't want what she said getting into print."

"But you said it wouldn't. Allison wouldn't be able to finish the story."

"I don't know," Mercy said. "Maybe Sarah didn't want to run the risk. She wanted to help everyone, didn't want to leave any loose ends. Maybe that was in her mind."

"And it was Sarah knowing about computers that made you realize she was the killer?"

Fitzgerald said, "Calvin knows Sarah best. He made the connection."

Calvin shrugged. "It came to me. Then we beat our butts over to Sarah's place, dragging Max through the woods, thinking the worst. What we find is Mercy in the kitchen, gun and one of Cam's bamboo rods on the table, having coffee with Sarah."

"It was the gun she killed Allison with," Mercy said. "Sarah didn't want to use it again, but she couldn't let me see Lucille, let the same thing start up again, leave her without a friend again. Maybe it wouldn't have but she couldn't take the chance. When she saw I'd break Cam's rod—I think it gave her an excuse. She crumpled like a leaf."

"We used Mercy's vehicle," Calvin said, "hauled Sarah and Max in here, turned them over to Zack. Same time Zack gets a call from Bonnie. She's at the bakery with Max's wife, having coffee."

"I know," Stroud said, "happy as clams." Then he looked from Mercy to Fitzgerald. "Ringwald's wife had nothing to do with either killing. That right?"

"She didn't pull the triggers," Fitzgerald said.

"But she was the reason," Mercy said, "both times."

STROUD SAID HE WOULD need statements from everyone but they could wait until morning. He sent Zack Cox to the Six-Grain Bakery to bring Bonnie Pym and Lucille Ringwald to the city-county building—and another deputy with Calvin to pick up the canoe left on the mainstream. Calvin didn't want to leave it overnight.

"Another one's stashed there," Calvin pointed out. "Red Oscoda."

Fitzgerald said, "Probably Gus Thayer's."

"In that case," Stroud said, "let it rot."

"What will you do with Lucille?" Mercy asked him.

"Get a statement. See if everything checks out."

"Then?"

"No reason to hold her. We'll take her home."

"She'll be alone."

Stroud nodded. "You have to write something for the paper?" he asked Fitzgerald.

"Phipps gave me the story. I'll call him. He's got it back."

"You certain?"

"I only wanted to find out about Allison. I never meant to write anything. I told you that."

"True," Stroud said. "You told me that. But you didn't tell me what you and Calvin were up to with Max Ringwald." He turned, looked at Mercy. "Or you with Sarah."

Mercy said, "Heard you were going to retire, Stroud."

"I was."

"Goes to show you. Never do a good deed."

"IT'S ALL OVER TOWN," Sandy said the moment Bonnie, Mercy, and Fitzgerald took stools at the bar of the Borchard Hotel, waiting for Calvin to return from the river. "The sheriff's got everybody in jail."

"He solved the case," Fitzgerald said.

"Max Ringwald I can understand. But Sarah Nunemaker—boy, that takes the wind out of your sails."

"It does," Mercy said.

"But you know what they used to say," Sandy went on, her voice lowered, "back when old Dawes was shot. So maybe it was so. Sarah did him in, too."

"Why bother reading a town newspaper," Fitzgerald said after Sandy moved down the bar, "when you've got this place?"

Bonnie said, "Try the Keg O'Nails, sugar, you want a real scoop."

Beyond the bar the dining room was beginning to fill up with retirees out for the early-bird specials. Nils and Wilma wouldn't appear until later. "Anyone hungry?" Fitzgerald asked. When neither Bonnie nor Mercy answered he said, "You just want to drink?"

"Not even that. I've had so much—"

"You say coffee," Bonnie said, "I'll puke."

"Would you have done it," Fitzgerald asked Mercy, "broken the rod?"

"Are you kidding? In a flash."

"Then what?"

"I never thought that far ahead, what Sarah might do afterward. She had a bunch of Cam's rods in his workroom. I kept wondering if she was willing to waste one."

"She wasn't willing to waste Allison's computer."

"What?"

"Stroud told me before. The way she shot Allison, the bullet passed through her head but missed hitting the monitor. Sarah must have calculated the angle."

"Good Lord."

"I suppose I can understand that, sparing good equipment even though Allison wouldn't be there to use it. I suppose that makes some twisted sense. But shooting Allison the way she did, back of the head, point-blank range. How could Sarah do that to someone she cared about?"

Mercy shook her head. "Maybe because she did care about her. Maybe she thought she was sparing Allison, too—sparing her needless suffering. She must have told Allison she had more militia information, something she'd remembered, so Allison sat at the computer, ready to enter the information, her head turned away from Sarah. Then—" Mercy shook her head again. "I don't know."

"I know one thing," Fitzgerald said to her. "You risked your life with Sarah."

"So did you with Mysterious Max, sneaking around his property, neither you or Calvin armed. That was dumb."

"Dumber than facing down Sarah with a flyrod?"

"Hey," Bonnie said, "you two get married and didn't say?"

"I'VE BEEN THINKING about Lucille," Bonnie said after Mercy changed her mind and Sandy brought them schooners of beer. "What's going to happen to her out there, big old barn of a place, all by her lonesome? She won't have Max."

"Or Sarah." Then Mercy said, "I've got a confession to make. Right in the middle of everything I had this thought about buying Sarah's place—buying it someday. The things that go through your head. It's strange."

Bonnie looked at Mercy and said, "About making a confession—"

"What?"

"On second thought," Bonnie said after a glance at Fitzgerald, "tell ya later. It's *real* strange. The thing between Lucille and Allison," she went on, "it was over when Lucille found out Allison was pregnant. Lucille told me at the bakery. She never wanted to see Allison again."

"For Lucille," Mercy said, "I suppose pregnancy meant rejection. But Sarah never knew that—knew the affair was over. She didn't need to kill Allison to protect Lucille."

Fitzgerald said, "And Max didn't need to kill Ray to protect her."

"Wow," Bonnie said, "makes you think. You know, about relationships."

"Out in the woods," Fitzgerald said, "Max told us that getting involved with Allison, involved with her story, was the second biggest mistake of his life. He must have meant that marrying Lucille was the first."

"But he wouldn't let her go," Bonnie said.

"Catch and keep." When Bonnie and Mercy looked at him Fitzgerald said, "You find someone, you try to hold on."

"It seems the way," Mercy sighed. "Sarah thought Allison should be free of Ray, but there's no evidence she wanted to be. It's what Sarah wanted. For her own reasons Allison was holding on to Ray. Maybe that's why she helped with the bootlegging business. It tied them together all the more."

"Maybe," Fitzgerald said. "But she wanted to hold onto her newspaper career, too. She wasn't willing to let that go."

From behind them Calvin called out to Sandy to bring him an O'Doul's, then took a stool at the bar and said he found his canoe. It was in the back of his pickup, safe and sound. "You got a canoe you're familiar with," he explained when no one responded, "you don't want to lose it."

"We understand," Fitzgerald said.

Elizabeth Gunn

FIVE CARD STUD

A JAKE HINES MYSTERY

It's a frigid winter in
Minnesota, but detective
Jake Hines has bigger
problems than keeping
warm. The body of a
man, nearly naked and
frozen solid, is discovered
on a highway overpass.

As Hines probes the last days of the victim's life, a
grim picture of betrayal, greed and fear emerges. But
for Jake, solving a murder is a lot like playing cards—
figure out who's bluffing and who's got the perfect
hand, especially when one of the players is a killer.

"This series gets better and better. Gunn keeps her
readers absorbed in the exciting case throughout…"
—*Booklist*

Available July 2001 at your favorite retail outlet.

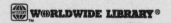

MYSTERY WORLDWIDE LIBRARY®

WEG389

J. R. Ripley

Skulls of Sedona

Struggling musician and amateur
sleuth Tony Kozol heads for
the Crystal Magic of the Skulls
Conference in Sedona, Arizona, to
play guitar at the request of an old
college friend, a New Age music guru.
But when his buddy is found sitting at his piano—dead from
the crushing weight of the piano lid—Tony finds himself
investigating a murder.

A Tony Kozol Mystery

"**Wacky characters, liquid prose, frequent humor,
and a decidedly light plot place this in the fun,
breeze-to-read category.**"
—*Library Journal*

Available July 2001 at your favorite retail outlet.

 **WORLDWIDE LIBRARY®**

WJR390